Quintin Jardine gave up the life of a political spin doctor for the more morally acceptable world of murder and mayhem. Happily married, he hides from critics and creditors in secret locations in Scotland and Spain, but can be tracked down through his website: www.quintinjardine.com.

Praise for Quintin Jardine's novels:

'Perfect plotting and convincing characterisation . . . Jardine manages to combine the picturesque with the thrilling and the dream-like with the coldly rational' *The Times*

'The perfect mix for a highly charged, fast-moving crime thriller' *Glasgow Herald*

'[Quintin Jardine] sells more crime fiction in Scotland than John Grisham and people queue around the block to buy his latest book' *The Australian*

'Remarkably assured . . . a *tour de force*' *New York Times*

'There is a whole world here, the tense narratives all come to the boil at the same time in a spectacular climax' *Shots* magazine

'Engrossing, believable characters . . . captures Edinburgh beautifully . . . It all adds up to a very good read' *Edinburgh Evening News*

'A complex story combined with robust characterisation; a murder/mystery novel of our time that will keep you hooked to the very last page' *The Scots Magazine*

By Quintin Jardine and available from Headline

Bob Skinner series:
Skinner's Rules
Skinner's Festival
Skinner's Trail
Skinner's Round
Skinner's Ordeal
Skinner's Mission
Skinner's Ghosts
Murmuring the Judges
Gallery Whispers
Thursday Legends
Autographs in the Rain
Head Shot
Fallen Gods
Stay of Execution
Lethal Intent
Dead and Buried
Death's Door
Aftershock
Fatal Last Words

Oz Blackstone series:
Blackstone's Pursuits
A Coffin for Two
Wearing Purple
Screen Savers
On Honeymoon with Death
Poisoned Cherries
Unnatural Justice
Alarm Call
For the Death of Me

Primavera Blackstone series:
Inhuman Remains

Quintin
Jardine
INHUMAN REMAINS

A PRIMAVERA BLACKSTONE MYSTERY

headline

First published in 2009
by HEADLINE PUBLISHING GROUP

First published in paperback in 2009
by HEADLINE PUBLISHING GROUP

1

Cataloguing in Publication Data is available from the British Library

ISBN 978 0 7553 4899 2 (B format)
ISBN 978 0 7553 4023 1 (A format)

Typeset in Electra by Avon DataSet Ltd,
Bidford-on-Avon, Warwickshire

Printed in the UK by CPI Mackays, Chatham, ME5 8TD

Headline's policy is to use papers that are natural, renewable and
recyclable products and made from wood grown in sustainable forests.
The logging and manufacturing processes are expected to conform
to the environmental regulations of the country of origin.

HEADLINE PUBLISHING GROUP
An Hachette UK Company
338 Euston Road
London NW1 3BH

www.headline.co.uk
www.hachette.co.uk

This book is dedicated to the village of St Martí d'Empúries, and all who sail in her, especially Dominic, with a nod also to Sunny and the boy Canelo

Acknowledgements go to

The inimitable, incredible, indestructible, in . . . (you name it, she's 'in' it) Sue Scarr.

The legendary Eddie Bell, for a fleeting guest appearance.

Mike, for letting me almost borrow his name.

One

What do I like most about my village?

It's this: nobody asks any questions.

In St Martí d'Empúries they don't want to know what brought you here, or why you choose to live here. Okay, maybe they do, but it's not in their nature to ask. If you want to tell them, they'll listen, but they won't push you to it. If you have a past that you need to leave behind you, that's where they'll let it stay . . . even if, now and then, it still shows in your eyes.

Our house is on the Catalan coast, on the north of what you might know as the Costa Brava. It overlooks the sea, with nothing obscuring the view. It's set on the highest point in the village, alongside the church. I've no idea how old it is, but some of the outer walls must date back for hundreds of years, maybe even a full millennium. It wasn't built, as such, it evolved through the centuries into its present form, with successive owners leaving their stamp upon it, until finally, it came to us . . . or, rather, we came to it.

I can't begin to tell you how beautiful this place is. You'll have to see it for yourself. Often, when the year is starting to

1

bloom and the weather is set fair, I leave my bedroom shutters open at night so that I'll waken at first light. Then I go out on to the east-facing terrace and gaze at the horizon, waiting and watching as the red sun rises from the still waters of the Mediterranean.

I've tried to persuade Tom to share the experience, but he's not at his best in the morning . . . not that early at any rate. One day he'll come to appreciate it.

How did we get here, Primavera and Tom Blackstone? That's a *looooong* story, too *looooong* to get into now . . . but I'll give you the shortened version.

They thought I was dead, you know, my dad, my sister, my son (although Tom didn't understand 'dead' then: I'm not sure he does even now); everybody in the whole damn world thought I was gone from it.

They even held a memorial service for me, thirty-nine years old and gone to Jesus, at my family's parish church in Auchterarder. It was full, with people standing in the boneyard outside, the sound from within relayed through loudspeakers. The Scottish media were unanimous, for once, in their reporting of the gig next day. (I know this because I read all the coverage on-line. I wish I could have been there to hear what was said about me, in disguise, hidden somewhere at the back of the crowd, but that really would have been pushing my luck.) They found it moving in the extreme, made all the more poignant by the fact that my body had never been recovered from the swamp in New Jersey into which the aircraft had plunged.

They agreed on something else too, that my ex had given the performance of a lifetime in his eulogy. The lady who wrote the colour piece for the *Courier* newspaper was convinced that, at its end, he had real tears in his eyes.

He wouldn't have fooled me, though. I've always known Oz Blackstone for the consummate actor that he proved himself to be, even back in the days when he was two-timing me with his supposedly ex-girlfriend.

I wish I could look back on Oz without a trace of bitterness. Maybe I will, some day, but I'm not close to it yet, even though he was the only man I ever loved.

He owed it all to me, you know, everything that he became.

I don't say that lightly. But for me, he'd never have met Dawn, my actress sister, and Miles, her film-director husband, who in a drink-fuelled moment decided to give him the break that he seized with both hands, both feet, and that almost prehensile cock of his.

Hah! That's something about him that I do miss: I have to admit that from the day we met he and I were, metaphorically and often literally, joined at the groin. There was always that thing between us, indestructible, even after the second time he dumped me for another woman. I had power over him, and now I'm a little ashamed to admit that I used it whenever I could, even though it got me into bad trouble and, for a while, cost me custody of Tom.

Yes, I had my own share of guilt in our relationship but, still, I can't call it quits and look back on him with kindness. Why not? Because the bastard tried to kill me, that's why not!

If I had fronted him up about it, I'm sure he would have denied it. Christ, he might even have made me believe in his innocence, as everyone else does, for long enough for him to make a proper job of it second time around. But I know I'm right; nothing has happened since to make me change my mind.

He never got on the damn plane, you see, the private jet he had chartered to take us from Trenton to Newark to catch a transatlantic flight. Four passengers were listed but only three got on board; Oz stayed behind, with a Chinese messenger girl who had turned up to collect a package. I didn't hear the story he spun the pilot, but I'm damn sure she was part of it, part of the set-up.

He was standing there as we began our taxi. I looked at him through the window, and our eyes met. He had the strangest expression on his face. It puzzled me then but now I can describe it as anticipation, mixed with a little fear, and fear was something Oz didn't show too often. I wondered about it all the way through the flight, right up to the moment when we heard the bang and Scott, the pilot, told us through the speaker system that we had a problem, and that he was going to attempt an emergency landing.

I knew then, for sure, what that look had been about. He had decided to get me out of his life for good. When he wanted to be, Oz was lethal, and like many very wealthy people, he could get things done.

The 'emergency landing' wasn't: it was a crash, pure and simple. We came down hard, with a crunching, tearing bang, and that's all I remember, until I came to among the wreckage and found that everyone else on board was dead.

How did I survive? That's a little embarrassing, but it's true nonetheless.

I was on the toilet, wasn't I, perched on the tiny bog at the back end of the plane, when Scott read us all our death warrant. There was a little speaker in there too. I thought about going back to my seat, but decided that if Elvis had met his Maker with his knickers round his ankles, that was good enough for me. On the way down, I hung on tight to the hand-grips and concentrated my thoughts on Tom, banishing everything from my mind but his face, until we hit the swamp and everything went blank.

I don't imagine I was unconscious for more than a few seconds; a minute at most. When I came to I was waist-deep in brown, smelly water and my head hurt like hell. I glanced in the cracked mirror and saw a big lump in the process of forming above my left eye, as if a baby alien was trying to chew its way out. For a moment, I had visions of the flood rising until it filled the compartment, but it seemed to have found its own level. I kicked my way out of my underwear and tried to open the door, fearful that it might have been jammed shut by the impact. I had to push hard against the water, but I made it, and stepped outside.

I saw, at once, what had saved my life. At some point during the disaster, the tiny tail section of the aircraft had been ripped off and had soft-landed in an open area, while the rest had smashed through a stand of trees. The main fuselage was yards away, still ablaze, although the swamp water was doing an effective fire-fighting job.

I thought about Oz again, and knew for sure that he had taken himself out of this. No one, not even he, was that lucky. Accident or sabotage? With him involved, the odds were way in favour of the latter. I considered my two companions on the flight, the man and the woman: both of them had been trouble in their own way, and I reckoned that Oz had simply seen them as expendable. To this day, such an idea might shock his millions of fans, but trust me, that's how he was.

As the flames subsided, I took a look inside the main cabin; it didn't take long to appreciate that nothing was alive in there. I was in a fair old panic, I admit . . . I have never done 'unnaturally calm' very well . . . but I was thinking clearly enough to decide that the best thing I could do was get the hell out of there. As I looked around, I saw three black objects floating on the surface, and recognised my cabin bag among them. I grabbed it; then I looked around, at my surroundings.

The area was heavily wooded; I had no idea where I was but I guessed that the plane had been heading more or less north. So I headed more or less south, trudging heavily, barefoot, through the marsh water, hoping there was nothing nastier down there than the odd tree root.

My exceptional luck held: within ten minutes I had reached a broad spine of dry land that seemed to run through the morass, and saw on that a path.

I stopped and opened my bag. The seal must have been as good as the manufacturer claimed, for the clothing inside was dry. I stripped off what I had been wearing and used my upper garments to dry myself, then put on a fresh shirt, jeans and trainers. I found a mirror, comb and usable makeup in my very soggy handbag. When I had made myself look half normal, and arranged my hair so that it covered the creature in my head, I set out to follow the path.

America never ceases to surprise me with its contrasts. Less than half an hour later, I stepped out of the wilderness, and into a quiet suburb of what I guessed was a dormitory town for the nearest city. The streets were as empty as the swamp had been, save for a few cars parked in driveways. I walked on, aimlessly, until a black and white taxi slowly turned a corner and pulled up outside a house thirty yards away. A middle-aged woman paid the driver, then climbed out. She had barely reached the stone path that led to her front door before I flagged the guy down.

'Where to, lady?' The cabbie looked disconcertingly like Big Pussy, the *Sopranos* character who went to sleep with the fishes, but I forced myself to look at him casually and reply, 'Into town.'

'A little more specific?'

I searched for an answer that would mask my ignorance of my surroundings, and came up with 'Sorry, Wal-Mart.' In the USA, those are everywhere.

That Wal-Mart turned out to be in the centre of a community that seemed to have no obvious industry; my dormitory conjecture had been correct. I paid the man . . . happily, he was not gabby, and just as happily, the cash in my purse was still dry . . . and looked around. Straight across the road, I saw a car lot, the New Jersey equivalent of the sort of place you might find in *EastEnders*. It was evening, going on for eight o'clock, but it was still open.

I checked my cash reserve. I had six hundred dollars in my purse, and ten thousand in a compartment in my case . . . emergency money that I'd never thought I'd need. Around a third of that bought me an elderly but serviceable Chrysler Voyager, from a dealer who probably thought all his Christmas Days had come early. I gave my name as Mary Edison, and an address I also made up on the spot. He asked no questions. He even threw in a free map and a tank of gas.

I was fuelled by adrenaline: I found the nearest Interstate, and drove through the night without a break, apart from a couple of pit-stops, till early next morning, when I reached the city of Buffalo, and with it, the Canadian border. I ditched the car in a public car park, found the station and bought a ticket for the evening train to Toronto.

I had most of the day to wait; I bought a big floppy hat and a huge pair of sunglasses that covered most of my face, and spent it looking at the Niagara Falls, and thinking.

What was there to think about?

Are you kidding? Plenty.

First, had I done the right thing in committing what was probably a federal offence by leaving the scene of a fatal air accident? If I was certain that Oz had staged the crash, shouldn't I have stayed right there and denounced him?

A quick glance at that morning's *Buffalo News* was all it took to convince me that I'd done the right thing. As far as the media were concerned, Oz was a victim himself. Rescue teams were searching for his body as well as mine. I knew damn well that when he surfaced there would be a wave of public relief. I knew also that if he had sabotaged the plane . . . and the media were already alluding to suspicious circumstances . . . there was no way it would ever be traced to him. If I spoke out, I'd be a mad woman, a bitter and twisted ex-wife, with a track record of trying to harm him. Not a soul would believe me and I would still be in his sights.

No, much better to go along with playing dead for a while.

I was confident that I wouldn't be traced to the car lot in that New Jersey town, the name of which I still don't know, simply because nobody would be looking for me there. The riskiest part would be getting into Canada, but since the press seemed to be calling me 'Mrs Blackstone', and I was travelling on my Primavera Phillips passport, I reckoned I'd get through without leaving a trace.

The second big consideration was what to do next. My dad and my sister would be in agony, I knew. Was it right to allow that to continue? Much as I hated it, I told myself I had to, for a while at least, if I was to keep Oz off my trail. The word 'stoic' could have been coined for Dad, but Dawn was flaky. If she knew I was alive, she'd never keep it to herself . . . and she, Miles and Oz were still close. Then there was Tom, but at that stage I couldn't bring myself to think about him.

Finally, I asked myself the toughest question of all. What was I going to take from the experience?

I looked back over the time since I had met Oz, and thought of the person that I'd become, that he had helped to make me. It didn't take me long to realise I was having trouble blaming him for trying to bump me off. In his shoes, I'd have been tempted to do the same thing. Whatever happened, as the Niagara's white water thundered down I promised myself that I would emerge from the wreckage of my life as a better person, as the daughter David and Elanore Phillips had raised, not the woman she had been for the best part of a decade.

Crossing the border wasn't a problem. The Canadian immigration people looked at my passport and thought, 'Tourist,' as they took my entry card and filed it with the rest, where no American FBI investigator was ever likely to look.

I spent the night in the smallest hotel I could find in Toronto, to lessen the chances of being spotted. Next morning I went back to Union Station and bought myself a transcontinental train ticket for Vancouver. It seemed like a good place to kick off my new life, for a couple of reasons. My time with Oz, and our divorce, had left me very well fixed financially, thank you, and most of my money was stashed there, invested through a private bank. And so were some other items, in a safe-deposit box, chief among them being my two extra passports.

In the brief period when I was married to Oz, I'd applied for a passport as his wife and had managed, by a discreet lie, to hold on to the one it was supposed to replace, the one I was still using. But I'd done more than that. I'd obtained another, as

Janet More, the birth name of my predecessor, the first Mrs Osbert Blackstone. She was dead, and it was before the days of biometrics, so it was easy. Why did I do it? Because I was a devious, cunning bitch, always looking for an advantage, and thought that I might find it useful some day. That was how being with that guy made me think.

I checked into a hotel in Burrard Street, and holed up in Vancouver for a week, hanging around Granville Island and Stanley Park, breakfasting in Starbucks (I like Starbucks, okay?), dining in the Sandbar, Joe Fortes and Earl's, and reading every newspaper I could find. When I was sure that my disappearance had lost its news value, I booked a flight to Las Vegas in Jan's name, and rented an apartment through an Internet agency. Las Vegas, you ask? Trust me: it's one of the best places in the world to hide. The population changes all the time as the casino hotels fill up and empty, fill up and empty, weekend in, weekend out. If you need to, you can be truly anonymous there.

And so I set up my hopefully temporary home, and began to consider how I could get back into my own life, and into Tom's. It didn't take long for me to realise that it wouldn't be easy. In truth, I didn't have a clue about how I was going to do any of it.

But as it happened, six months after my 'death', all the subterfuge became irrelevant. I'll never forget how I found out.

I was having lunch in my favourite bar on the Strip; as always the place was busy, full of half-pissed rednecks having fun. Most of the television monitors were showing a country-music video, but there was one that was tuned to CNN. I happened to glance at it, just as a shot of a smiling Oz appeared. I couldn't hear what the anchorman was saying, but from the look on his face, one thing was certain: it wasn't a good news story. I left my chilli unfinished, went straight home, and switched on the telly.

They said, after the autopsy, that it was a ruptured aorta, a time-bomb in his heart that had been waiting to happen, the same condition that had almost killed his father a few months earlier. It had caught up with him on the set of a movie, during a stunt that he had insisted on handling himself.

At that moment, I didn't care what it was: all I knew was that the man who had tried to kill me was dead, that my unforgettable lover, my ex-husband, was dead, that Tom's father was dead. I cried for two days, and very little of that was out of relief.

Briefly, I thought about getting a flight home to Scotland and turning up at the funeral, which I knew would take place in Anstruther, his home town. Again, it didn't take me long to abandon that idea; it would have caused a sensation, and been desperately cruel to Susie, Oz's widow, and to the rest of his very nice family. Also, it might just have got me arrested if it had led to someone finding out that I'd entered the US under a fraudulently obtained passport. So instead I sat tight in Vegas until I saw coverage of the send-off on *Entertainment Tonight*. Next day, I called my father.

At first, he didn't believe it was me. He thought I was a malicious caller, until I told him that his middle name was

Montgomery, spelled like the soldier, not the golfer, and that he had a birthmark on his shoulder in the shape of the mouse that had scared my grandmother when she was carrying him. When he was convinced, he asked me the obvious question.

'Because, at the time, being dead seemed like my best option,' I told him. 'I think that's what was meant to happen.'

Dad's a very clever man. He knew what I was saying to him, not least because of the timing of my call. The line was silent for a few moments, and then he said, 'When your mother was alive, I became rather used to telling her, "Primavera knows best." I've always believed it too. What are you going to do now?'

'Come home, if I may.'

Two days later, I flew back to Vancouver as Jan More. I burned her passport, very casually, in an open fire in the Sandbar restaurant, and continued my journey as Primavera Eagle Phillips. I kept the Blackstone passport, but I didn't want to use the name at that point. Dad met me at Glasgow Airport.

On the way back to Auchterarder, I told him the story I've just told you, and much more too; I told him the truth about all of my life with and around Oz. He's a very slow driver, yet I had only just finished by the time we arrived at the great false-Gothic pile that is Semple House.

He dealt with the Dawn situation, thoughtfully and very well: instead of speaking to her, he called Miles, who was in the US at the time, and told him what had happened. Two hours later my sister phoned back; by that time she had calmed down and didn't give me too much grief over the pain I had caused them. Miles handled the inevitable American aftermath of my reappearance; he's a powerful guy, with political contacts, and so all I had to do was sign an affidavit, describing what had happened and saying that I had left the scene in a state of shock, a statement close enough to the truth for me to live with.

My reconciliation with Tom was down to me alone; that was less than plain sailing. The newly widowed Susie went ballistic when I called her at her home beside Loch Lomond. I wondered why her reaction was so extreme until, later, she told me that Oz had been so completely shattered by my disappearance that he had barely spoken to her for the last few months of his life. I could guess why that was, but I didn't tell her, not then at any rate.

'I suppose you want to see Tom,' she said, eventually.

'I want more than that, Susie,' I told her, as gently as I could. 'He's my son.'

As I spoke, I had visions of an expensive legal battle. But Susie's a good person, through and through, better than I've ever been, and she's a mother too. 'Come and see him,' she replied, 'and let's take it from there.'

We did. A month later legal custody passed to me, with the proviso that Tom would always be able to visit his half-siblings, Janet and Jonathan. He moved into Semple House with Dad and me, while I considered where our permanent home would be.

The choice, when I made it, surprised even me.

Early in our travels together, when we had only just started on the road to badness, Oz and I, *nouveaux riches*, pitched up by chance in a tiny village called St Martí d'Empúries, just along from the town of L'Escala, a fishing village that's become a family holiday resort. St Martí goes back to the Greeks and Romans, and maybe even before them. It's like a snapshot of history, and yet it has moved easily into the twenty-first century, catering for northern European tourists in summer and for Spanish weekenders and expats in winter. We were happy there, until he left me. After that I stayed on for a bit, content on my own, until he reappeared and took me back to Scotland. Of all the places I've ever been, St Martí is where I've been most at peace with myself.

I took Tom out there for a week, in early summer, before the place got too busy; Mrs Blackstone and her son, as we will always be from now on. He wasn't quite five then, so I had no school problems in Perthshire. We stayed in a hotel near the village; it opens on to a beach and Tom thought that it was paradise. My friends in St Martí remembered me . . . they never forget a face . . . and welcomed me back. After a couple of days I asked a few of them if anything was for sale. Property there is never advertised; the word is put about, that's all. Someone told me about the house, that it might be on the market, at the right price, and I bought it, there and then.

That's a couple of years ago now. Tom's turned seven and he goes to the local primary school; we speak English at home, but with his pals he speaks Catalan, Castellano or both, and he's retained the French that he picked up when he was in Monaco with Oz and Susie.

He couldn't be happier, and neither could I . . . even after all that bloody drama with Frank!

Two

Frank? Of course, you haven't heard of him before. He wasn't part of my back story with Oz. He'd dropped out of my life five years before the two of us ever met . . . not that he'd ever really been in it, not in any meaningful way.

Frances Ulverscroft McGowan was my cousin, the product of a fleeting union between my mum's older sister Adrienne and a Japanese deep-sea trawlerman named Kotaro whom she met on a winter holiday in Las Palmas. By the time she discovered that she was pregnant, at the age of thirty-six, she was back in London, at the helm of her successful literary agency, and the unfortunate mariner was at the bottom of the Atlantic, his vessel having foundered in a tropical storm. (Or so the story went: Auntie Ade has always been seen as a tiger in business, but in her younger days she liked drink and men, in no particular order. I wouldn't put it past her to have made up the sailor's name after the event, having neglected to ask for it before.)

So baby Frances was born without a dad. I didn't make a mistake there, by the way: his name is indeed spelled in the girlie manner, his birth having been registered by Auntie Ade's then secretary, a dimwit who paid for the howler with her job. That's why he was called Frank from the cradle. He grew up without even a surrogate father, my aunt being a firm believer in short-term relationships, sometimes as short as two or three hours. He was seven years younger than me, a lot when you're a kid. I remember being mildly excited when Mum told Dawn and me about his birth, but he was a messy three year old when Auntie Ade finally brought him to Auchterarder for the official viewing, and so he registered with the pair of us as little more than the sticky thing on the kitchen floor.

After that introduction we all got on with our growing for a few more years, until eleven-year-old Frank was sent north for a summer holiday. I was eighteen by then, just finished school and getting myself ready to embark on my nursing degree, so the job of looking after our cousin fell mostly to my younger sister, but I did spend some time with him. With his Asiatic features, he was an attractive boy, small for his age but advanced in other areas, or so I judged from the way I caught him looking at Dawn in off-guard moments. He was polite, but self-confident and glib-tongued, in the way that prep-school children can be.

I didn't see him again for another seven years, when I stopped off in London to spend a few days with my aunt, before beginning a contract as a theatre sister at a hospital in Dubai. This time Frank was the one putting his schooldays behind him ... and how. He hadn't stretched that much, being no taller than me, but his self-assurance had been boosted by a clutch of A levels, enough to win him entry to Cambridge to study economics. He had become a charismatic lad, and when he flashed me one of the looks he had given Dawn in his prepubescent days . . . let's just say it was my turn to be caught off guard.

There was something underlying it, though, something about him that I didn't like. I couldn't put my finger on it at the time, but when the trouble erupted, I might have professed shock to my parents, but I can't say I was surprised.

When it happened, Frank was twenty-six. I was in Glasgow with Oz, helping him get over Jan's death as best I could and working in the investigations business we had set up together. His court case wasn't hot news, but it made headlines big enough to embarrass Auntie Ade and my mum. Dad never said anything about it, but he keeps his own counsel most of the time.

Essentially, my cousin's own ego tripped him up. He had come out of Cambridge with a good degree, a two-one, had done a couple of years as a political researcher in the House of Commons, then schmoozed himself into a job in a merchant bank. From what the papers said, backed up by the account Mum had from Auntie Ade, he had done a Nick Leeson; in other words he had traded without authority in high-risk markets. But unlike Leeson, he had been consistently successful.

So why hadn't the bank regarded him as a hero, rather than a criminal? Simple answer: he had diverted a proportion of the profits he had generated into a personal account. When his unorthodoxy was discovered he had claimed that he had been risking his own money as well as the bank's, drawing what he called 'advances on salary and bonuses' totalling just over eighty thousand pounds to fund his own short-term investments. Unfortunately for Frank, just as no senior officer had given his trading the okay, neither had anyone approved the advances. The bank, its auditors, the police, the Crown Prosecution Service, and ultimately twelve jurors all agreed that they had in fact been theft.

He might have got off with just the sack, and no prosecution, if he had coughed up all the money he had made before the police were brought in. The bank wasn't thrilled about the publicity that prosecution was going to bring. But he wouldn't: all he ever returned were the so-called advances, arguing that however he had come by his stake, the profits he had generated with it had been the result of his skill and, as such, were his. By that time they were also well hidden, in an untraceable offshore account.

He was sentenced to nine years, much more than Leeson's six and a half, as a salutary example to other City slickers, I suppose. I felt a little sorry for him when I heard that, as the bank had made much more from his trading than the amount of the 'advances' for which he went to jail. The Parole Board may have had some sympathy too, for they sprang him after only five.

If anyone held a coming-out party for him I wasn't invited, not least because I'd just emerged myself from a short spell as a guest of the Mountbatten-Windsor Hotel Group, the fall-out from an ill-judged plot against Oz. (I must stop talking about him, or you'll get the impression that I still love him, that I remember every moment of the last night we spent together, in the Algonquin Hotel in New York, and that there hasn't been a day since he died when I haven't shed a mental tear for him. And I wouldn't want you to get that impression.)

It's not something I'm proud of, and nobody in my family will ever broadcast the fact that we had two members in the nick at the same time, but looking back I see that time as the start of the healing process that brought me to where I am today. I wasn't thinking about Frank at that time, even though his mother was the only person who came to visit me in HM Prison, Cornton Vale. I'd forbidden my dad and my sister to come near the place, but I hadn't thought to extend the ban to Auntie Ade, whom I hadn't seen in years until my mum's funeral a few months before. I held myself together pretty well in jail, but when she turned up I did lose it for a few minutes. We didn't talk about my cousin at all; she didn't mention him and I didn't ask, being much too wrapped up in my own situation to be bothered about someone I barely knew.

Not long afterwards, I was out and getting on with my life, with every intention of being a fit and proper mother to my son, even if his father (I'm getting better: I didn't mention his name) had obtained legal custody during my enforced absence. It wasn't that easy, though: before long I found myself caught up in the fateful last adventure that led to New York, to that night in the Algonquin and, two days later, to my 'death'.

Three

There's one problem about an earthly paradise. After a year or two, it can become a little stale, a little . . . what's the word? . . . yes, a little boring. (I suspect that's also true about the Other Side, but I'm in no hurry to check it out, not least because I doubt that my CV would get me past the first interview. As Jim Steinman wrote, and Meat Loaf sang, beautifully, 'Heaven Can Wait'.)

When we moved here Tom was in the process of becoming five, and looking after him was more or less a full-time job, but once he had started school in L'Escala, things started to change. I had time on my hands during the day, and my recent history indicates that when I'm in that situation I don't always fill the hours as constructively as I might. That doesn't mean I drink too much: if I over-indulge in anything, these days, it's coffee. No, my tendency has been to get myself engrossed in projects, wild schemes that usually lead to disaster.

At first, my intentions were pretty good. I enrolled on distance courses in Spanish and Catalan, so that I could keep up with my son's developing language skills, but I found pretty quickly that I had already progressed beyond the stage where they could do me much good. I looked into going back to nursing, part-time, and went so far as to enquire about job vacancies at the local primary-care clinic, but I bottled out when I saw a section on the application form that required me to declare criminal convictions. I thought about starting an estate agency, until I looked at a copy of the local *Yellow Pages* and found that there were almost fifty such businesses operating already in that one small town. I did a few afternoon waitress shifts in one of the four restaurants in the village, but that came to an abrupt end when a fat tourist groped me as I walked past his table and I buried a paella, still in its pan, in his face. (He shouted something from the floor, in French, about suing, until the proprietor called his bluff, and the police, and he legged it.)

My problem, all that time, was a lack of motivation. I have enough money invested to afford my son and myself a very nice lifestyle, without ever needing to work again, and the apartment I sold in London more than paid for the house in St Martí. Looking back, I reckon that my efforts to fill my days fruitfully owed more to my Scottish Protestant (I'm not discriminating here, I just happen to have been born one, so don't get on my case, okay?) work ethic than anything else. So, after a while, I settled for my new life as a home-maker, and a full-time mum.

The house was spotless. I didn't have the heart to lay off the cleaner, but everything she did I did over again as soon as she'd gone, and a bit more besides. The rest of my time was spent exercising (swimming in the sea, or running on the country roads), reading, and messing about on my computer. That was when Tom was in school; when he was home I concentrated on giving him the best time I possibly could. He got a bike; so did I. He asked for a PlayStation for Christmas; now I'm a gamester too. Soon we added a dog to the family: my son assured me that we were the only household in the village without one . . . a distinction that was okay by me . . . and kept on raising the subject, until I raised a hand in surrender. His name is Charlie, he's a golden Labrador retriever and he is, I swear, the only dog I've ever known with the ability to frown when he's puzzled about something, which, being essentially thick, he is quite often.

The one thing I did not go looking for was a man. Tom's a good boy in many ways, not least in that he doesn't talk much about his father. Whatever his current level of understanding about death, he knows that he's not coming back, and he's come to terms with it. I'm sure he was helped by the fact that Oz was only in his life for around a year, but still, he keeps his picture by the side of his bed, and that's nice. I don't know if he's waiting for me to fill the vacancy, but if he is, I'm afraid I'm going to have to let him down on that one. Two people, one dog: that's our family and that's how it's going to stay. Sex? Twice in all that time, and the first time barely counted. Emotionally, I still haven't left the Algonquin; maybe I never will.

Unlike my auntie Ade; she's spent her life moving from one ship in the night to another. She passed the seventy mark a couple of years ago, and yet she insisted that the fancy still took her until she hit that number. It may have been all in her mind, but somehow I doubt it.

Her phone call, six months ago now, took me by surprise, and her announcement even more so. My son answered, when it rang: most of the calls we receive are for him. He keeps nagging me about a mobile, but I don't reckon he's quite ready for that yet. After a few seconds he switched to English. 'Yes, this is Tom. Yes, Mum's in.' He passed me the handset with the Catalan raised eyebrows and the shrug he's picked up at school. The boy's going native.

'Primavera,' the voice at the other end boomed.

'Yes?' I replied, tentatively.

'For Christ's sake, niece!'

'Auntie Ade? Is that you?'

'Unless your mother had another sister I've never heard of, it bloody well has to be, does it not?'

'It's great to hear from you,' I told her, meaning it at the time. 'How are you?' I paused, as a small spasm of dread gripped my stomach. 'This isn't bad news, is it?'

'That depends on you. Does that house of yours have a spare room?'

'Three, actually.'

'That's good. I'm coming to visit. That okay?'

'Of course it is. Where's the fair?'

'What bloody fire?'

'I said "fair", Adrienne, as in book fair. Barcelona, is it?'

As I understood it, since the Las Palmas adventure that had

led to Frank's arrival, every trip she had made outside London had been work related, to book fairs in Germany, Australia, Prague and the US.

'This isn't business, girl. I'm going into semi-retirement, and I plan to celebrate by coming to visit my niece and great-nephew for a few days. At my age, I can't afford to ignore any members of my family any longer. I got your number from your father: he said you'd be pleased to hear from me. Bugger didn't give me your address, though, just in case.'

Good for Dad, I thought. 'It's all right, really. When are you coming?'

'In a couple of days, I thought. How do I get there?'

'Find yourself a peanut flight from London to Girona. Let me know the date and number and I'll pick you up.'

'I don't do cheap flights, dear. I always travel business class.'

'Not to Girona you don't. But don't worry: at this time of year and with that sort of notice it won't be all that cheap.'

Auntie Ade sighed. 'If I must, I must. I'll have my PA book for me, and give you the details. Will it be hot?' she asked.

'Don't pack the mink,' I told her. Adrienne had turned up at my mum's funeral dressed all in black, and encased in a fur coat that she made a point of telling me was 'Wild, dear, not ranch. As with salmon, the farmed variety just isn't the same.'

'That sounds promising,' she said. 'I look forward to seeing you. By the way, what strange tongue did young Tom speak just now?'

'Catalan.'

'Ah, that explains why I didn't understand a bloody word of

it. There's no market for book translations in anything other than Castilian Spanish. Can he read and write?'

'In four languages.' Actually he's not very literate in French, but I wasn't going to tell her that.

'Bloody hell, that's as many as me.'

We said our farewells and I tossed the phone back to Tom, to replace in its cradle. 'We're having a visitor,' I announced. 'Your great-aunt.'

'Is she as great as Auntie Dawn and Uncle Miles?'

'In her own special way.'

'She sounded funny.'

'She's all that.' He frowned. 'You don't mind if she comes to stay, do you, Tom?'

He shook his head vigorously. 'No, I don't mind. I like it when we have visitors. I liked it when Grandpa Phillips came to see us, and Auntie Ellie and Uncle Harvey, and Auntie Dawn.' My dad had come to Spain twice in the time we had been there, and Dawn once. Oz's sister and brother-in-law had called in too, on the way to a legal convention in Barcelona, to see Tom, of course, not me.

I looked at him, suddenly concerned. Had I missed something? Had I screwed up his young life by uprooting him from the rest of his family and bringing him to yet another country, the fifth in his short life? 'Tom,' I asked him nervously, 'if you didn't like it here you would tell me, wouldn't you?'

'I love it here, Mum,' he replied, without a pause for thought. 'I like visitors because when we have them you're never sad.'

I stifled a gasp. 'Tom, I'm not sad.'

'But you're lonely. You don't have anyone.'

He'd made me want to cry. 'Son,' I told him, 'I'm not lonely. I have you, and I promise you, you're all the company I'll ever need.'

Four

Those expats who have lived in St Martí and L'Escala for a while tell me that there was a time when Girona Airport handled nothing but charter flights and closed in the winter. That was before a low-cost airline decided to establish its northern Spanish hub there; now it handles scheduled services to upwards of forty destinations.

Four aircraft seemed to have landed in quick succession on the Saturday afternoon that Tom and I went to collect Auntie Ade, rather a lot for the chuckers . . . sorry, baggage-handlers . . . to work their steady way through, and so we had to wait for almost an hour before she strode out of the hall. She was wearing white cut-off pants and a T-shirt that declared 'Happy to be here', and was pushing a four-wheeled case big enough to make me wish I'd pinned her down on her definition of 'a few days'.

I should tell you right now that I don't recall Adrienne ever looking her age, except maybe one time. She's tall, about five ten in her heels, and her hair has always been shoulder length, and dyed a shade of auburn that verges upon red. She drew a few glances from other unofficial taxi-drivers and from a couple of security guards as she spotted us, and headed our way.

'Darling,' she exclaimed, reaching out to hug me. 'I thought I was going to melt in there. I must look bloody frightful.' (Her makeup was immaculate: I could tell that she'd just spent some time in front of the mirror in the baggage-hall toilet.)

She took a step back from me and looked down at Tom. 'My God, Primavera,' she said, 'what a handsome boy.' She wasn't wrong there: the older he gets, the more he looks like his dad, dark haired and blue eyed. For a moment I thought she was going to bend and hug him too, which would have been a wrong move, but instead she reached out a hand for him to shake. 'We haven't really been formally introduced,' she murmured. 'I'm your great-aunt and I'm very pleased to meet you.'

My son is a very open kid. He hasn't developed one of the less-endearing male traits, the charm button that can be switched on and off at a second's notice. I hope he never does: right now you can look into his eyes and know exactly what he's thinking, and I pray that nothing ever happens to change the fundamental honesty with which he's been blessed. I hadn't been sure how he'd react to our visitor, but when he took Adrienne's hand, said, 'Hello,' then gave her a smile that turned into an awkward laugh, I knew she'd cracked it with him.

He took charge of her case as I led the way out of the terminal into the heat of the late-June day. At first Adrienne thought it might be too bulky for him, but he's tall for his age, over one metre thirty already, and strong from all the swimming, running and cycling that he does, so he could handle it easily, although I had to give him a little help to lift it on to the back platform of our Jeep. (No, I'm not out to kill the planet. It has low carbon emissions, and it's a necessity where I live. I gave up on the BMW Compact last April after the silencer was ripped off by a tree root that had pushed its way through a badly laid black-topped road.)

'This is nice,' said my aunt, as she slid into the back seat. 'I haven't had a car myself for twenty-five years. There's no point in London any more, especially not since that awful man became mayor.'

'It suits us,' I told her, as we headed out of the airport car park, towards the northbound N11. 'The roads can be a bit rough in the smaller towns and villages, plus it takes us up into the mountains whenever we feel like it. We can do that while you're here, if you like. It's a bit cooler up there.'

'Heat doesn't bother me, dear, the opposite, in fact. Are you far from the beach?'

'The house backs on to it.'

'You two must do a fair bit of sunbathing, from the colour of you both. Do you, Tom?'

He looked back at her. 'Mum does, sometimes. I don't. It's boring: I like swimming.'

'Are you a good swimmer?'

'I suppose so.'

'He is,' I chipped in. 'I taught him when he was a toddler.

He's always swum, in the sea and in the town swimming-pool, and with his brother and sister when he's with them.'

'Does he see much of Oz's other family?'

'Janet and Jonathan,' said Tom, firmly, giving them their names. He's very proud of them, and protective.

'Oh, yes,' I added. 'I've promised him that he can go on holiday with them in August. They've been to stay with us, too.'

'But not . . .'

I guessed what she was about to say. 'Their mother? No, not for any more than a night at a time. She brings them, then leaves them, and it's the same with me when Tom goes to them. Susie and I are on friendly terms, but you know what they say about two women in one kitchen.' There was more to it than that, too many memories, too much shared pain, but I didn't want to get into it with my son in earshot.

'One woman in one kitchen is too many as far as I'm concerned.' Adrienne laughed. 'I'm a stranger to cooking.'

'My mother did tell me as much,' I admitted. 'But surely, when you were bringing up Frank . . .' I knew at once that I'd said the wrong thing. There was a tightening of the mouth, a tensing of the eyes behind the shades. It only lasted for a second or so, but in that time she looked close to her real age. '. . . but maybe not,' I added quickly, and as lightly as I could. 'I have to admit that Tom and I eat out as often as not, especially in the summer when all the restaurants in St Martí are open for business, and all the beach bars. Isn't that right, son?'

'Yes,' he said. 'But I like it when it's just us.'

'What's that over there?' Adrienne asked suddenly, pointing at a castellated building on the top of a distant hill.

'It's a castle,' Tom told her. 'There's lots of them here, even more than in Scotland.'

The rest of the drive home was taken up by my aunt quizzing my son about the local landmarks. His answers usually consisted of two words, 'Another castle,' until we passed the first of the roadside prostitutes, and Adrienne asked, innocently, I have no doubt, why she was standing there, in the heat, well away from the nearest village. I sighed with relief when he replied, 'She's waiting for a bus.' He and I had had that conversation a year before, but I couldn't be sure that one of his little friends hadn't put him right since then. Before long he's bound to ask me why no men ever wait there for buses.

Our garage lies below the house, and its entrance is actually outside the village itself, off the narrow road that runs above the beach. I guess that, in the past, it was a cellar or a stable. It has an automatic opener, and I drove straight in. Tom cancelled the alarm, led the way up the internal staircase, and set out to give his new aunt a tour of the house, as I lugged her case behind them. He finished by taking her out into the front garden to introduce her to Charlie, left dozing in his kennel while we had gone to the airport.

I had given our guest a room on the first floor, with access to another terrace from which she had her first proper sight of the village, and of the summer people in the square.

'This is beautiful,' she said, 'remarkable. You should write,

Primavera,' she declared. 'The ambience is perfect for a creative person.'

'I'll pass on that, Adrienne.' I laughed . . . although I've changed my mind since then. 'All my stories are staying locked up in my head. Come on. If you like, I'll show you the beach.'

'Please do, dear.'

I went to my room and changed into a bikini. My aunt took a little longer, but when she emerged she was similarly dressed, with a diaphanous garment wrapped around her. Tom had gone on ahead, saying that he had arranged to meet some French kids down below. We left by the front door this time, after refilling Charlie's water-bowl (dogs are barred from the beach in the summer), walking past the church and the old, restored foresters' house, then down the sharp slope that leads to the sand.

I have a deal with the nearest beach bar, a season ticket of sorts that lets me have all the sun-bed and parasol time I need. I grabbed a couple of loungers and hauled them over to an available sunshade. Almost before I knew it, Adrienne had lost the drape, stretched herself out and whipped off her top.

'Bloody hell,' I heard myself murmur. I'm rather proud of mine, but I don't expect them to look like that in thirty years.

She smiled as she caught my glance. 'Silicon, dear, the finest silicon, not those awful water-filled things.' She tapped her perfect teeth. 'Crowns, all of them; steel-bonded porcelain set on gold posts. Nature needs some help from time to time,' she said. 'If one can afford it, why not?'

Five

Tom rejoined us at seven o'clock, his cut-off time for reporting back to Mum. (When he gets to be eight, it'll be eight o'clock, when he's nine it'll be nine, when he's ten . . . we'll see.) In fact he had never been out of my sight, since he had spent his time swimming with his friends on the guarded beach, playing a slightly over-ambitious game of volleyball, and tidying up empties around the cabin bar, a labour of love for which he and his mates are rewarded with the odd free soft drink. Tom never goes off on his own: he's a gregarious boy, and when he's not with me he's with friends. He always tells me where he's going, and if it's too far for him to cycle, or involves the public roads, I take him there and pick him up. We may have a relaxed lifestyle, but I'm a responsible mother, and nowhere near the soft touch for him that some people may believe I am.

We let Adrienne decide where she wanted to eat, and what. From the options we laid out she chose a takeaway paella (I always leave those to the experts) from Mesón del Conde, to be eaten on the east-facing top-floor terrace that's accessed from my bedroom. That suited me, since all the restaurants are jammed on Saturdays in the summer and also since there was stuff I wanted to ask her.

I didn't get round to it, though, until after ten, when Tom had gone off to bed with Charlie, and his new friend Harry Potter (I plan to allow him only one a year: I reckon that the later books are a bit too dark for pre-teen kids), leaving us old folks in the candlelight, looking out across the bay and starting on our second bottle of Palacio de Bornos, from El Celler Petit, our local wine shop.

'So,' I began, settling down into my chair, 'what's this crap about semi-retirement? You don't look ill. Are you?'

'Of course not.' Adrienne snorted. 'Why shouldn't I ease off? I've passed the age I will not mention, Primavera. Am I not entitled to enjoy my golden years?'

'Yes, but last time we met you told me you were fit as a tick and that you'd die in harness. It's not in your nature to ease off. You and my mother may have lived your lives in very different ways, but you're cut from the same genetic cloth. She worked until she died. If she'd gone on till she was ninety it wouldn't have been any different. She couldn't do inactive. She wrote six days a week, then dragged my dad down to church every Sunday, but it was to fill her spare day, rather than to commune with her Maker. What do you do at the weekends, Auntie?'

'I review my clients' royalty statements, and I catch up on some other book-keeping. But I go out a lot, to Tate Modern, for example. And I'm a regular at the NFT,' she added, proudly but a little defiantly also.

'Exactly. You aren't capable of sitting on your arse and doing nothing, any more than Mum was, any more than I am, if I'm honest. So what's behind this sudden and irrational decision?'

'I have an assistant in the agency, Fanette. You remember her: you met her last time you came to see me in London. I felt it was time to give her more responsibility, with a view to her taking over from me completely.'

I laughed as I topped up her glass. 'Adrienne, she must be pushing fifty-five by now. She'll be ready to retire before you are. Come on, straight answer. I'm my mother's daughter: you couldn't bullshit her, and it won't work with me either.'

She frowned as she looked across the wide bay, at the lights of Santa Margarita. 'It seems that it won't,' she murmured. Her eyes snapped back towards me. 'I had decided that I wasn't going to broach the subject, you know; after this afternoon, after seeing what a nice life you have now, I realise I have no business interrupting it.'

'With what?'

'A mad idea I had. But forget it: it's quite inappropriate. Your father would go berserk if he knew I had even thought about it.'

I chuckled again. 'Dad doesn't do berserk. Dad does "Primavera knows best", meaning that if your idea is that crazy I'll be the first to tell you. So out with it.'

'If you insist. It's Frank.'

Why hadn't I guessed that? I should have known from the off that the only person in the world who could divert Auntie

Ade's attention from her agency and her clients was her precious wayward son.

'What about him?' I asked, trying to stay casual. 'He's not in trouble again, is he?'

'I don't know. The fact is, Primavera, I don't even know where he is.'

'Is that unusual? I mean,' I added hurriedly, as I saw her eyebrows start to knit, 'does Frank always make a point of letting you know where he is?'

'Yes, he does,' she said, mollified. 'He always keeps in touch.'

'How?'

'Mostly by email: he says he has a lap-top and that he's on-line virtually all the time. We live in a virtual world now, my dear.'

'But when did you see him last?'

She thought about her answer. 'Fifteen months ago, on the first anniversary of the day that I reached the age I never mention. I thought I'd got away without anyone twigging I was a year older, but Frank turned up out of the blue and took me to dinner at the Savoy.'

'And you haven't seen him since then?'

'No.'

'You said "out of the blue". Does that mean he wasn't living in London at the time?'

'He hasn't lived in London since they gave him his passport back, and that was going on for three years ago. When he got out of the pokey he had to report to a probation officer for a year and have a registered address, so he moved in with me. But as soon as he was free to travel, he was off. A pity: when he was with me he got involved with the agency. He did very well: for a while I entertained hopes that he'd come in with me as a partner, but when I made the offer, he told me it wasn't what he wanted to do.'

'And what did he want to do?'

'He was rather vague about that.'

'Where did he go when he moved out?'

'Switzerland. He got a job as a chalet maid in Davos, in an international ski facility called Cinq Pistes.'

'As a what?'

'Chalet maid. I'm not kidding. He filled out an application on the Internet, using his proper name, Frances. The company who owned the resort assumed he was female and took him on.'

'What happened when he turned up?'

'He showed them the name on his passport and pointed out that he had ticked the "M" gender box on the form, so any misunderstanding was theirs. They huffed and puffed, but in the end they agreed that he could give it a try.' She smiled. 'He lasted two weeks as a cleaner: that was how long it took them to work out he was rather over-qualified for the job. They moved him into the office, into the publicity department at first, but within six months he was head of sales and marketing.'

'Is he still there?'

'No. When he took me to the Savoy, he told me he was

being moved to another company within the group. He was to become a director and sales manager of a new hotel and casino complex that's being readied for construction just outside Seville. A few days later, he called me to say he was in post, and to give me his new business address. After that I heard from him, or I got in touch with him, every couple of weeks or so. He told me he was very busy, and kept apologising for never coming to see me. I understood, of course: business has always been my priority too. He sent me flowers at Christmas and on my last birthday. Everything seemed to be going fine, until suddenly . . . it all stopped.' Her voice faltered, and she did her best to bury her face in her wine glass for a few seconds.

I waited for a moment. 'When did you hear from him last?' I asked, when I judged she was ready.

'In the middle of May,' she replied. 'Around six weeks ago. He sent me an email saying he'd be in London on business, and that he'd stay with me for a few days, but he never arrived. I had his room ready, and the fridge stocked with all his favourites, but he didn't show up. I called him and asked where he was, but his phone was on voicemail. I sent him a text, but got no reply. So I sulked.'

'Weren't you worried then?'

'Not really. Frank's never been all that reliable when it comes to keeping dates with his mum.'

'How long did your moody last?'

'About a month. I'd planned to sit it out until he got in touch with me to apologise, but it got too much for me. So I sent him an email, asking how he was, as if nothing had happened. Again, no reply. I texted him and called him, but it was the same. Finally I called the office number he'd given me, and asked to speak to the sales manager. I was put through to a woman. I told her I didn't want to speak to her, but to Frank McGowan.'

'And?'

Adrienne's carefully drawn eyebrows rose. 'And she said, "Who?" I repeated myself. She said, "Who's he?" in a dry way, and in a mid-European accent that I didn't care for. I told her that he was her sales manager and my son, and advised her to mind her tone, to which she told me that she was the sales manager, that her name was Lidia Bromberg, and that she had never heard of any Frank McGowan.'

'So it was bullshit: the big job in Switzerland, the promotion to Spain, it was all crap?'

'No!' my aunt protested. 'It was real. I visited him in Davos. I had a week there, in the resort, as his guest. So was the casino; the number I called was on his business card, plus he sent me some literature on the place.'

'Then he's been fired, Auntie. He's been up to something, he's been caught and they've sacked him.'

'If that's so, why not tell me? Why would that woman deny his very existence?'

I didn't have a snappy answer for that one. 'What have you done about it?' I asked instead.

'Nothing that's worked. I contacted the embassy in Madrid, but they had no knowledge of him. The man I spoke to assured me that if he'd been arrested, or involved in a serious accident, they'd have been informed by the Spanish authorities. He checked with all nine consular offices, and he even contacted the Guardia Civil, to see if they had any unidentified . . .' She paused. 'But there was no one.'

'How about his friends? Lady friends?'

'There was a girl in Davos, Susannah. I met her when I was over there: she was head receptionist at the resort. I called her. She told me that they kept in touch after Frank moved to Spain, but there was nothing between them any more. She'd had a Christmas card from him, but nothing since. She did say she thought he was involved with someone else, but she couldn't give me a name.'

'How about London? Anyone there?'

'Not many. His business colleagues dropped him when the trouble arose, and so did most of his school chums. There are still one or two, though, people who stayed loyal. Justin's the closest, Justin Mayfield. He and Frank worked in the House of Commons, in the dying days of the last Tory government. They were both researchers: Frank worked for a junior minister and Justin was with an opposition back-bencher.'

'What does he do now?'

'He's a junior minister himself; number two in the Culture department. He's been an MP for seven years. I called him, of course; his assistant said he was busy, and that he would get back to me. He hasn't though; not yet, at any rate.'

Some long-buried instincts started to murmur within me. I pushed myself out of my chair. 'Let's get this right, Adrienne,' I said. 'You're telling me that Frank's vanished into thin air, and that the company he was supposed to be working for has denied all knowledge of him.'

'That sums it up.'

'What about the bird in Davos, Susannah? If she and Frank had a thing going, she must be concerned too. Can't you get more out of her?'

'Maybe. I don't know.'

'Then it's time you spoke to her again. And it's time you rattled the man Justin's cage again. If he's Frank's closest friend, it's time he was told about the situation, if nothing else. As a government minister he'll have clout.'

And then a thought struck me, like a car I hadn't seen coming. I found myself grinning at her. 'But that's why you're here, isn't it?' I exclaimed. 'You want me to find him for you.'

'No, no, no.' She shook her head, but not quite emphatically enough. 'How could you do that, really? You have Tom, you have a dog. Your hands are quite full enough, Primavera.'

'I have a computer with a broadband Internet connection.'

'So have I, but even today, there are limits to what the web can achieve. I need a hands-on approach.' She sighed heavily. 'And, yes, I admit that when I decided to visit you, I did have in mind the fact that you and Tom's father ran an investigation business a few years ago, before all the later stuff happened to you. But now that I've seen how you live, I can't possibly expect . . .'

'No, you can't, Adrienne.' I picked up my glass from the table and took a sip of sauvignon blanc. It was warm, so I refreshed it from the bottle in the ice bucket. As I leaned against the terrace rail, ostensibly looking down at my aunt, I found myself seeing other things, scenes from times past, from affairs that might have been described as adventures, with a tall figure by my side, one whose smile and good looks were a match for a much darker persona. Old thrills, old dangers, all in the past. Compared to which, asking a few questions about my crooked, probably recidivist cousin . . . 'But now that we've established that,' I continued, 'if you were able to look after Tom and Charlie for a few days, I suppose I could catch a flight down to Sevilla.'

She stayed poker faced: I made a mental note never to play cards with her. 'I couldn't possibly allow that, Prim . . .'

There were men out on the bay, in boats, fishing for squid. I could see, like fireflies in the night, the bright lights they used to draw their catch to the surface. I grinned at her, aware that she was luring me into her net. 'Cut the crap,' I retorted. 'We both know that you could, and that you will.'

Six

Tom was very good about it, when I told him I had something to do for Aunt Adrienne and that she'd be house-sitting with him and the dog. If he'd been upset in the slightest, I'd have aborted the mission there and then, but he assured me he didn't mind a bit. In truth I was the one with reservations; my son's early years had been a little nomadic, thanks to me, and I didn't want him to form the impression that history might be repeating itself.

Once I was fully committed, mentally, I booked myself a flight on-line, from Barcelona to Sevilla for the next day, Monday: the regular schedules were full, but I found a seat on a budget operation called Clickair. That done, and having despatched Tom and Charlie to give the great-aunt a guided tour of the nearby Greco-Roman ruins of the city of Empúries, I sat down to review the situation.

Ade had given me a small glossy strip of paper with the logo of the Hotel and Casino d'Amuseo, Sevilla, a telephone number and a web address. I turned back to my computer and keyed it into the address bar, then sat back, impressed.

The home page showed a complex that wouldn't have looked out of place on the Las Vegas Strip, with a Y-shaped, ten-storey building sitting on top of what I took to be a vast gaming area, an assumption confirmed when I read the detailed description. A lake guarded the front of the building, while the rear opened out on to an eighteen-hole golf course. It was impressive, but it would have been even more so if it had been a photograph. What I was looking at was all artwork, apart from photography of the Andalucían countryside and the Sierra Nevada.

I scratched my head absent-mindedly as I studied it, feeling myself frown. There was something about the place that I couldn't put my finger on. I thought about my time in Vegas, and as I did it came to me. I was looking at an amalgam, a blend of things I'd seen there; it was as if the architect, or artist, or whoever, had looked at an aerial shot of the place and had nicked pieces from it to form his grand design. Yes, for sure, the lake had been taken straight from the Bellagio, and the golf course from the Wynn. The building itself was more or less identical in shape to the Mirage.

That said, I had to admit that the presentation was first class. Okay, the design might not have been original, but imitation is the sincerest form of whatever, and if you're imitating the best, that's not so daft. Still, I found myself wishing that I'd asked more questions about the people behind Frank's big job. My aunt was no fool, but her son was her blind spot.

The d'Amuseo project might still be at the planning stage,

but one thing did exist: the ski resort where my cousin had worked his way through the ranks, in short order. Its number was there, on a business card of Frank's that Adrienne had given me. I picked up the phone and keyed it in, then paused as two truths struck me: one, it was Sunday, and two, it was July, hardly the time to be calling a winter-sports complex. I almost hung up, but it was ringing so I let it, and was surprised when it was answered.

'Bonjour, Cinq Pistes,' a male voice announced.

'Hello,' I replied. 'I don't suppose Susannah's working today, is she?'

'Susannah Gilpin? I imagine so, but let me try Reception. Who shall I say is calling?'

'Tell her it's Primavera Blackstone, Frank McGowan's cousin.'

'Hold on.'

I held on, for around a minute, listening to the theme from *Ski Sunday*, until a female voice broke in. 'You're for real,' it exclaimed. 'So Frank didn't make you up. He told me he'd two glamorous cousins, that one had been married to a movie star, and the other still was, but he wouldn't tell me any names, so I assumed it was a touch of bullshit, the same as the stuff about the big-name authors he said his mother represents. He wouldn't say who they were either. But if your name's Blackstone . . .'

'That's right,' I confirmed, 'and it's true about his mum as well.' *It's nice to know*, I thought, *that Frank has a little discretion after all.*

'How can I help you?' Susannah Gilpin asked, then paused. 'You're not calling to give me bad news, are you?'

'No, I'm not. You had a call from my aunt a few weeks ago.'

'Yes, that's right. But I can't tell you any more than I told her. I haven't heard from Frank since Christmas.'

'When you had a card.'

'Yes.'

'Did you send one to him?'

'Of course.'

'To the hotel?'

'No, to his home address . . . that's to say, his private post-office box number.'

'His private number? All my aunt has is his business address . . . and come to think of it, that's a box number too.'

'XC2301?'

'That's it.'

'I have that too, but the one I use is XE0142.'

'What's the street address of the complex?'

'I have no idea, Mrs Blackstone. Frank didn't give it to me.'

'But can't you find out through your group? Frank told his mother that he'd been promoted within the organisation.'

'We don't have an organisation; Cinq Pistes doesn't have any subsidiaries, or a parent company for that matter. Forgive me, but I suspect that he didn't have the heart to tell your aunt what really happened. The year before last, at the start of the season, we had a guest at the resort. He was a Lithuanian, and his booking was made by a company in Kaunas. His name was George Macela. He and Frank struck up a friendship straight away. Frank never said as much, but I got the impression from a couple of things he let slip that Macela might have come to Davos to meet him. He used to go off on sales trips during the summer, and that year, one of them was to the Baltic states.'

'Miss Gilpin,' I interrupted, 'can I ask you something personal? How close were you and my cousin?'

'As close as you probably suspect. Nothing too intense, but he's a very attractive little guy.'

'He's all that. Apart from his family connections, did he tell you anything else about his background?'

She gave a soft laugh. 'He never stopped. He made up such wonderful stories. He told me that his father was a Thai pirate who'd kidnapped his mother when she was on holiday in the Far East, and that he'd been hanged for that and other crimes. He told me that he had an economics degree from Cambridge, that he'd worked in your Houses of Parliament. Oh, yes, and he told me that he'd done time for a multi-million-pound investment scam. Is any of that true?'

'The part about the pirate's pure fancy . . . as far as I understand, although I wouldn't put much past my aunt . . . but the rest is pretty much accurate. He was an MP's gofer and the scam wasn't quite that big but, yes, it's mostly true.'

'And what about you? You are the cousin who was married to a movie star, aren't you?'

'Not for long but, yes, I was.'

'He talked about you more than anything else. He said you were a few years older than him and that he'd met you a few times as he was growing up. He told me his mother went to your funeral, only you turned out not to be dead after all.'

'Also true. Did he say anything else about me?'

'Yes. He said there are two people in the world who scare him stiff. His mother's one, and you're the other, because you're so like her.'

Jesus! A cold shiver ran through me. If Adrienne had given me a glimpse into the future, I wasn't sure I fancied it. I made another mental note, to ask Tom if he found me scary, hoping he'd laugh at the very idea.

'Let's go back to the Lithuanian,' I said, cutting that discussion short. 'You thought his meeting with Frank might have been prearranged.'

'Yes. It was pretty clear that they knew each other. Macela spent more time talking with Frank in the bar than he did on the ski slopes. He stayed for five days, two fewer than he'd booked, then checked out. Three days later, Frank was gone also.'

'Just like that? Was he fired?'

'No, he left. We were together in his chalet, the night after Macela left, and he asked me if I would consider going away with him. I said no, I couldn't do that.'

'You didn't fancy him that much?'

'Not enough to leave my husband. It's Madame Gilpin, not Miss. Frank acted as if he was a little disappointed, but he said he understood. A couple of days later, I came into work and the managing director asked me if I knew where he was. His office was cleared, his chalet was cleared, the keys of his company car were lying on his desk, and he was nowhere to be found.'

'He did a moonlight?'

'That's a good way of putting it.'

'Why, for God's sake?'

'That's what I asked him, when he contacted me a couple of weeks later, in an email, using a hotmail address I'd never seen before. His answer was that if he'd told the boss where he was going he'd have been released without notice. There was more to it than that, though. As well as being head receptionist, I'm Cinq Pistes IT manager. Frank had a PC, as all the management-level staff do, but he also has a personal laptop. When I looked at his computer, I found that all his files, all the information he had gathered while working for the company, had been cleaned out. This is a very prestigious resort, Mrs Blackstone. You would not believe some of the clients who have passed through it. Pop stars, presidents, prime ministers, plutocrats, we've had them all; the rich, the famous and the infamous. Frank took all their contact details with him when he left. He transferred them to his lap-top.'

'How do you know?'

'Because when I asked him in my reply to his email, he admitted it. We also have a central terminal where everything is backed up. The copies had been deleted also. When I challenged him about that he owned up to that also; he told me that the data would be useful to him in his new venture. I asked him what that was, and he told me: a huge new complex called Hotel Casino d'Amuseo, just outside Seville, with a satellite ski lodge in the Sierra Nevada. That's why he cleaned out those files, he said: rather that than leave them with a company that was now the opposition.'

I was thinking as she was speaking. 'He actually said that it was his venture?'

'Yes. I asked him about that, and he said that he'd have "significant equity". Those were the words he used. When I asked him if the Lithuanian was involved, he said he couldn't name his associates in an insecure message, but I'm sure he is.'

'Did he ever mention the name Lidia Bromberg?'

'Mmm? No, not that I can recall. But then again, he probably wouldn't. I'm not sure Frank ever gave up on the idea that I might leave Hector and join him.'

'But my aunt said you thought he might be seeing someone else.'

'I said I assumed he was. I'd be surprised if he isn't; I don't see him staying celibate for too long. He's a horny guy.'

'Have you seen him since he left Davos?' I asked.

'Once,' Susannah admitted. 'Last September. I had to go to Paris, on a computer course. I told Frank about it and he met me there.'

'Did he say much about his project?'

'It wasn't at the top of our agenda, Mrs Blackstone. He mentioned it, though. He said that everything was going well and the civic authorities were eating out of their hands.' She hesitated. 'You're really worried about him, aren't you?'

'His mother is,' I confessed. 'I'm worried for her. I don't know my cousin very well, but I do know that he has an eye for trouble.'

Seven

I left all my contact details with Susannah . . . after she'd checked her records for the spelling of 'Macela'. She promised to get in touch with me the moment she heard from Frank . . . or of him, for that matter . . . just as I promised I would keep her informed.

I turned back to my computer. The Hotel Casino d'Amuseo website was still on screen: apart from the description of the project, its menu was short and sweet. There were only four items, the normal 'About Us', 'Our People' and 'Contact Us', plus another 'Investment Opportunities'. I hit the first, and waited as the page loaded.

The Hotel Casino d'Amuseo [*I read silently*] will be the new heartbeat of Andalusian culture, offering the classic mix of twenty-four-hour gambling and high-quality year-round entertainment. Our highlights include

- A state-of-the-art American no-limit gaming hall, featuring roulette, blackjack, craps and slots.

- Two theatres featuring spectacular shows and concert appearances by global entertainment stars.
- A championship golf complex designed by Ryder Cup legend Syd Hoylake.
- An associated ski-lodge in the Sierra Nevada with a private transport link for our winter guests.
- A five-star, two-thousand-bedroom hotel with a hundred opulent suites, and restaurant options to suit all tastes.

Your pleasure is our only concern.

'I'll bet it is,' I murmured, as I clicked on 'Our People', 'but there's more to it than that.'

We are an international team of professionals in the leisure industry, with almost a century of combined experience. Our principals are

- Alastair Rowland, chairman of the board. An internationally renowned hotel impresario, who has led successful ventures in Italy, France and the US.
- George Macela, chief executive officer, with experience of similar ventures in Reno and Florida.
- Lidia Bromberg, director and sales manager.

Doesn't tell you much about the last two, I thought. *Come to think of it, it doesn't tell you much about any of them.*

I switched from the website to a search engine, and keyed in each name in turn. How many hits did I have? None. Not one of these leading professionals in the leisure industry had left a single footprint on the Internet. On the trail of George Macela, I visited sites in Reno and in Florida, where the Seminole Indian tribe have casino interests. The name drew no results on either of them. Then I realised something else: the searches didn't even lead me back to my starting point. The 'new heartbeat of Andalusian culture' had yet to be detected by the worldwide web.

I returned to the d'Amuseo site and clicked on 'Contact Us'. I found no more than the details on the slip that Adrienne had given me: no street address, only the post-office box and telephone numbers. Nothing, except . . .

The phone was a land-line and so it had to be sitting on a desk somewhere. I went back in my mind to the days when Oz and I were in the investigations business, when we were at our happiest and when our lives were at their least complicated, and I recalled finding out then that while reverse telephone directories did exist, they were restricted, and that their use was even illegal in some countries . . . unless you were a cop.

Once upon a time I knew a policeman whose territory took in St Martí d'Empúries. His name was Ramón Fortunato, and I use the past tense deliberately. Like too many men in my past, he wasn't altogether nice, but he did have a sergeant, Alex Guinart, whom I'd met on occasion and whom I do like and trust. He's a sub-inspector now, and since I've been back in town, our paths have crossed: we started by having a beer or two together . . . when he was off duty, since the restaurants don't like people in uniform sitting at their tables . . . and soon I grew close to him, and his new family, his wife Gloria and their baby, Marte. I can turn to Alex for advice when I need it, and I did.

I called him on his mobile: from the background noise I guessed that he was in the small Mossos d'Esquadra station in L'Escala. 'Primavera,' he answered, having read my number as he took the call, 'how goes it?' He and I converse in Catalan. (I don't use English unless I have to; for example, with another Brit. We move to Spain in our thousands, but we're so damn clannish that most of us don't bother to learn the languages.)

'I'm fine, thanks, Alex,' I replied. 'Can you do me a favour? I've got a phone number, and I need to tie an address to it. It's a business in Sevilla that my cousin's involved with, but I only have a *poste restante* address. No problem if you can't do it.'

'For you I can do it. You got me your sister's signed photograph: you're my heroine.' That's true. Alex is a movie fan: he keeps the photo in his office, and makes damn sure that all his colleagues know of my family connection, even if Dawn's career has been on hold since she and Miles had their second kid, Eilidh, a wee sister for Bruce. It does no harm to have every cop in town keeping a special eye on my son.

It didn't take him long. 'The address is Calle Alvarez Quintero forty-seven. I checked the local property register. But it's not a business, it's a residence, right in the city centre, near the town hall. It's listed as belonging to a lady named Benitez.'

Maybe that disclosure should have taken me by surprise, but

it didn't: I was beginning to catch a faint scent of fish. 'Thanks, Alex. Give me a call next time you're heading this way and I'll buy you lunch . . . but not for a few days. I'm off to Sevilla.'

I was frowning as I ended the call. A multi-million-euro rural complex operating from a city-centre house? That didn't sit right with me. I decided to dig a little deeper, and to set up a reason for my visit.

I can hear you asking something. Since I have a friend in the police, why didn't I report Frank as a missing person and leave it to them? Good question. Right now, I wish I had, but then I didn't because, given Frank's record, I was concerned that criminality lay behind his disappearance, and I reckoned that my aunt had suffered enough public embarrassment at his hapless hands.

Instead, I went to the final section of the d'Amuseo website, 'Investment Opportunities', and clicked on it. I was greeted by a short, encouraging statement.

While the bulk of the equity in Hotel Casino d'Amuseo will be held by leading financial institutions, a number of shares in the holding company have been reserved for private investors. In addition to unrivalled growth potential, these carry with them the benefits of discounted rates in the hotel and ski-lodge and membership of the golf club. For further information, contact Lidia Bromberg, director and sales manager.

'Why not?' I said, and dialled the number Alex had checked

out for me. It rang four times, then a solicitous automated voice told me, in Spanish, that my call was being diverted. The sound changed to a double tone, which I heard a further six times until finally, in a lousy accent, '*Sí?*'

'Is that Lidia Bromberg?'

'Yes?' She switched to English; there was a degree of caution in her voice.

'The same Lidia Bromberg who's marketing director of Hotel Casino d'Amuseo?'

'Yes.' Instantly, she sounded more comfortable and more confident. 'And you are?'

'A potential investor in your complex,' I replied. 'My name is Janet More.' The decision to use my previously borrowed identity was made on the spur of the moment. If Frank had let slip the celebrity names in his family when he was in Switzerland, there was a better than even chance he'd done it in Spain.

'What level of investment did you have in mind, Mrs More?' Her accent was definitely not British; if I'd had to name it on the spot I'd have said middle rather than eastern European, German probably.

'It's Ms More, and that's not something I care to discuss over the phone. Let's just say that I have access to substantial funds.'

'Our starter level is around two hundred thousand US.'

'Is that all?' I asked. 'Your club doesn't sound too exclusive.'

'Ah,' she said, a little too quickly, 'but that is only our starter level. Once potential investors take a look at what we have to offer, in terms of benefits and capital growth, invariably they go way above that.'

'And what do you have to offer?'

'A piece of the biggest and most exciting leisure development ever undertaken in Europe.'

'I thought that was Disneyland Paris.'

'Kids' stuff, literally. Let me send you our prospectus. I'll include a share application form because you'll be hooked as soon as you see it.'

'Let me tell you something, dear.' I laid on the Scottish accent. 'I've never bought anything off the page in my life, not so much as a pair of knickers. Your website's full of nice pictures but, with respect, it tells me little more than bugger-all.'

I could almost hear the wheels as the sales pitch was cranked up. 'We don't have anything on the ground yet, Ms More, but I can assure you that the authorities in Sevilla are co-operating with us fully. As of last month, we have all the necessary licences and permissions in place and we'll be ready to begin the construction phase soon.' She paused. 'Of course, once that's under way, the investment opportunities will either dry up or become much more expensive.'

'I told you before; cost isn't an issue, but timing might be. My partner and I have money we need to get invested soon, if you get my drift. The UK isn't an option for us; your operation might be, but I need to see something more attractive than a pile of bullshit.'

My obvious hint at money-laundering didn't faze her in the slightest. 'Then come to Seville,' she invited. 'I'll show you models, I'll show you the ground where the complex will stand, and I'll take you up to the mountains and show you where the ski-lodge will be. I'll even take you to the town hall and introduce you to the people we're working with there.'

'Okay. Now you're saying what I want to hear. I'll be there the day after tomorrow. Where's your office?'

'Let's meet somewhere more interesting than that,' she proposed. 'Let's say the San Fernando Bar, in the Hotel Alfonso Thirteen. Two thirty in the afternoon, yes?'

'Fine.'

'Dress light when you come. It's very hot here at this time of year.'

'I'm used to heat. I've lived in Vegas.' I hung up on her, leaving her pondering, no doubt, about a Scotswoman with a Las Vegas background, a partner and a pot of money that needed investing in a hurry.

That left me with two things to do, before I was ready for my trip. The first was to find a hotel. That was easy: I logged on to a travel site, searched for hotels in Sevilla and found one called Las Casas de los Mercaderes, in Calle Alvarez Quintero itself, and so not far from the house where Lidia Bromberg's land-line phone was located. I booked myself in for three nights, Monday through Wednesday, as Primavera Blackstone, not Jan. I had – still have – an unexpired MasterCard in that name, but the hotel would almost certainly have wanted to see some back-up ID.

My second task took me back to Google, where I entered the name 'George Macela'. I came up with two footballers, nothing more. Another faceless mystery man . . . but maybe not quite.

I called Cinq Pistes again, and was put through to Susannah. 'When your guests check in do you ask for their passports?'

'Of course.'

'By any chance, do you photocopy them?'

'No, but we scan them.'

'Do you still have an image of George Macela's passport?'

'Sure. That's where I checked the spelling of his name.'

'In that case, would you be breaking any Swiss laws if you sent me a copy as an email attachment?'

'Probably, but I'll do it anyway, for Frank's sake.'

I gave her my email address, and four minutes later it hit my in-box. I can't read Lithuanian, but the numbers are the same. George Macela was forty-eight years old, and one metre seventy-four tall. The photo showed a man with an oval face, a sallow complexion and brown hair that was either greying, or so greasy that it had reflected the flash. I opened some software and edited Susannah's scanned image, isolating the picture and blowing it up as much as it would take without losing clarity. When I was done I printed myself half a dozen copies, to go with those of Frank I had done earlier.

At least I knew what one of my potential targets looked like. Maybe some other people in Sevilla would too, once I'd showed them around.

Eight

So there I was, all my meticulous groundwork done, and ready to go in search of my disappeared cousin, ready to step back into some of the excitement of my past life . . . only to discover that I wasn't.

As soon as I heard the front door open, and went through to find Tom fetching an isotonic drink from the fridge for a distinctly frazzled Auntie Ade, who was slumped in one of the kitchen chairs, all my resolve seemed to drain out through the soles of my bare feet. 'Are you all right, Adrienne?' I asked, anxiously.

'Fine,' she replied, unconvincingly. 'Those ruins are more exposed than I realised. I must have become a little dehydrated. I felt a little faint, that's all. Luckily, Tom knew one of the people there, a very nice young man called Jordi. He put us in his van and ran us home.'

'I'm sorry, Mum,' said my son, frowning anxiously. 'I should have taken more water with us.'

I looked down at them. The trip to Sevilla was predicated on Adrienne looking after my seven year old; what I could see at that moment was him looking after her. As I've told you, he's a very sensible, resourceful lad for his age, but . . .

'This won't do, Auntie Ade,' I declared. 'You take Tom for an outing and you come back a basket case. I can't leave you.'

I stalked back to my office, picked up Frank's old Swiss business card and dialled the mobile number, which his mother had told me was still active. I had called it earlier, to find it on voicemail, as Adrienne had said. This time I left a message: you could say it was a little terse. 'Frank,' I began, 'this is your cousin Primavera. I have your mother with me, here in St Martí, worried out of her skull because you've disappeared from your so-called job and aren't answering her calls. If you pick this up, then ring me at once. Otherwise tomorrow I'm on my way down to Sevilla to find you. I have a strong feeling that you're messing her around, you little sod. If you do not stop, then I will personally give you a double orchidectomy, and if you don't know what that means, look it up!' I recited my mobile number, then slammed the phone down.

When I turned, I saw my aunt standing in the doorway. 'What have you just threatened to do to my son?' she asked, with a weak smile.

'Rip his balls off.'

'This may sound unmaternal, but I really hope you have the opportunity to do that soon. I fear you won't, though. I fear . . .' Her voice broke, her shoulders slumped and she started to cry. To say that it took me aback is putting it mildly: in all my life I never saw my mother shed a tear, and her sister's a pea from the same pod.

I held her to me and let her dampen my shoulder for a while. 'I'm sorry, my dear,' she whispered, when she had composed herself.

'What the hell for?'

'For being so soppy, for making a complete tit of myself in front of my nephew at those ruins, but most of all for being so damn presumptuous. It was outrageous of me to ask you to get involved in this. I'll go to Seville myself, and find out what's happened to Frank.'

It was as if her weakness had restored my strength. 'Auntie Ade,' I reminded her, 'you're that number you never use plus two years old, and if the heat gets to you here, it will kill you in Sevilla. My arrangements are made. I'll go, and I'll trust you not to do anything silly. If you do need anything, you can go to any of the people in the restaurants or shops: they're all chums of ours. If something comes up when they're closed, I have a friend called Alex Guinart. He's a police officer, and you can rely on him.'

When she smiled again, the mischief was back. 'A friend, eh. How close?'

'Fairly. I'm godmother to his baby daughter, Marte.'

Nine

I had another blip in my resolve early next morning, when the time came to set out. If I had seen the slightest hint of a wobble in Tom's chin when I told him to be a good boy and to look after his aunt as carefully as he looked after me, I swear I wouldn't have gone.

But he was fine. It was as if he was looking forward to being shot of me for a few days. I backed the still-new Jeep carefully out of the garage, then saw him waving a brief goodbye before he stepped back inside to let me close the door with the remote.

I had been slightly wary of the airline called Clickair, but it was okay. I've never been a fan of on-board catering, so its absence didn't bother me. The aircraft was clean, the flight was on time and that was all I cared about. My sister had asked me recently whether my near-death experience in New Jersey had made me a nervous flier. I told her that the opposite is true. The odds against being involved in a major incident (and that's the bet we all make when the wheels leave the ground) are long enough to make us all feel secure, so the odds against one person being involved in two of them must be astronomical.

The airport in Sevilla is pretty compact for a major city, but I only had cabin baggage so I didn't have to get involved with the carousel. Instead I walked straight out and found a line of taxis waiting. I climbed into the leader. The driver's name was Tony; he made a point of telling me that all the cabs charged a flat fare from the airport to anywhere in the city, and that it was thirty-five euros. There was a notice in his cab that contradicted him by about ten euros on my side of the deal, but he was chatty and friendly as he drove me, through some very narrow streets, right to the door of Hotel Las Casas de los Mercaderes, so I handed over two twenties without a murmur.

I'd picked the place on the basis of its location, not stars, but it was central and pretty well appointed, even if there was a steel pillar in the middle of the room. (A design feature, I hoped, rather than a structural necessity.) I put thoughts of pole dancing to the back of my mind as I unpacked.

It was early afternoon, almost a full twenty-four hours before I was due to meet Lidia Bromberg, and I had a couple of things to do. The first involved a short stroll along the narrow Calle Alvarez Quintero, which was signed 'For pedestrians only', from the hotel on, although local rules seemed to extend that definition to take in cyclists and kids on roller-blades and skateboards. The number forty-seven wasn't hard to find. It was above a double wooden door, painted a dark green. I rapped on it with my knuckles, and heard a hollow sound, but nobody came to answer. I tried the handle, but it was locked: a layer of dust gave me the impression that it wasn't opened all that regularly. I looked, but saw neither bell-push nor knocker. There was a small brass rectangle that might have displayed the occupier's name, but it was empty; no mention of anyone called Benitez. A letter slot was set into the door to the left: I knelt, raised its flap and peered through, into the total darkness of what I assumed was a mail-box.

Undeterred, I glanced around and saw a shop directly across the street, offering the usual tourist stuff that you find in the heart of every city. It was open and devoid of customers so I stepped inside. The man behind the counter was in his forties, not too clean, and with an appearance that was generally . . . well, 'crumpled' is the kindest description that comes to mind. He gave me a bold, curious look, the kind that a certain type of man might direct at a lady, the one that starts at the legs and works its way up.

'I wonder if you can help me,' I began. 'I have an appointment to meet someone this afternoon, and the address I was given is that one over there.' I pointed at the dirty green door. 'But it's locked and it's pretty clear there's nobody in.'

'That doesn't surprise me,' he said. 'That door is always locked when I am here. I guess the people who live there work during the day.'

'So you don't know them?'

'No.'

'That's too bad. Thing is, I've never met the people I'm supposed to see. But I was given photographs.' I took the images of Frank and George Macela from my bag and showed them to him. 'I don't suppose you recognise either of them.'

He looked at them, then shook his head firmly. 'No, I don't.' He paused, then grinned, unexpectedly and lasciviously. 'But don't be too upset. I'm about to close. Maybe you could spend some time with me instead.'

Bloody hell! The guy thought I was a hooker. I said nothing, but stared at him long enough and hard enough for him to realise that he had made a big mistake. 'No,' he said again, a lot less comfortably. 'But I have seen another man go in there once or twice. He never stays long, though.'

'I guess I've been set up.' I sighed. I turned to go, but paused as I opened the door. 'Incidentally,' I told him, 'you couldn't afford five minutes with me.' He called me a rude name as I left.

There was a tapas bar two doors further on, with an empty window table that offered a clear view back towards number forty-seven; I occupied it and ordered coffee, with some croquettes and a little octopus salad. I had no real expectation that Frank might put in an appearance, but I had some thinking to do, and that was as good a place to do it as any.

I was toying with a piece of tentacle when a dark-haired man, dressed in a lightweight cream suit, and carrying a plastic supermarket bag, walked past the window, coming from behind so that his back was always towards me. He stopped, then stepped up to the drab door. I watched him as he unlocked it: he was about to open it when he looked over his shoulder, as if in response to a call. The creep from the shop

72

sidled alongside him. As he spoke, I saw the newcomer's right eyebrow rise, in profile, and then he shrugged. I still couldn't see all of his face, but he was too tall to be Frank and looked about ten years too young to be George Macela.

I was trapped at my table, in clear view if the shop-owning lecher had glanced my way, but he didn't. Instead, the visitor to number forty-seven patted him on the shoulder, as if he was thanking him, then watched as he went on his way in the opposite direction, mission accomplished. I had no doubt that he had been cliping on me. (That's Scottish for 'grassing me up'.)

Left on his own, the newcomer opened the right half of the double door and stepped into the building. I was in a bit of a quandary. I had no idea how long he'd be staying, but if Shopman had described me, and he saw me on the way out, I'd be well exposed, there in my goldfish bowl. On the other hand, I still hadn't seen his face.

I had a sun-hat in my bag. I put it on, and my shades for good measure. There was a newspaper on the table, a *Herald Tribune*, discarded by a previous Anglo customer. I picked it up and gave a fair imitation of reading.

I hadn't got past the first page before he reappeared, closing the door behind him and locking it once more. As he did so I noticed that he was no longer carrying the supermarket bag. He turned, and I had my first clear look at his face: he was cleanshaven, with high cheekbones and dark eyebrows, and a look about him that reminded me faintly of my late ex-husband. He glanced at the tapas bar . . . although not at me . . . and seemed to hesitate in his stride, as if he was considering coming in. I stared intently at the *Herald Tribune*, and breathed a sigh of relief when he carried on his way.

'So who was he?' I wondered softly. 'Which of the mystery men might that have been?'

Ten

As soon as the visitor to number forty-seven was out of sight, I paid my modest bill and went back to the hotel. There was a lounge just behind the reception area; I took a seat there, had another coffee and read another newspaper . . . *El Mundo* this time . . . but I found I couldn't settle, and that I was on edge.

I knew what the problem was, of course. My head was back in St Martí, with my son. I had been gone for just a few hours and I was missing him. That's how it is with Tom and me. That's how it was with his dad and me. Oh, shit, there I go again! Stop it, Primavera!

I decided that the best thing I could do was to keep active. But how? After a couple of minutes spent glancing at a town map, it came to me. Not far from the hotel was a square called Plaza Nueva, and taking up one side of it a building labelled '*ayuntamiento*'; that means 'town hall', in English. Lidia Bromberg had promised to take me there, but it wouldn't do any harm to pay it a visit in advance. Would it? I checked my watch; it was ten to four and odds on they'd be closed, but you never know.

I strode out of the hotel, more in hope than anticipation, map in hand. I followed its directions, round a corner then down a slope. Within two minutes I found myself in Plaza Nueva . . . actually, it was more rectangle than square . . . a paved area with the traditional equestrian statue in the middle, this one on an ornate plinth that was three times the size of the king on the horse, and with big modern sculptures decorating its perimeter.

The town hall was easy to spot: the flags of Spain, Andalusia and Europe flew . . . or, rather, hung limply . . . from three poles set on a balcony above its main entrance. As I approached, I saw that the place was still open, and so I strolled casually inside. There was a dark-haired, late-twenties man behind the reception desk, upon which I spotted a sign that told me his name was Ignacio Gallardo i Blazquez. (Why do Spanish people often use two surnames? First one's Dad's, the second is Mum's. Women don't change their names on marriage.) He was dressed in a grey suit, and he wore a tie, a clear indicator in Spain of a public official: no other bugger wears one. As I approached, I realised I had no idea of what I was going to say to him, and so I settled on the truth.

'I'm trying to find someone,' I began, in my accented Spanish, after we'd exchanged courtesies and he had welcomed me to Sevilla. 'He's my cousin, we've lost touch, and I need to find him because his mother is anxious. He's English, although he doesn't look it, and he's involved with a project in this area: the Hotel Casino d'Amuseo. I'm wondering if he's known here.'

He nodded. 'I've heard of that development,' he told me.

'Could one of your colleagues help me?'

'I'm sure of it.' He glanced up at a wall clock. 'Unfortunately, our planning department is just about to close. Maybe you could come back tomorrow?'

'I suppose.' I frowned, and he took pity on me.

'Look,' he continued, 'everyone who comes into this building has to pass me. Do you have a photograph?'

I found it in my bag, and showed it to him.

He studied it for a few seconds, then nodded. 'Yes, I have seen him here. Mr Urquhart, yes?' He stumbled over the name, but I got his meaning: some Scottish names are impossible for Spanish people to pronounce . . . for that matter, few English people get close.

'That's him.'

'Mr Roy Urquhart.' The second try was no better. 'Yes, he's been here.'

'Recently?'

'No. I haven't seen him for a while.'

'Weeks? Months?'

'Weeks, certainly. Maybe two months.'

'Do you know any other people from the project who come in here?'

He mused for a moment. 'I can't think of any.'

'How about this man?' I showed him the Macela print. 'He's my cousin's colleague.'

'Mr Macela? Yes, he's been here, but not for a while now.'

'Have they visited here often?'

'Yes, but they don't need to any more. They have all the permissions.'

Just as Lidia Bromberg told me they had, I thought. That much was true, at any rate. Maybe I was damning the whole operation out of sheer mistrust of my cousin.

'So they're building?' I probed.

'No, I don't think so. A friend of mine in the licensing section told me they haven't started construction yet, although everything's been approved since May.'

'Maybe they're waiting for their contractor to be ready. Do you know where I can find them?'

'Sorry,' said Ignacio, shaking his head. 'You'll need to ask my colleagues.' He paused, looking towards the main door. 'Ah, too bad,' he exclaimed. 'The co-ordinator of planning, Mr Caballero, would have been able to help you . . . that's him . . . but he looks as if he's in a hurry, and I'm afraid he's too important for me to interrupt. You should come back tomorrow, and ask to speak to him.'

I followed his gaze, and saw a tall, dark-haired man, with high cheekbones, in a lightweight cream suit. *Now there's a coincidence*, I thought.

Eleven

Why was a council planner calling in at a sleeper address for Hotel Casino d'Amuseo? Damn good question, I reckoned, as I wandered idly along the narrow shopping streets off the Plaza, and it was one that I couldn't answer. When it came to it, there was precious little I knew for certain at that point.

But I was learning. Frank McGowan was known locally as Roy Urquhart. That would explain why he hadn't given his mother a business card, but why would he need a false identity? And what about George Macela? Was that his real name, or was it phoney too?

No, the only thing I had established was that the whole project was well thought of in the town hall and that there was nothing to back up my instinctive suspicion. The friendly Ignacio at the town hall had told me they had all the permission they needed to start construction. I'd be interested to hear what Lidia Bromberg had to say about the timetable when we met. I was going to see her as a potential investor. How many others had they drawn into their project and where had their money gone? But should I meet her, or should I call a halt there and then and report my cousin's disappearance, and his use of a false name, to the Guardia Civil?

I suppose that was the first real test of the new Primavera, the one I'd set out to be. Maybe I failed it. Maybe that's exactly what I should have done, report it to the authorities. But I didn't: I decided against it, for reasons I believed were legitimate. For a start, I'd have been shopping Frank, putting my cousin in the frame as a convicted criminal operating in Spain under an alias, and raising large sums of money into the bargain. That didn't bother me of itself, but it would have bothered my aunt, and I had to consider her feelings. The clincher, though, the possibility that stopped me from trotting off to the Guardia Civil, was a real fear that I might be held myself, not as a suspect, but as a witness, and that I might find myself stuck in Sevilla, cut off from my son.

I felt exposed, though, no mistake about that, and just a little bit nervous about my meeting with Lidia Bromberg . . . if that was *her* real name. I've become pretty self-reliant, in all things, over the years, and I've got out of the habit of turning to others, even my dad, for help and advice. That's not to say that I don't have a Mr Fix-it. Miles Grayson, my brother-in-law, is a very influential man. Trouble is, he's also straight as a die and I knew that any advice he gave me would involve the police, and might even be conditional upon it.

And then I thought of Mark.

Back in the old days, Oz had a . . . How best to describe him? Let's call him an associate. His name is Mark Kravitz, and he describes himself as a security consultant. But he's one of the very few consultants I know who doesn't have a website, and if you Google his name the only hits you'll make will be a rock musician and an American judge, neither of whom are related to him in any way.

I paused in my stroll. 'Lady,' a voice called to me.

I turned, to see a café called the Gallego, and a white-shirted waiter beckoning me towards an empty table. *Why not?* I thought. It was hot as the approach roads to hell, and I was beginning to feel parched. I thanked him as I sat down; a badge on his chest told me that his name was Carlos.

'You're not Spanish,' he said. (I'll never pass for one, no matter how fluent I become.) 'English?'

'Not quite,' I told him. 'Try Scottish.'

'Ah, Scotland.' He sighed. 'Football. Rangers, Celtic?'

A thousand years of history, and that's all they know about us, but I went along with it. 'In my case, St Johnstone,' I confessed.

He smiled, then extended his left hand towards me, displaying an embossed signet ring. 'What is that, do you think?'

I peered at the crest: it was familiar, but out of place. 'Barcelona?' I suggested.

He nodded, in a way that told me I had made his day, and made a friend too. 'I am the only Barca supporter in Sevilla. I never speak of it at home. You like some tapas? For you I have a special selection.'

I thanked him, but settled simply for a beer. When it arrived it was full to the brim, with a normal head, not the usual kind they give you, with a layer of foam so deep that a bloke could shave with it. I took a mouthful and went back to my thoughts.

Some years ago, I acquired a PDA, a personal organiser, and it's been one of my best buddies ever since. Among other things it holds just about every phone number I've ever known, including two for Mark Kravitz. I found his mobile and dialled it.

He answered curtly: 'Yes.' His tone was all business, making me guess that he had a second number for personal calls. I realised that I had no idea if he had a personal life or if he was consumed by his round-the clock job.

'Mark, this is Primavera Blackstone. Do you remember me?'

His reply was instantaneous, without a pause for thought. 'Yes, Prim, of course I do. Still alive, I'm glad to hear.' That was as close to a joke as I'd ever heard him come. 'What can I do for you?'

'A favour?'

'I don't normally do those,' he shot back, then continued, 'but just this once, for old times' sake. *In memoriam*, let's say. What is it?'

'I'm on the hunt for a missing person, my cousin, Frank McGowan. Recently he's been in Seville, calling himself Roy Urquhart, and involved with an enterprise called Hotel Casino d'Amuseo; his title was director and sales manager and he was responsible for recruiting investors for the project. He has an associate, George Macela. There are two others involved. They are listed on the company website as Alastair Rowland and Lidia Bromberg.'

'This is the same cousin who did time for illegal dealing?' he asked.

I was taken aback. 'Yes, that's the boy. You must have a hell of a memory for names. That was a while back.'

'Oz called me when he was released. He asked me to make sure that he wasn't going to be a problem for you or Tom.'

Even in the heat of the afternoon, I felt a shiver run through me. 'Did he give you any specific instructions?' I asked.

'He asked me to talk to him, that's all, to make it clear he was very protective of your interests.'

'You mean Tom's?'

'No, both of you; he was quite specific. He was really broken up when you disappeared, Prim. He never really accepted that you were dead. He spent a lot of money having me try to find you,' yes, and I could guess why, 'but I couldn't.' He paused. 'As a matter of professional interest,' he went on, 'where did you go?'

'Las Vegas, via Vancouver.'

He whistled. 'Then you can really trust your Canadian lawyer. I went to see him and he flat out denied any knowledge of you. I asked him what would happen to your investments. He told me that was between him and your son, and Oz, as his legal guardian.'

'And what did Frank say to you when you went to see him?'

'He promised me that he had no intention of going anywhere near you.'

'And if he hadn't?'

'I'd have had to go back to Oz for further instructions.'

'Which you'd have carried out regardless?'

'Absolutely. I loved that guy, Prim; there was something about him. But I don't have to tell you that.'

You surely don't, I thought.

'These people Frank's mixed up with,' he said. 'If they're bent, as you think they are, and he's missing, you'd be as well to stay clear of them.'

'I'm meeting Bromberg tomorrow afternoon, as a potential investor, using the same alias I had in Vegas, Janet More.'

'In that case, I'll check out those names right now and get back to you.'

'Let me give you my number.'

'That's okay: my phone's picked it up. Just make sure yours is charged up. Something else: I'll run another check for you, just in case.'

'On what?'

'Unidentified male stiffs in Spain. Juan Does, you might call them. Frank would be mid-thirties, yes?'

'Yes, five feet seven, with an Asian look to him.'

'I've met him, remember.'

'Of course. I have a photo; I can probably get it to you through my hotel fax.'

'Leave it for now, until I need it to identify him.'

'I'm sure you won't.' As I spoke, I realised that I wasn't nearly as confident as I sounded.

Twelve

It didn't take Mark long; less than an hour in fact. I had only just returned to the hotel when he called me.

'I'll give you the good news first,' he began. 'There is no one answering your cousin's description currently lying in a morgue anywhere on the Iberian peninsula.'

'That's a relief,' I said. If there had been, I wouldn't have fancied telling Auntie Ade.

'But that's all it means. Sorry to be blunt, but if Frank's upset someone badly enough to have been taken out, they may have done a proper job and cleaned up afterwards.'

'And that's the bad news?'

'No, or not all of it. None of the names you gave me is kosher. Yes, there are people who answer to Rowland, Macela and Bromberg, but none of them could possibly be linked to this casino project.'

My original doubts returned. 'Are you telling me that the thing's a phoney?'

'No,' he replied. 'The company behind it is real enough, and that brings me to something significant. It's registered in

Luxembourg and the directors of record are your three friends. However, Lidia Bromberg only joined the board two months ago, following the resignation of Mr Roy Urquhart.'

'Where did you find this?'

'Certain records are public in Luxembourg, up to a point. The office of record of Hotel Casino d'Amuseo SA is hosted by a local corporate law firm called Pintore and Company. They were obliged to give me the information I asked for.'

'Did they say why Frank resigned?'

'That wasn't minuted, but I did find out some other stuff. The authorised share capital of the company is one hundred million euros, one euro per share, and more than three quarters of it is issued, seventy-seven million, two hundred thousand shares to be exact. The directors' personal shareholdings are . . .' He paused, for effect, I guessed. '. . . one hundred shares each.'

'So whose is the seventy-seven mil?'

'The shareholder register will tell us that. Luxembourg law requires that it be kept at the company's offices, but I'd have to turn up there in person to inspect it. One thing looks certain, though: your cousin was very good at his job, until he quit.'

'What do you think's happening, Mark?' I asked.

'The investors may well be about to make a shedload of money. On the other hand, the lack of information on its principals gives cause for concern. If the company is operating under a false prospectus, then the shareholders' funds are going to vanish, and probably pretty soon. They're approaching the date by which they must have an AGM, the end of August. If the plan is to cut and run, they'll do it before then. However, your meeting with Bromberg shows that they're still fund-raising. It's probably legit, but possibly bent. Can't say for certain.'

'If it is crooked, can the money be moved that easily?'

'On the chairman's authority, that's all it takes. His signature, stamped by the company seal. That's what the guy at Pintore told me.'

'We can't let that happen,' I said. 'We should dig a bit deeper.'

'We? Prim, you should back off this. You're only there to look for your cousin.'

'Maybe I should, but it's just become even more personal. It's one thing that my cousin's vanished without trace, but now I find that I have a meeting tomorrow with someone who might be out to steal my money.'

'I can't talk you out of going?'

'No chance.'

'Then make it as useful as you can. See if you can get me a photograph of Bromberg, even if you have to take it with your mobile.'

'Will do. I can give you one of Macela right now, if you like.'

'Do I ever like? How will you do it?'

'I have an image of him on my computer back home. Give me your email address, and I'll call my son and have him send it to you. He's only seven, but he's as computer literate as I am, probably more so.' As he spelled the address out, I patched it into my PDA. 'This is getting beyond a simple favour,' I told him.

'You've got me curious. Plus . . .' he hesitated '. . . maybe Oz had a premonition. I don't know, but when he asked me to find you, he said something else: that if anything happened to him, and you turned up afterwards, I should take care of you.'

I didn't have an answer for that. I was too busy thanking my lucky stars that he had misunderstood the instruction totally.

'Now,' he continued abruptly, 'is that everything?'

'Well, not quite.' I told him about the mysterious address near my hotel and about the city planner's furtive visit.

'Now that doesn't sound too kosher,' he declared. 'It would be good to get inside. There might be an outside chance that Frank's holed up in there . . . or being held.'

'Yes, but how? I can't go back there. The lecher in the shop would spot me for sure.'

'I appreciate that, but maybe I can arrange for someone to kick the door down.'

I was still wondering what he'd meant as I called Tom to ask him to send the image.

It was Adrienne who answered, not him. It took me a while to convince her I wasn't covering up any bad news about her only-born. What I told her was essentially the truth, that he seemed to have resigned from the company at around the time she'd been expecting his visit, and that I was trying to find someone who could tell me where he'd gone. The someone might be the bloke whose photograph I wanted Tom to pass on, or it might be Lidia Bromberg.

She put my boy on the line; he was chuffed when I told him there was something important I wanted him to do for me. He still sounded brave and cheerful, but hidden in there I detected a hint that he might just be missing me. Just as well, for I sure was missing him.

Thirteen

The evening seemed to pass so slowly it made me think back to my time in the nick, when every day dragged. My hotel didn't offer an evening meal, or I'd have settled for room service in front of the telly. The receptionist did recommend a few nearby restaurants, but I didn't fancy sitting at a table for one in a formal setting.

In the end I decided to go back to the Gallego, and my new-found buddy Carlos, the only Barca supporter in town, since the evening was hot and humid, and I didn't want to walk far. When he saw me coming, and caught my nod, he chased away four back-packers, who had been making a beeline for the only available pavement table, and ushered me straight to it. I asked him to use his imagination and bring me a selection of tapas. He did just that, coming back with a tiered arrangement that looked like an old-fashioned cake stand, with a nice bottle of albariño to wash the lot down. I had packed an English-language novel for my trip. It was called *Death's Door*, and as I ate I pretended to read it, as a barrier against intrusions as much as anything else.

That said, I'd probably have been pissed off if nobody had tried to talk to me all night, so when two American guys took over the next table and said, 'Hello,' I didn't blow them out. Their names were Sebastian Loman and Willie Venable, they were around thirty, about the age I was when I stopped being normal, and it didn't take me long to realise that they were travelling as a couple and I was as safe as houses with them. They told me they were from Topeka, Kansas, and preferred to holiday in Europe than in their staunchly Republican home state.

We spent a pleasant evening together; they helped me finish the albariño and I helped them through a jug of beer. They told me their life stories: they were former teachers who had become computer programmers after they found themselves unemployable in modern America because of their sexuality. I gave them a heavily edited version of mine: I said that I was a divorcée with a young son, taking a break for a few days, thanks to my aunt, who was minding child and dog at home. When I revealed where that was, they announced that they were heading north to a resort (they didn't say 'gay' but I was sure that's what they meant) they knew in Catalunya, so I gave them my mobile number and my address, just in case their onward travels took them anywhere near St Martí.

The encounter drew to a natural end around nine thirty. The guys went on their way, towards Plaza Nueva, and I went on mine, back towards the hotel, stopping off at another pavement café for the last coffee of the gently cooling day.

I've always been good at going to sleep: insomnia and I are

strangers. But that night I was afraid we would become acquainted, given the facts that I was away from familiar surroundings for the first time in a few years, and that I had a significant meeting next day, one for which I had no concrete agenda.

Over that final latte I had given some thought to what I might say to Bromberg, how I might handle her, armed as I was with Mark's very useful information about the status and possible purpose of the company she was trying to sell me. There were two ways of playing it, as I saw it. One, I could carry on with my Jan More act, let her hit me with her sales pitch, and ask a few gentle questions, leading up to one about Roy Urquhart, whose 'name was mentioned when I first started looking into this investment opportunity'. Two, I could abandon any subtlety, and tell her exactly who I was and why I was in town, threatening to make a hell of a loud noise unless she told me damn quick what had happened to Frank and where I could find him.

Inevitably, I asked myself, *What would Oz have done?* It didn't take me long to come up with the answer. He'd have kept well out of it. He'd either have commissioned Mark, or he'd have sent Conrad Kent, his aide-cum-bodyguard, to resolve the situation. I was pretty sure that if I asked Mark to do the same for me, he'd take the job on. But I was on the ground, I had my meeting with Bromberg in my diary, and I saw no harm in going through with it, especially as it was to be in such a public place.

Still, as I slipped under a single sheet that was all the

bedcover I needed, I hadn't decided whether I was going to be Ms Gauche, or Ms Blunt. The final choice could probably wait until I saw the woman and could size her up.

I was still wide awake as I returned to *Death's Door*, but I hadn't read two short chapters before my eyes grew heavy and I found myself reading the same paragraph twice. I laid the novel on the bedside table, switched off the light and let myself sink.

Although I find it easy to nod off, that doesn't mean I'd sleep through an earthquake or, in this case, a rush of feet so loud that, in the seconds after I awoke, I thought it was happening right there in my room. I sat upright, eyes wide open, disoriented until I remembered where I was. Heavy boots were slamming on the walkway outside my window, or rather outside the french windows that opened on to a minuscule patio, and which I had left slightly ajar for extra ventilation. As I listened it dawned on me that the noisemakers were heading along Calle Alvarez Quintero in the direction of . . .

It was then that I made a big mistake. As I jumped out of bed, in the dark, heading for the curtained window, I forgot all about the special design feature that was part of my room, the painted metal pole running from floor to ceiling. (Why it was there, I still have no clue.) I remembered its existence as soon as my right big toe slammed into it, followed almost instantaneously by my shoulder.

When Tom's around I try not to swear, but even if he'd been in the room's other bed, I reckon I'd have let go with the same mouthful I did then. I bounced off the wall, then hirpled across to the window. As I did so, I heard a loud, splintering bang from outside. I parted the drapes, opened the twin doors, and was about to lean forward into the street, when I remembered I was buck naked.

By the time I had found the courtesy bathrobe and put it on, the post-midnight runners had gone (I checked my watch; it was just after three a.m.), but I could still hear noise. There was just enough light in the narrow street for me to guess that some of it might be coming from the newly opened door of number forty-seven. 'Bloody hell,' I murmured, 'what did Mark say about getting someone to kick it in?'

I stood there watching for at least ten minutes. For a while I wasn't the only onlooker: there was a guy in an apartment opposite my room, leaning out of a window. He asked me if I knew what had happened, but I didn't want to be involved in a conversation, so I lied and told him in English I didn't understand him.

A couple of minutes after he had drawn himself back in and closed up for the rest of the night, three uniformed cops emerged from the house. Two of them stood at the door, as if on guard, while the other walked back towards me, heading for the entrance to Calle Alvarez Quintero.

'What's the noise about?' I asked him as he passed beneath me. He couldn't have seen me for he almost jumped out of his steel-capped boots, before recovering himself and donning the superior expression that some young police officers adopt before the world teaches them that life isn't Hollywood or *vice versa*.

'Police business,' he said.

'Son,' I told him, feeling a momentary chill as I used the word and realised that I was indeed old enough to be his *madre*, 'when you waken me up in the middle of the night, it becomes my business.'

He looked at me and decided to take me seriously. 'There's a dead man in there,' he said. 'In that building along there.'

'Was he dead when you smashed the door down, or did that happen afterwards?'

He didn't get the irony. 'No, he was dead already,' he replied, straight faced.

'So what made you go there?'

He shrugged. 'All they tell me is we had a call that there was a deal going on there, and that we should get in. But it's a con.'

'What do you mean, a deal?'

'Drugs. That's what my team does.'

'You're telling me that my hotel is next to a drug den?'

'No; that's why I say it's a con. There's no drugs there that we can see, only whisky bottles and maybe some pills . . . and the dead guy.'

'So why's he dead? Was he old? Heart-attack?' I was doing my best to sound casual.

'Heart-attack maybe, but he's not that old. Maybe my father's age.' He smiled up at me, without any idea of the relief I felt. I realised that the bathrobe had loosened, and jerked it tight. 'You should go back to bed, lady,' he advised. 'I have to go, to show the medics where to find us.'

I watched him as he walked away. As he took up position at

the junction, fifty yards away, I glanced back towards the raided house. The two guards were still at the door; both were smoking, and I could hear the faint sound of their conversation, but not its detail. They did not give the impression of men on high alert.

I stepped back inside my room but left the wood-framed doors ajar. As I did so I realised that my right big toe was hurting like hell from its vicious assault on the base of the defenceless pillar. I went into the bathroom, filled the bidet with cold water and bathed my foot for a while, then limped back through and lay on my bed, waiting for the pain to subside. It didn't. It occurred to me that I might have broken the damn digit. If that was the case there was nothing to be done, other than taping it to my second toe as a splint and taking painkillers as necessary. My nursing training has led me always to travel with a basic first-aid kit, so I patched myself up there and then.

I had just finished when I heard two vehicles pull up outside, one after the other. I rolled off the bed, limped carefully past the pole, and peered down into the street. Below, I saw a woman in plain clothes with a great frizzy ponytail that looked in the streetlight as if it might have been red, and two paramedics, one male, one female, pushing a trolley, with an empty stretcher on top. Ponytail carried a bag; it made me think, *Medic*. The young cop was ambling along behind them. He glanced up at my window, but didn't appear to see me.

As they reached the door I saw that the two officers had

become three. The new arrival was older than they were and wore what looked like significant braid on his shoulders. The door guards had stubbed out their cigarettes and were standing to something that might have been attention, so I assumed that he was the brass.

He greeted Ponytail with a handshake and a smile. I heard her call him something that might have been Pablo, but as she had her back to me I couldn't be sure. He led her inside. As soon as they had gone, the male paramedic produced a pack of cigarettes and offered them to the three remaining cops. I watched, unobserved, as all four guys smoked; they chatted quietly among themselves. Suddenly the youngest, my informant, glanced round in my direction, grinning. The phrase 'her right tittie falling out' floated up to me. I must have been leaning further over than I'd thought. Happily, he added, 'It looked like a pretty nice tittie, too.' The night was getting better.

But not for long. After less time than it took to finish the fags, the doctor's head reappeared in the doorway, together with a hand, beckoning. Her team took the stretcher from the trolley and followed her inside.

It took no time at all to load up, and I saw why as soon as they arrived. I've heard it said that the Spanish are less hot on dignity than us Brits. In general terms I don't believe it, but in the middle of that night in Sevilla it was certainly the case. There was no sheet on the body as they rolled it past under my window. They took him out as they had found him, dressed in a shirt that was as grey as his face, and crumpled cream trousers that might have been linen. From the way the body was lying I could tell he had been dead for a few hours, as rigor mortis had set in.

One of his eyes was half open, staring up at the night sky. His face was a couple of days short of a shave, and his greying hair hung lankly. He was middle-aged, northern-European in appearance, and he was the spitting image of one of the pictures that still lay in my bag, that of George Macela, or whoever the hell he really was.

Fourteen

At first I wasn't going to call Mark: it was still the middle of the night and an hour earlier where he was. I had no idea of his domestic situation, but I knew that if he was married with kids, he wouldn't appreciate having them roused.

I lay there, my resolution firm and my toe throbbing, until four o'clock. That was when I picked up my mobile and called his number; I supposed there was a fair chance he'd be switched off and that all I'd be able to do was leave a message. But he wasn't. He picked up after five rings and he sounded just as sharp and business-like as ever.

'Prim,' he said, before I'd had a chance to announce myself. 'Are you okay?'

'I am,' I told him, 'but someone isn't. Did you have anything to do with the Sevilla cops breaking down the door of Calle Alvarez Quintero forty-seven an hour or so back?'

I heard a light chuckle. 'They bought it, did they?' He paused. 'Yes, that was me. I have an associate in Madrid. I had him make an anonymous call.'

'Not only did they buy it, they woke me in the process

of following it up. Did you get that pic of Macela?'

'Yes, I surely did, and it got results. His real name's Hermann Gresch, German, not Lithuanian, with a distinguished past in the fraud business.'

'A past is all he's got now, I'm afraid. I've just seen them carting him out of number forty-seven, stone ginger.'

'Jesus!' Mark shouted. 'Prim, I really must urge you not to go any further with this.'

'It may have been a heart-attack, nothing more sinister than that. They were kind enough to wheel him under my balcony, so I had a good look; there wasn't a mark on him.'

'That means nothing, and you know it. I need to find out how he died, but I don't buy natural causes or misadventure, given the circumstances.'

I was touched by his urgency. 'You've done enough already. Look, I'll meet Bromberg tomorrow, and if she doesn't give me what I need I'll go to the police.'

'Prim,' he countered, 'I'm not leaving you in the middle of this situation. If this is a multi-million-euro scam, as it might be, you could put yourself in danger. You told me you saw a man go into that house this afternoon, and now Gresch has been carried out of it dead. Think about it.'

'But that guy's a public official.'

'So was Saddam Hussein.'

'Mark, I'm going to meet Bromberg.'

I heard him sigh. 'If you insist. If you're that reckless. We still have a few hours till your meeting. I'll use them as best I can.'

'Doing what?'

'Finding out as much as I can about Hermann Gresch; past known associates, see if a woman shows up among them. Also, I'll do some digging into Señor Caballero. What did you say his job was?'

'The lad at the city hall described him as the planning co-ordinator.'

'Okay. Let's see what that means, and how important it makes him.'

'He's too important for Ignacio to interrupt when he was leaving; he sounded very deferential.'

'In that case, I'm even more worried about him. Once more, I'm going to ask you, get on a plane and go home.'

'As soon as I've seen Bromberg and got a lead to Frank.'

I heard him draw a breath. 'I didn't want to say this,' he murmured, 'but given what's just happened to his associate, there's every chance that by now Frank's helping to fertilise a small part of Andalucía.'

'You didn't have to say it either. I'd worked that out for myself. But one way or another, I need to know.'

'Then take care for the next few hours. Don't hang around your hotel. If Gresch was murdered, the police will start asking questions in the area. Chances are the guy you told me about, in the shop, will tell them about you asking questions yesterday. As soon as you decently can, get out of there. Do one of two things: go somewhere very noisy, where you'll be lost in the crowd, or somewhere very quiet, where nobody's likely to find you.'

Fifteen

I considered Mark's two options and chose the second. My time in Las Vegas had been my version of hiding out in a crowd and, to be honest, it never made me feel entirely comfortable. Although I tried not to, I always found myself looking over my shoulder, or trying to be aware of every face, just in case there was one who might remember me from the old days. Once or twice I convinced myself that I recognised someone, and found myself taking evasive action.

Having decided on the quiet approach, I sneaked out of the hotel just after nine. My toe hadn't got any better, but I could walk, after a fashion. I headed down towards Plaza Nueva, then along the Avenue of the Constitution towards the Cathedral of Sevilla.

Maybe I had the romantic thought that I might find sanctuary there; I can't remember now. What I do recall is seeing the queues at the admissions desk (yes, in Sevilla you have to pay to get into a church), and realising that I was back at option one. So I turned my back on what they say is the biggest cathedral in Spain and looked around for a better idea.

Across the square, I saw a sign pointing to the entrance to the Real Alcázar, the royal palace. Surprisingly there was nobody waiting. I strolled across, paid my money and, after one last glance over my shoulder, stepped inside. There was hardly anyone there, just me and a few security people. The downside to that was that I had all their attention focused upon me, and in what I now recognise as my increasing paranoia, it dawned on me that they'd be bound to remember me if the police, or anyone else, decided to trawl the tourist spots in search of the suspicious woman who had been trying to gain entrance to Calle Alvarez Quintero forty-seven the day before.

Eventually I limped into an empty gallery, empty, that is, but for a display of wall tiles. (People go to Sevilla to look at wall tiles?) On the far side, there was an open door. I stepped through it and into a vast, spectacular garden. Trees towered on both sides of long pathways that seemed to be set out in a grid. Walls that seemed to be boundaries in fact divided sections with different themes. As I stepped into it, a jet of water arced from a pipe on my left into a pond below; Mercury's Pool, I learned, when I was close enough to read the sign.

As I made my steady way towards its heart, I passed several gardeners, none of whom, I was delighted to see, displayed the slightest interest in me, or even looked my way. I began to relax, strolling around, exploring and enjoying my surroundings, in spite of everything that had happened, and was, perhaps, still to happen.

After half an hour, during which I had seen only a handful

of visitors, I came upon a small arch, set against a wall, with a single seat beneath, placed before a water feature upon which a few ducks swam. I sat; the stone was cold beneath my bum, as the morning sun had still to reach the spot, but the weight was off my feet so I didn't mind that. I had found the solitude I had been after in the middle of one of the busiest tourist cities in Europe.

I had brought my book with me. I dug it out of my bag and started to read, finding my way back into a story that made my situation seem nothing at all.

I had gone through four chapters and was starting the next when my mobile sounded in the pocket of my shorts. I took it out and looked at the number displayed: my own, in St Martí.

'Adrienne?' I began.

'No, Mum, it's me.'

My heart seemed to swell at the sound of his voice; at the same time I felt very lonely, and very far away. 'Hello, Tom,' I said. 'Are you checking up on me?'

'No, Mum.' Even in those two words, I sensed from his tone that something was wrong. 'I can't find Auntie Ade,' he continued.

'What do you mean, love?'

'She's not here. I took Charlie for a walk, down along the beach path before it got busy with people. Auntie Ade said she'd make the breakfast, but when I got back there was nothing, and she's not here. The cereal box is on the table, and the kettle's boiled. I've looked all through the house and so has Charlie, and we can't find her. The door was open, though.'

I didn't like the sound of any of that, especially not the open-door bit. Tom knew very well, and I'd told Adrienne specifically, that that was a no-no, with all the strangers in the village through the summer. 'Are you sure she's not in the bathroom?' I asked him.

'Yes, I'm sure. And she's not in her bedroom either, or in the laundry room, or watching television, or on the computer.'

'She's probably gone to get bread, or fruit.'

'I got toastie bread from the freezer before Charlie and I went out, and there's plenty of fruit.'

I felt myself start to shake, and had to make damn sure that my voice stayed calm. 'She'll have gone somewhere for something, love. You get your own cereal and juice and wait for her to come back. Or if you'd rather, if you want more to eat than that, take some money from my dressing-table drawer,' I always keep a few hundred euros about the house, 'go to one of the cafés and get something there.'

'Don't want to go on my own,' he grumbled, giving me a major guilt spasm. 'I'll have something here and wait for her to get back.'

'Okay,' I replied, as casually as I could manage. 'Whatever you want. But when Auntie Ade gets back, you tell her to phone me right away.'

'Yes, Mum. Have you found Frank yet?'

'No, but I expect to today. Either way I'll try to get home tomorrow.'

'Promise?'

'Promise. Now go and feed yourself. Love you.'

'Love you too, Mum,' he said. As he hung up I suspected that he was trying as hard as I was to sound cool.

I felt my heart thump as I leaned against the wall. However positive I might have sounded, I did not like what Tom had told me. I looked at my phone. I'd forgotten Mark's stricture, and the battery level was down a couple of notches; I'd have to use it carefully. That said . . .

I went into my phonebook and called Adrienne's office. Fanette, her middle-aged assistant, picked up on the fifth ring, just as the answer-machine kicked in. I introduced myself. 'I'm looking for my aunt's mobile number,' I told her.

'Sure,' she replied, with a trace of a French accent, and recited it. I made her do it again, more slowly, and noted it on the title page of my book. 'You haven't heard from Adrienne this morning, have you?'

'No, but I'm only just in. I haven't heard from her since she left for Spain. But,' she continued, 'I was going to phone her myself this morning. Someone called last night, asking for her. It was a woman, Swiss or German accent, I'd say, and she said that she was ringing on Frank's behalf, trying to locate his mother.'

'Frank?' I exclaimed.

'That's what she said. I told her that Adrienne was with you in Spain, and suggested that she call her mobile. She said that Frank hadn't given her the number, so I did. The woman knows where he is. That's good news, isn't it?'

Not to me it wasn't. 'You told this woman where Adrienne

is,' I said. 'You had no idea who she was, but you gave her my address. Is that what you're saying?'

'Yes. What's the harm in that?'

'Maybe there's none,' I snapped, 'but if there is, then heaven help you. Frank's been missing for weeks, in God knows what circumstances, you get a call out of the blue and you give a stranger my home address, my son's home address. And now Tom says that Adrienne's vanished while he was out. If you put them in danger . . .' I slapped the phone shut, ending the call before I got round to telling her what I was going to do to her.

I waited for a few seconds, until my temper and my breathing were back under control, then called the number the woman had given me. It rang four times, and . . .

'Hello?' said a young voice.

'Tom. It's Mum. You're on Auntie Ade's mobile. Where was it?'

'On the kitchen table. And so's her bag. And she's not back yet.'

'Okay, love. Switch it off and it won't bother you again.' I paused. 'But . . .' I continued. 'Listen, son, I'm going to phone Alex Guinart.'

'The policeman?'

'Yes. She might not look it, but Auntie Ade's an old lady, and sometimes old people can do . . . funny things. I shouldn't have left you with her; I'm sorry.'

'Auntie Ade's nice, Mum. And she's not that old.'

In spite of it all, I laughed at his protest. 'You're a gentleman, no question. But I'm still going to call Alex. Then I'm going to figure out what to do about you . . . and Charlie, of course.'

My cop friend's number was the first entry in my book. I must have sounded tense because he was business-like from the very start. I told him where I was, gave him a potted version of why I was there, and explained what had happened at home. 'I don't like it, Alex. Either she's got far fewer marbles than I thought and she's wandered off, or . . .'

'Or what?'

'Or she's been taken. Her son's involved in a business scene, with some other people. One of them died here last night, and now Adrienne's gone missing. That's a big coincidence. I'm concerned about the whole operation, but most of all, I'm concerned about them.'

'I agree,' he said, firmly. 'Give me a description and I'll have our people look out for her, maybe stop cars at roundabouts, like we do often as routine.'

I did the best I could with the description: tall, dyed auburn hair, busty, looks early sixties although she's not. 'Okay,' he said. 'What about Tom?'

'Can you look out for him?'

'Of course, Gloria will look after him. Tell him to go and sit in Esculapi. I'll call and ask Pep to keep an eye on him. As soon as I can I'll get up there and take him to our place. When will you be home?'

'Soon as I can. If I can get a flight this afternoon, I will, but . . .' I paused as I thought. 'I may be able to make another arrangement for the wee man. I'll let you know.'

I phoned Tom again, told him to go down to the pizzeria, and to treat himself, then found another mobile number in my directory, almost at the other end of the alphabetical list. I hit the green button and heard a familiar Scots voice. 'Hi, Prim,' said Susie. 'Que tal in Spain?'

'Dodgy at the moment. Where are you?'

In Oz's final years, he and Susie had become tax nomads; it wasn't just to shelter his money either. Before he got his lucky breaks, she was an established businesswoman, running the family building and property empire with considerable success. She had backed off a little after having her two kids, but after his death she had taken the reins again, albeit mostly from a distance. She had sold one of their three homes, in Los Angeles, but had kept the other two.

'I'm in Monaco,' she replied. 'What's up?'

I gave her the bones of the story, speaking as quickly as I could for fear that my battery would give out on me. She whistled as I finished. 'Trouble still comes looking for you, doesn't it?'

'Don't, Susie,' I pleaded. 'I've managed to keep my head down for the last couple of years.'

'I suppose it's the old story. We can pick our friends, but not our relatives.' I heard her take a deep breath. 'Right, this is what's going to happen. I'm going to get Conrad Kent into a car right now, and on the road to L'Escala. He can do it in five hours, easy. He'll pick up Tom and bring him here. Janet and Jonathan are looking forward to him coming to visit in August, so this will be an extra treat for them. Once he's here, you don't have to worry about him.'

I sighed my relief, for that was very true. Conrad is ex-military, and not the man you mess with. 'Thanks, Susie, thanks a million. I'll make sure he's ready to go.' A further thought struck me. 'This is pushing it,' I added, 'but could you take the dog as well?'

Susie laughed out loud, lightening my mood. 'For Tom, anything. I'll tell Conrad to take the SUV. I know what's going to happen, mind. My kids will want a bloody mutt too!'

Sixteen

My battery life didn't look good as I called Alex Guinart, and told him of the arrangements I had made for my boy and his dog. He promised that he would help them both pack: clothes and Game Boy for Tom, harness, lead and food for Charlie, and passports for them both.

I asked him to tell Tom that I would come to Monaco for him as soon as I could, although I had no idea of what that meant in real terms.

'There is no sign of your aunt, I'm afraid,' he said, as I was about to hang up. I hadn't even thought to ask him: if there had been, that would have been the first thing he'd have told me. I could feel no optimism on that front. Adrienne would not have walked off on an errand without her bag or her phone, far less her great-nephew, and if she'd had an accident or a stroke anywhere about the house, Tom or Charlie would have found her.

I'd neglected to tell him before about Fanette's mystery caller; I filled in that gap in his knowledge.

'A woman, she said?'

'Yes. German or Swiss accent. But if it was who I think it might have been, don't go looking for her in your neighbour-hood. I'm supposed to be meeting her here in a few hours.'

'And you're still going to?'

'That's my plan.'

'Primavera . . .'

As he began to protest my phone gave an ominous 'beep'. 'Got to go,' I said. 'My battery's dying.' I ended the call.

I sat in my stone alcove, watching the ducks and thinking about where I was at. I looked around. The garden was still almost deserted; away in the distance I saw a man, tossing chunks of bread to the geese, but apart from him I was alone. It had just gone eleven thirty, three hours before I was due to meet Lidia Bromberg, and the sun was about to reach my refuge. Once it did, I wouldn't be able to stay there for long.

Just as its first rays fell upon my feet, my mobile surprised me by ringing again. It was Mark Kravitz. 'I've got some news for you,' he began, 'courtesy of a journalist contact of mine. The man that the police in Seville have now identified as Hermann Gresch died from a massive overdose of morphine, some time yesterday afternoon. They've got it down either as accidental death or suicide. Apparently there were empty capsules all over the place; on the face of it, Gresch was an addict with a big habit.'

'And two different identities.'

'The local police don't know that yet, although they soon will. I've tipped a contact in the Guardia Civil to the fact; they should be getting in touch with Seville any minute now. If this is a scam, then it's about to blow up, Prim. If it is, then for the sake of the investors we can only hope they haven't moved the money yet.'

My phone beeped again. 'Mark, my battery's going dead.'

'And so might you if you keep that date with Bromberg. You really mustn't do it.'

I yielded to his judgement: by that time it was in line with my own. 'Okay, I give in,' I said. 'Things have happened back in St Martí to help persuade me.'

'What?' he exclaimed.

'It looks as if my aunt's been snatched.'

'And your son?'

'Tom's okay. He's under guard and Conrad Kent's on his way to get him and take him to Susie's.'

'That's good; you've done something sensible at last. Now let me think. If Frank's mother's been kidnapped, that means . . .'

My phone beeped again and he was cut off in mid-sentence. I looked at it and saw that the battery indicator was solid red. 'Bugger,' I swore softly.

I checked my bag, to confirm that my passport was there, plus my cash and credit cards. Clickair had been the sort of operation that requires photo ID: although I'd booked only a one-way flight, it hadn't been full and I was pretty confident that I'd be able to get on one that day, back to Barcelona. As I'd said to Mark, I had definitely given up on the idea of meeting Bromberg, or of looking any further for Frank in Sevilla. His mother had become my priority, although God alone knew what I was going to do about her.

With a degree of regret I left the gardens of the Real Alcázar. They had been truly peaceful, and I made myself a quiet promise that I would take Tom there one day, when he was old enough not to wonder where the play zone was. Heading out of the palace I shuffled down the side of the cathedral into Constitution Avenue, then across, into a maze of side-streets. It didn't take me long to find what I was after: an Internet café. I took an empty terminal, logged on to the Clickair website and bought myself a ticket on the six o'clock flight to Barcelona. Then, on a whim, I switched over to the electronic edition of *Diario de Sevilla,* and checked the latest entries.

There was a brief story on the discovery of a man's body in a street near the *ayuntamiento,* following an anonymous tip, but that was all. I went to the newspaper site's search facility and entered the name 'Lidia Bromberg': I drew a complete blank. I tried again with George Macela, but once more came up with nothing. Finally I entered 'Roy Urquhart' . . . and made a connection. The piece that appeared on screen was a year old, a feature about the Hotel Casino d'Amuseo project, built around an interview with my cousin. Yes. It was Frank, no doubt about it: his unmistakable image stared out at me from the centre of the article, those Asiatic eyes, that smile, managing to be modest yet dazzling at the same time.

I read it slowly. It was the same pitch that Bromberg had given me when I had called her two days before, only more so.

Frank . . . or Roy . . . was selling it as the greatest thing to hit Sevilla for the last hundred years and more, and the journalist who had written the puff seemed to be buying it, and him, hook line and sinker. Lidia Bromberg hadn't said anything about the golf course, but he had. This wasn't going to be just another flat course for hackers and old men. Oh, no, they had the agreement of the European golf tour to staging an event within three years, and to taking the Ryder Cup there in 2018. I found myself wondering if anyone had told the European tour officials. Overall, though, the piece was wonderful publicity for the project. I couldn't help but admire Frank's natural ability as a salesman, and wonder at his ability to pitch so effectively a proposition that I feared more and more was a total fraud.

I was still smiling at his effrontery as I closed the window. There was one more thing that I wanted to do. I found the official website of the city council, entered 'Caballero' in its search facility, and clicked.

And there he was, Señor Don Emil Caballero i Benitez, the man I'd seen going into number forty-seven just before Hermann Gresch had taken his last and fatal fix: he wasn't an official, he was a member of the bloody council, and a pretty senior one, by the look of it. He was thirty-eight years old, a 'retail businessman' by occupation, with a record of involvement in civic government that stretched back for nine years, and currently held responsibility for planning matters. 'And as bent as a corkscrew, I'll bet,' I whispered, as I closed the window and shut down the terminal.

I paid the clerk, and checked my watch: it was half past twelve, and I was done in Sevilla. I needn't have gone back to the hotel. I had left nothing there that was irreplaceable, and they had a print of my credit card to take care of my room charges. There was nothing stopping me hailing a taxi and heading straight for the airport, except, when I thought about it, that my phone charger was still on the dressing-table. It might be difficult to replace that at short notice, and I was beginning to feel out of touch already, after only an hour without my mobile. I decided I could afford to go back, give it a quick charge, then check out properly.

I took a circuitous route to the hotel, one that didn't take me past the *ayuntamiento*, where I might just have bumped into friend Caballero, or past Calle Alvarez Quintero forty-seven, where that greasy bastard of a shopkeeper might have spotted me and shouted, 'Policia!', 'Puta!' or something equally inconvenient and embarrassing. Given my slow rate of progress, it was well after one when I got back, and by that time the streets were quiet, the shops having closed for lunch and the punters having gone home or off to a tapas bar. I looked around as Las Casas de los Mercaderes came into sight. The entrance to the narrow, pedestrianised street was all but blocked by a big black car, but at that hour it wasn't causing any problems; even if it was still there when I called a taxi, there was plenty of room for it to get past.

Mind you, I thought, as I picked up my key, *that's if I go to the airport*. The idea of fronting up Bromberg hadn't gone away completely. But as I considered it afresh, I decided that there would be precious little point. Frank was gone, and possibly dead, as Macela/Gresch certainly was. As I saw it, the chances might even be that Councillor Caballero was tying off all the loose ends and that Lidia could be running for her own life.

Only . . . As I stepped out of the lift, Mark Kravitz's final words came back to me, those he had been in the middle of forming when my mobile died on me. *'If Frank's mother's been kidnapped, that means . . .'*

I had just realised what it meant as I opened my door, and saw that decisions on my immediate future had been taken out of my hands.

Seventeen

For some reason, I'd been carrying a mental image of Lidia Bromberg as a Nordic type, a leggy blonde. I couldn't have been more wrong. She was small, five-two tops without the heels, voluptuous but edging towards fleshy, and with a head of thick, jet-black hair, razor-cut, I guessed, as I stared at her. She wore white shorts that ended just above the knee, and her formidable bosom was crammed into a sleeveless pink top that was barely fit for purpose, to quote a former politician.

She wasn't alone. Caballero was standing beside her, still in his lightweight cream suit, and in his hand he had a brutish-looking gun, made even uglier by a silencer. Okay, so they hadn't come to sell me a share in the casino project.

If I'd been more alert, and if I hadn't been hampered by a toe that I was not certain was cracked, maybe I'd have slammed the door shut and legged it, but staring down a gun barrel does have a certain hypnotic effect. So, instead, I stepped into my room.

That's not to say I was completely stunned. 'Who the hell are you?' I demanded. 'There's no wagon outside so you can't be chambermaids, and you don't fit my image of hotel-room thieves.'

'I think you know who I am, Mrs Blackstone,' Bromberg replied. 'I believe we have spoken, yes? The way things stand, it looks as if you are going to be late for a meeting with me, yes?'

'I'd decided to give that a miss. I had you checked out, you see, by a friend of mine, a security consultant, so I know that the whole project's a con. I don't really fancy pouring my money into a suitcase for you bastards to run off with.'

'You're totally off your head,' said Caballero, angrily, in Spanish.

'That's been remarked upon before,' I told him, in his own tongue, 'but it's never proved to be true. I'm clever enough to have made sure that my friend knows exactly where I am right now. I'd guess that in the last hour he's tried to call me a couple of times on my mobile.' I took it from my bag and held it up for him to see. 'The battery's dead; I only came back here for the charger, but he's not to know that, is he? By now, he's either called the police, or he's about to.'

'In that case, we'd better not delay,' he said roughly. In that moment, I believed, truly, that he was going to shoot me. Instead, just as I felt my legs start to give under me, he picked up the charger from the dressing-table and tossed it to me. I caught it, one handed. 'You'd better take this. We might want you to call your friend, to reassure him, and it'll be most convincing if you do it on your mobile. Now this is what we'll do,' he continued. 'We use the service lift and we go out of the side door, to my car, which is parked outside.'

'Maybe it's been towed by now,' I suggested helpfully.

He treated me to a small smile; he wasn't a bad-looking bloke and I found myself reacting to it, clinging to it in the hope that he wasn't all that bad in any respect. 'My car doesn't get towed in Sevilla,' he advised me. 'Now be good and come with us quietly. Killing you would be a last resort, but you have been a Goddamned nuisance, so I won't feel too bad if I have to.'

So long, Mr Nice Guy! I looked at the gun, and considered it. Of course it could have been a replica, but it looked real enough, and when it comes down to it one doesn't bet one's life on such chances. There was also the silencer; it occurred to me that I'd seen fake firearms often enough in shops in L'Escala, and real ones in shops in the US, but I'd never seen a silencer, real or pretend, on display. The thing was like an exclamation point, emphasising my peril.

That was when I realised that I can't do the Wonderwoman stuff any more. I have known a couple of moments . . . and I'm not including the plane crash . . . when my life could have come to a sudden, painful conclusion. On each occasion I took my chances, and came through. But things are different now. No reward could ever balance the risk of not seeing my son grow up, watching him turn from a boy into a man through his teenage years, feeling my chest swell with pride as he becomes a doctor or a scientist, or whatever. I realised in that room how much I'm looking forward to crying at his graduation, and at his wedding, and later on, to holding my grandchildren in my arthritic, stiffening fingers while I still can. No reward could ever make up for all that, and I hadn't even gone south in search of one. I was doing a favour for an aunt I had barely known for much of my life and for a cousin who didn't bloody deserve to have her as a mother. Bugger it! I was even paying my own air fare and hotel bill.

'Okay,' I said submissively, tucking the phone charger away in my bag. 'You're the dealer, whatever you say.'

'Smart woman,' Bromberg sneered. I really didn't like her, I decided. She reminded me of someone I'd seen in a TV sci-fi drama a few years before, a character who'd worn an attractive human skin to conceal the voracious creature within. That wasn't the moment to tell her, though. That wasn't the moment to say anything more.

Instead I stood quite still as they came towards me, flanking me as she opened the door and took a quick look into the corridor. 'Okay,' she murmured, then took my elbow, pulling me roughly after her. I will tell you at this point that in the second half of my twenties, when I signed on as a nurse in an African war zone, I decided I should learn how to take care of myself, so I took up mixed martial arts. I was quite good, and trained with a couple of the UN soldiers in my base while I was away. They also taught me to shoot. Since then I've kept up my skills at classes, whenever I could. Maybe I was exaggerating with the Wonderwoman claim, but at another time, I might have broken a couple of Lidia's fingers for the way she grabbed me.

At another time, when I didn't have Caballero on the other side, and the gun, which I saw him tuck into his belt. I went with them meekly. They led me along the corridor, then to the right to a lift door that I hadn't seen in my time there. Lidia pushed the call button. Nobody spoke as we waited; they had what they wanted and I knew there was no point in winding them up.

When the lift arrived, it was occupied by a chambermaid, with her trolley. She looked at us in surprise as she pushed it out. 'This is the staff lift,' she said, in a hard accent that told me she was from Ecuador, Guatemala or another of the Latin countries that provide Spain with much of its cheap labour.

'City council,' Caballero snapped, and she backed off, cowed. I guessed that she had read it as a threat, since not all of those migrant workers have legal status.

We rode the lift down to the ground floor. It opened into an area of the hotel that seemed to be closed to the public; the floor wasn't carpeted and cleaning implements were propped against the wall in a corner. My captors must have studied the place on a plan in the city offices, I guessed, for they seemed to know exactly where they were, and where to go.

They walked me to a door and through it into another corridor, wider and with a fire exit at the other end. As we reached it Caballero raised his right foot and kicked the crash bar, releasing it and opening the door outwards into the street. It was still deserted. Just my luck to be snatched at the hour when all of Sevilla was eating or asleep.

The big black car was almost directly opposite us: I was close enough to recognise the Chrysler badge on the back, and the model number, 300C. At least I was being kidnapped in style,

I thought . . . until Caballero reached into his pocket, produced a key and pressed it. The boot popped open. 'You get in there,' he said.

'Wait a minute!' I protested involuntarily.

'Don't worry, you won't suffocate. I don't want you to see where we're going, plus I'm not having you wave at every police car we pass on the way there.' He dropped the key into his jacket's right-hand pocket, took the gun from his belt, handed it to Bromberg, on my right, and grabbed my upper arms, as if he expected me to resist being put into that dark oven.

I probably would have too, even if things hadn't started to happen very fast. Suddenly, I was aware of a new shape, moving just at the edge of my peripheral vision, and behind Lidia. I saw a hand clamp on the wrist that held the gun, and then a flash of metal. She screamed and dropped the weapon. As she did, Caballero loosened his grip on me, enough for me to wrench myself free and to dig my left elbow into the pit of his stomach. I heard him gasp as I spun round on my undamaged foot, dipping a little to allow me to bring my right forearm up, hard, between his legs, and to a very firm conclusion. The gasp turned into the sort of squeal of pain that I'm told no woman can make, or even understand. As he began to fold into himself, I snatched the pistol from the ground, dropped it into the bag that, by some miracle, was still slung over my left shoulder, and then grabbed him. Quickly, I retrieved the key from his pocket, along with a cell phone I found there, then pushed him, bundling him into the car's capacious boot, the prison he had planned for me. 'Sorry, mate,' I hissed, as I slammed the lid shut, 'but I'm told you won't suffocate.'

Bromberg was on the ground, writhing and whimpering, her hands clasped to her right buttock, from which blood was seeping, turning her white shorts a deep red. The idea of helping her didn't even occur to me. Instead, I looked at the Chrysler's key, saw which button released the locks and pressed it.

As I slid behind the wheel, I called to my rescuer, 'Get in!' He had become a spectator, but he did as I ordered, while I found the ignition slot, and looked at the controls. I was vaguely aware, from an audible thud, that he had tossed something heavy into the back, but not of him, not at that point: all my concentration was devoted to flight.

By happy chance, my Jeep's a Chrysler too, and automatic, so everything was familiar. I fired up the engine, hit the brake-release pedal, slammed the gearstick into drive rather more firmly than is necessary and drove off.

'Thanks,' I said to my passenger, then turned to take a proper look at him, as the first thumps and muffled shouts came from the boot.

He smiled back at me; a modest smile, yet one that was on the edge of being dazzling. 'No problem, cousin,' said Frances Ulverscroft McGowan.

Eighteen

'Frank!' I screamed. 'What the . . .'

That was what Mark Kravitz had been saying when my phone went dead. If Frank's mother had been kidnapped, that meant he was still alive, and on the loose.

'Take a left at the end of this street,' he said firmly, before the volcano I felt building within me had a chance to erupt. 'We have to get out of the city centre and dump this thing before that woman sends the police, or anyone else, after us.'

'I think you could find that the police are after her,' I told him, 'but you're right in principle. I have to get to the airport: I've a plane to catch.'

'It's best if you miss it,' he said. 'Okay, go straight ahead till you get to the next junction, then left again, right at the lights and across the river.'

I concentrated on the road and on his instructions until we were on the other side of the Río Guadalquivir and well on our way into the southern suburbs. I could drive without too much discomfort, I'd discovered, if I made a point of keeping the pedal pressure on the ball of my foot.

'Who was that creature?' Frank asked, breaking the silence.

'You don't know?'

'Never seen her before.'

'She's your replacement as director and sales manager of the Hotel Casino d'Amuseo. Where is it, by the way, the site of this mythical playground for the rich and famous?'

'We're on the way there now. Jeez,' he mused, 'that's Lidia, is it? And I just stabbed her in the arse.' I was reminded of something I'd forgotten, that he had inherited the vestiges of a Scottish accent from Auntie Ade.

'Why did you do it, Frank?' I demanded. 'Why did you get involved with another fraud? Did you like being in jail? Do you like torturing your mother? For that's what it amounts to.'

'Please, Prim, later. I'll tell you the whole story later. For now, take a right at this next fork then keep on that road for twenty-five kilometres or so.'

'Where will that take us?'

'I've told you, to the land where the casino was supposed to be.'

'Whose land is it? Yours?'

Frank laughed. 'As if I'd be that dumb. No, it belongs to him in the boot. There used to be a chemical works on it, in his father's time, until there was an accident and it was shut down. The site's been contaminated ever since, no use for agriculture or anything else.'

'But all right for a leisure complex?'

'That was the idea.'

132

'And a great one it was,' I retorted sarcastically. 'Now here you are on the run, you've pulled me into it, I've had to send my son to safety and, to cap it all, your mother's been kidnapped.'

He sat bolt upright. 'Mum? Kidnapped?'

'That's how it looks. I left her at my place, with Tom. He went to walk the dog this morning and when she came back she was gone. The house was like the *Mary* bloody *Celeste*.'

'Oh, Jesus!' He closed his eyes and leaned his head back on the rest behind him. Another indistinct shout came from behind us. 'Shut up!' Frank yelled. He picked up the gun from the central console, where I'd laid it, and fired a shot into the back seat, behind me, more or less in line with where Caballero's feet must have been. Twin sounds echoed, from the silencer and from the upholstery, as the bullet ripped through it. All the way through? I waited for a scream but none came, only silence. I found myself hoping that the space wasn't big enough for the guy to have twisted himself round.

I drove in silence after that, for I had something new to consider. I had marked my cousin down as something of a wimp, but it was all too clear that I'd been wrong. He'd bladed Bromberg without hesitation. He'd fired a shot that might have killed Caballero, for all we knew at that point, without even thinking about it. There was a dangerous side to him, and no mistake.

'There's a turning just ahead,' he said, plucking me from my thoughts, 'on the right. The road gets a bit bumpy after that, but follow it. It won't be too comfortable for our passenger, but he's asked for more than that.'

He was right about the track. The big car had luxury suspension, but even with that we were bounced about in our seats.

'I'd have been back there if he'd had his way,' I growled, through clenched teeth. Then I frowned as the obvious question finally forced its way out. 'Frank, how come you showed up at the hotel in the nick of time, so to speak?'

'I've been on the look-out for you,' he replied, 'since you left that ferocious message in my voicemail.' He chuckled. 'By the way, I do know what an orchidectomy is.'

'You picked that up? So why didn't you call me back?'

'I've been keeping radio silence on the mobile. These things can be traced, you know, as easily as you can pin down a land-line call, maybe even more so. I knew you'd be flying down, and I could guess from where, so I staked out all the incoming Barcelona traffic at the airport, spotted you, and followed you, right to your hotel.'

'So why didn't you do the obvious and come in? Didn't you want to be found?'

He shook his head. 'No, it wasn't that. I couldn't be sure they weren't following you too.'

'They?'

He held up a hand. 'Later, Prim. Like I said, the whole story, I promise.' He stopped, then pointed ahead. 'We're here. Draw up by that building.'

We were in flat, arid open country, several hundred hectares by the look of it, well enough for all the website claimed was going to happen on the site. All around there was nothing to be seen, save for a big brick barn, with sliding iron doors made of corrugated iron and a pitched roof. I parked beside it as instructed.

'You've been here before?' I asked, as we stepped out into the blazing hot afternoon.

'Sure, with him.'

'Why are we here now? This doesn't exactly look like a getaway route.'

'Ah, but it is, cuz.' He slid one of the barn doors open. It creaked, but moved easily, for its size. 'Caballero keeps a few toys here: he's got a quad bike, a few trail motorcycles and, of course, a four-by-four. I think we'll borrow that for the next stage of our trip.'

I looked inside. Sure enough, the barn contained an array of recreational vehicles. 'And what about him?'

'Let's see, shall we?' He reached inside the car and pressed a button. The boot catch popped and the lid swung open.

Caballero's eyes screwed tight as the sunlight hit him. His face was beetroot and he was soaked with sweat. The cream suit would never be the same again. He groaned, and made to get out until Frank waved the gun in his face.

'Stay where you are,' he snapped, in Spanish. 'You're getting no kindness from me, you bastard. Prim, do me a favour and get my rucksack.'

That was what he'd chucked into the back seat as he'd got into the car outside the hotel, a black bag with a single shoulder strap. 'Okay,' I said, 'I've found it.' It was weighty; I wondered what the hell he had in it.

'Give it to me, please.'

Again, I did as he asked. He unzipped it, took out a bottle of water, and held it up for Caballero to see. 'This is for you.' He placed it on the ground, then slammed the boot lid shut once more. 'Eventually.'

He walked round the car and shot out the tyres, one by one. 'Can't have him coming after us,' he explained, as if I was a simpleton.

The keys were in the ignition of the four-by-four, a silver Suzuki Grand Vitara. Frank took the wheel. 'No offence,' he said, as we reversed out of the barn, 'but I know where we're going, so I'll drive.'

'Fair enough,' I agreed. 'That was a nice trick,' I added, 'bursting his tyres. But won't he come after us on one of the bikes just as easily, once he gets out of there?'

'True,' Frank admitted. He stopped the car, got out and went back into the barn. I watched him as he picked up a container, as he splashed its contents over all of the machines inside, and as he took a book of matches from his pocket, lit one, used it to ignite the others, and tossed it on to the quad bike. Finally, almost as an afterthought, he threw the gun inside too. As he slid the door closed I could see the flames beginning to bloom like roses in an accelerated frame-by-frame nature film.

'He will get out of there, won't he?' I asked, as we drove off.

'Sure. Those things have a manual release inside the boot.

They're American made: I suppose they fit it in case you're snatched by Big Tony Soprano and the boys.'

'What if he doesn't know that?'

Frank gave me the smile again. I felt a tremor as I realised just how much it reminded me of Oz. 'Then that'll be just too damn bad for him,' he said.

Nineteen

'What's the game plan?' I asked, as we headed back towards the city. 'Indeed, do you have a game plan?'

'Oh, yes,' my cousin replied, 'and it's a good one. But rather than have me describe it, just watch, Primavera, watch and learn. Where did you get that name anyway?'

'From my mum.' I let out a small, outraged snort. 'And don't you go there with the names, Frances. At least mine was planned, not an accident forced upon me by an intellectually under-developed employee.' To my surprise, I found that even under all that stress I was laughing.

'I can only blame her for the girlie first one,' he confessed. 'The other, that was all dear old Ade's idea.'

'Ulverscroft?'

'Yes. It's a publishing company; they specialise in large-print books.'

'For the hard of hearing?'

He grinned. 'No, you're thinking of the taped version. Do you know,' he went on, 'that this has now become the longest conversation we've ever had, and probably the longest time we've ever spent in each other's company.'

'Not quite,' I advised him. 'The first time you came to visit us my dad took the three of us, you, me and Dawn, to the beach in St Andrews. I remember it, because I didn't want to go, but Mum persuaded me that he wouldn't know what to do when you had "little boy's needs", as she put it.'

'What the hell did that mean?'

'It meant that I had to take you to the ladies' toilet, and make sure you did everything properly.'

'You mean you got to watch?'

'And worse. You were only just three at the time.'

'You'll be glad to hear that I can go on my own now.'

'So could Tom, when he was that age. So can Charlie, and he's even younger.'

'You have two kids? I thought . . .'

'Charlie's a Labrador.'

'My God. Who was the father?'

'Shut up and drive, you idiot.'

He did, into a small commercial area to the south-west of the city, where he parked in a supermarket car park, well away from the store.

'Are we going to shop our way to freedom?' I asked.

'I told you. Watch and learn.'

He reached into his pocket and produced the most elaborate Swiss Army knife I'd ever seen. 'Is that what you used on Bromberg?'

'Yup. Specially sharpened to meet the need, should it arise. Three-inch blade, but that will do the job, as you saw. And, of course, it does many other things.'

From its many tools, he selected a Phillips . . . no relation . . . screw-driver, jumped out of the car and proceeded to remove the number-plates. 'Back in a minute,' he said, when he was done, and disappeared into the rows of parked cars.

Actually, two minutes had passed, but no longer, when he returned with two different plates, which he fixed to our stolen jalopy. 'There,' he declared, with more than a little pride, as he climbed back into the driver's seat. 'It's going to take the owner of the other car a couple of days at best to notice that he has a new registration. If Caballero does get loose, if he makes it to the road and stops someone, if . . . long odds against, in the circumstances . . . he calls the cops . . .'

'Then they're not going to find the number he gives them on a silver Suzuki.'

'Exactly. And just to confuse them further . . .' He switched on the engine and drove off, not out of the car park but round, closer to the store. He parked once more, this time in a space about fifty metres from a big sign that read 'Taxi'. I looked and saw a couple of cabs waiting for takers. 'Come on.'

We grabbed our belongings, Frank locked the Suzuki and we walked, unnoticed, across to the rank. I nodded to the first driver and he nodded back. 'Station,' Frank told him, as we slipped into the back seat.

'But what if they're watching the station?' I asked him quietly.

'That's a small chance we'll have to take, but I reckon that at the moment they . . . quote, unquote . . . will be looking for

Caballero's car, and for him. If they've found him by now, and I doubt that, they'll be looking for the Suzuki. Either way, we'll know in about ten minutes.'

That was more or less how long it took the taxi to drop us at the entrance to the big airy railway station. I paid the driver, and we headed inside. Frank found a timetable board and studied it. He smiled. 'Perfect,' he murmured. He turned to me. 'There's an AVE . . . that's high speed . . . to Madrid in twenty-five minutes. We'll take that.'

'Madrid? I want to go to Barcelona. That's where my car is.'

'We'll get there, eventually, when it's safe.'

'Safe? To hell with it, Frank, I've had enough of this. I can still catch my flight: I'm taking another cab to the airport, flying to Barcelona and driving to Monaco to join Tom.'

He looked at his watch. 'Primavera,' he pointed out, 'less than two hours ago, Caballero and that woman were about to cart you off somewhere and kill you.'

'That's an exaggeration. They weren't going to kill me. If they were they'd have done it at the hotel.'

'Listen, Emil Caballero is an extremely well-connected man in this city, but not even he could commit murder in a public building and expect to get away with it. You got in their way; you annoyed them. What use were you to them alive?'

'And your mother?' That didn't need saying at that point, and I regretted the words as soon as they were out. Frank had been olive-skinned before he acquired the permatan, but still he went pale.

'That's between me and them.' He shot me a piercing

look. 'There's no chance of a misunderstanding, is there? Your son didn't overreact or anything, did he? Could she have gone for a swim?'

'Tom was on the beach. He'd have seen her. She was in the middle of making their breakfast, Frank. She took nothing with her. Plus, she told me the other day she doesn't believe blue-flag beaches are any cleaner than the rest . . . "Shit doesn't know it's not supposed to wash up there," was how she put it . . . and that she wouldn't put as much as a toe in the Mediterranean.'

'That's my dear old mum for you. Okay, I'll grant you it sounds bad. But to answer your question, my guess is that she's been taken to put pressure on me.'

'So tell me. Why? What's this all about?'

'Soon, once we're settled. For now, you go and get us two tickets on the AVE to Madrid. How much cash do you have? You don't want to be using your credit card.'

'Four hundred and something.'

'That'll be enough.'

It was. In fact it was enough for me to buy club class, which let us use a very nice lounge for the fifteen minutes or so that it took for our train to be called. I took a glass of white wine from the bar, and spent the time doing women things, hair, makeup . . . not that I ever use much more than the lippie I had in my bag . . . and such. When I was finished I looked a little less like someone who'd just emerged from a fight to the near death, and a flight from danger. Or was that into danger?

Club class on the high-speed train was as close to the in-flight equivalent as Renfe could manage, with a hostess to show us to our seats and bring us drinks and nibbles. As soon as she had gone and we were settled in, I looked across at Frank, ready for the explanation he had promised. He was asleep, wasn't he? Like a baby, as if nothing had happened and we were just another couple of tourists. Except, we weren't: we didn't have any clothes for a start . . . at least, I didn't, for I had no clue what was inside Frank's rucksack. After the Swiss Army knife episode, there could have been a white tuxedo in there and it wouldn't have surprised me.

He dozed for a while, waking just as the train slowed and cruised past an establishment that looked suspiciously like a prison. I waited for it to pick up speed once more, but it didn't. Instead it eased its way into a station.

Frank jumped to his feet and grabbed his bag from the overhead rack. 'Come on,' he said.

'But this isn't Madrid. You've only been asleep for half an hour.'

'I know; this is Córdoba. We're not going to Madrid.'

I couldn't be bothered to ask why. I followed him, pausing as he dropped a word into the ear of the hostess, and a fifty-euro note into her hand. 'What did you say to her?'

'I told her that we were breaking the journey and that we'd be taking a later train.'

'And are we?'

'No. We'll stay here overnight.'

We climbed the stairs that led from the platform and walked

the short distance to the station concourse. Happily, I saw a row of shops. 'How much cash do you have?' I asked him. 'Those train tickets used up most of mine, and I need to buy some clothes.'

'I'm flush.' He delved into the magic rucksack, peeled off six fifties from a roll, and handed them to me.

'I take it you're okay.'

He nodded. 'Mostly I buy cheap basics from street markets and dispose of them as I use them.'

I wrinkled my nose. 'You were brought up that badly?'

The shops took care of my needs. I was able to buy three pairs of sensible knickers, another pair of shorts, two tops and a light, non-crushable skirt with Frank's cash, plus a small, cheap roller case.

'Why did you need that?' he asked when he saw it.

'I'm not sleeping rough, boy,' I advised him. 'We're finding a hotel, and not the kind that's used to guests arriving with their clothes in shopping bags.'

'In that case . . .'

There were plenty of taxis at the rank, as nobody else had got off our train. The driver of the first looked pleased to see us. When Frank told him, 'Mezquita,' he nodded, as if that was where everyone wanted to go. As it happens, that's probably true. The twelve-hundred-year-old mosque that became a cathedral is Córdoba's only serious tourist attraction. Our taxi dropped us near the entrance, outside a hotel called the Conquistador.

'This looks okay,' I declared, and marched up to Reception.

They had two rooms available, doubles for single use. 'How will you be paying?' the clerk asked.

'Credit card,' said Frank, and slapped a piece of plastic on the desk.

'Hey,' I whispered, as the man took it across to his terminal, 'how come I can't but you can?'

'I have resources they can't trace,' he told me.

I stared at him hard. 'The time has come, cousin,' I said, a little harshly perhaps, considering that he'd saved my skin, 'for you to tell me the whole story. Now, or we stay here and max out that card until you do.'

Twenty

'You're not going to believe this.'

Whenever somebody's said that to me in the past, my instant, if unuttered, response has always been, 'You're right about that.'

But when Frank said it, somehow I knew that I would, however strange the yarn he was about to spin me. We were sitting on the terrace off my room, under an awning, with a bottle of Pinot Grigio by our side, standing in a bucket of rapidly melting ice. I had showered and changed into one of the tops and the cool skirt I had bought. I took a sip from my glass and challenged him: 'Try me.'

'Okay.' He took a sip from his, then drained it, refilled it, and looked me in the eye. 'I'm a secret agent.'

I gasped, then laughed. 'You're a what?'

His face took on an expression that might have fitted the barely three year old I had taken to the toilet in St Andrews. 'See?' he grumbled.

I mollified him: 'Sorry, I didn't mean to laugh. Go on, but warn me properly next time you're going to say something like that.'

'Then be warned: I'm going to say it again. I'm a secret agent. I work for Interpol, but my parent organisation, if you care to put it that way, is the security service.'

'Whose security service?'

'Ours. Her Majesty's. Britain's.'

'MI5?'

'That's not our official title, but we answer to it these days.'

'Frank, you've got a criminal record.'

He winked at me. 'Chas and Dave have hundreds but they're respectable.'

'Cut the bad old gags and get on with it.'

'Yes, ma'am.' He tugged his forelock. 'They approached me when I was inside. I found out later that my mum was the indirect cause. At first I thought it must have been Arnold Thomas, the guy I worked for in Westminster, who put them on to me. He's on the Commons' defence intelligence committee. But it wasn't. Mum was punting a book around by a retired senior spook; she'd mentioned my predicament to him, and he had a word with the people in Millbank. I'd been in for three years, then one day at Ford prison . . . I was in open conditions for most of my sentence . . . I had a visitor, a smart-suited lady, about my age; not a glamour girl, very business-like. We had a roundabout discussion, and she asked me about my plans, post-nick. I said I didn't have any. She said that her company . . . that was how she put it . . . had an interest in people like me, guys with financial acumen who'd screwed up big-time and were looking for a way back. I said I'd be interested in hearing more, and she went away.'

'And you did hear more.'

He nodded. 'Yes, but not until they'd made me sit a series of tests; IQ, isometric, physical. I was interviewed by a psychologist too. When all that was done, the woman came back, all business, and told me who she represented. She also promised that if I breathed a word, I'd do my full stretch and never work again when I got out, or get anywhere near the money I'd stashed in Switzerland. She told me they were involved, with colleagues in other countries, in the detection, infiltration and subversion of major international fraud. This would involve the use of what she described as sleeper agents, with no official status, ready to be drawn into scams as they developed, to gather intelligence from the inside on them and on the people involved and, when the time came, to pull them down. She admitted that it would be risky, and that I'd be largely on my own. I told her that I'd been largely on my own all my life.'

'That's not fair. Your mum loves you.'

'I know, and I love her; but I had a solitary upbringing, Prim. I was a loner as a kid, and I stayed that way. Other than Mum, you and Dawn are my closest family, and I've spent no more than a few weeks with you in my entire life.'

'You must have friends, surely.'

He gnawed awkwardly at his bottom lip. 'Nobody close. Girlfriends, sure . . . I'm straight . . . but I've never had any boy buddies, not even at university.'

'What about Justin Mayfield?'

He frowned. 'Yes, there was him, I suppose, but like all the rest of my little circle, he cut me loose when I got banged up. That was the way it was.'

'So you took the Queen's shilling?'

'Yes. The deal was that I was transferred from Ford to another place. I was still a prisoner, in that I couldn't leave, but I wasn't in jail. I was in a training college, learning all the stuff that spooks need to know: intelligence gathering, surveillance, counter-surveillance, communications, and combat, armed and unarmed. I was there for over a year, save for a few weekend visits home to Mum, who thought I was still in Ford but preferred not to go there anyway. When I was ready, they paroled me. I did an induction course at Millbank, then I was transferred to Interpol headquarters in Lyon to be integrated into the international operation. After three months there, they sent me back to the British bureau, where they told me to go out and get myself a job, establish myself in the real world, and wait for an assignment.'

'You were on their payroll, though?'

'Yes. I was on what I suppose you'd call a retainer. And part of the deal was that I'd get to access the funds I'd stashed away from my private enterprise at the bank, without hindrance.'

'So the application to Cinq Pistes, that was for real?'

'Oh, yes, entirely.'

'And Madame Gilpin, she was for real too?'

'Susannah? You've spoken to her? Yes, she's the genuine article, in more than one way, as far as I'm concerned.'

'Did you really want her to come with you, or did you just say that to get back into her underwear in Paris?'

'I wanted her to leave her husband, still do. Not to come here, though: I'd have set her up somewhere, Madrid, maybe, or London, until the d'Amuseo business had run its course.'

'The d'Amuseo business. What's it really about?'

'You've been digging. What do you think?'

I told him that I thought it was an elaborate fraud, that the intention was to raise finance for the project and then, when there was enough in the kitty, to bugger off into the wide blue yonder with the funds, never to be seen again.

'Spot on,' said Frank. 'I reckon I could get you a job as an analyst with my outfit. Fancy it?'

'Not in a million years. How did you get involved?'

'Through Hermann Gresch. He was in the same boat as me; his criminal record was a hell of a lot longer and more distinguished than mine but, like mine, it was for real. He was recruited in a German prison, in the same way that I was, but instead of creating a new, respectable front for him, they let him carry on as a fraudster, making sure he was never caught.'

'What about the people he conned?'

'He focused on government agencies; they were always reimbursed on the quiet and Hermann never got to keep all the money. Interpol hung him out there as a human lure.'

'Did they know who they were after?'

'No, but they did know what. This type of hustle has been pulled before, in St Lucia in the Caribbean and in the Far East, in Thailand. In the second one, an American politician was done for four million dollars, and some very loud noises were made. The minor people involved in each case were caught and put away, but there were others who weren't and none of the money was ever recovered. The Interpol operation had several targets but the people who had pulled off those two were very high on the list. And then it fell into our hands.'

'How?'

'Hermann Gresch was approached in Lithuania, by a woman calling herself Lidia Bromberg. She told him she was putting together a team for an operation, built around a hotel casino complex in Spain. She said that the seed capital, twenty million euros, was already in place, and she needed salespeople to raise more.'

'Did she say where the seed capital had come from?'

'No, but I'll get to that. She told Gresch that she had vacancies for two people, who would be presented as board members and whose brief would be to sell the project to investors.'

'Did she say what was in it for Gresch and his eventual associate?'

'Ten per cent each of the money they raised. The target was . . .'

'One hundred million euros: I know. So potentially you and Gresch stood to pocket eight million each.'

'How did you find that out?'

'Basic company research,' I said glibly. I hadn't told him about Kravitz; Mark prefers to operate discreetly.

He swallowed that without a sign of doubt. 'Of course. The project had to appear legitimate, since we were dealing with legitimate people, mostly. Pintore, the law firm that registered it, is absolutely kosher. Anyway, Gresch agreed to go along with it, and said he could find the second man. He contacted his handler, and I was told to go to Kaunas to meet up with him, and eventually to meet Lidia Bromberg.'

'I know you went there; Susannah told me. So you did meet Bromberg? Why didn't you recognise her this afternoon?'

'Ah, but I didn't. Somebody else showed up in her place, a Canadian guy Gresch said he'd never met before.'

'How did you know he was Canadian, not American?'

'One, there's a slight thing about the Canadian accent: there's a bit of Scots in it, as in the way they say "house". Two, he wore a maple-leaf badge in his lapel. Honest to God, it was like a bloody job interview. He asked us about our backgrounds, and we told him. He asked how I swung so much remission, and I said that was how it worked in England . . . plus when I was in I'd given the prison governor stock-market tips that had done very nicely for him. He laughed at that.'

'Was it true?'

'Of course not. Those people are incorruptible.'

'I take it you passed.'

'Not there and then. The Canadian . . .'

'Rowland?'

'Eh?'

'Was he Alastair Rowland, the chairman of the board, according to the website?'

'Maybe. I've never met Rowland, not to my knowledge at any rate. Anyway, as I was saying, the Canadian guy, who never did give us his name, told us that they had some further checking to do on us. He told me to go back to Switzerland and wait for word. But he also made it clear that if the two of us didn't check out okay, that would be very bad news. In fact it would be hazardous to our health.'

'But you did, obviously.'

'Yes. A couple of weeks later, Gresch turned up in Davos, only he checked himself in as George Macela. He told me we were on board, and that we were moving to Seville. He gave me paper identifying me as Roy Urquhart. He said our new team would not be expecting me to serve any formal notice period in Switzerland, and that when I left, they'd expect me to trawl the Cinq Pistes records for potential contacts . . . as I did, but I imagine Susannah told you that.'

'Yes. So you and "Macela" changed identities and you started your new job.' Frank nodded. 'Did he ever describe Lidia Bromberg to you?'

'No, but it's a pretty fair bet that she's stocky, with dark hair, big bazookas and currently sporting a superficial stab wound in her arse.'

The thought amused me, I'm afraid. 'And Caballero, when did you meet him?'

'As soon as we got there. Gresch told me to report to Calle Alvarez Quintero forty-seven, and when I did, the council-man turned up. His mother owns the place, but she's in a care home, so he told us we could stop there.'

'Shouldn't this super-complex have had an office?'

'There wasn't any need. Hardly any of our punters ever wanted to come to Seville. When someone did, we met them in Hotel Alfonso Thirteen, and pitched the project to them in a meeting room there, videos, literature, the lot, then took them to see the site. They all went away happy, and we banked their cheques shortly afterwards.'

'Who controlled the money?'

'Ultimately? That's what Gresch and I were supposed to find out, but we never did.'

'Caballero?'

'Maybe, but I doubt it. At first I thought that he was a mug, the owner of the land and our fixer with local and national government, and no more than that.'

'I can tell you different.'

'Sure, but I found that out for myself a while back.'

'How?'

'I'll get to that too. Let me fill you in on the rest. For a start, I never trusted Gresch.'

'Why not?'

'Because I was told not to by my controller in London: she thought the Germans were taking a huge chance, thinking they could bring a recidivist criminal on to their side.'

'Hell's teeth, Frank, what are you?'

'I'm not a career crook. I'm a guy who chanced his arm and got caught, but unlike others I didn't rob anyone . . . okay, technically I did, but ultimately I didn't cost anyone any money. I was convinced that if this thing had played out, Gresch would have taken his cash and run with the rest of them. We were supposed to have three objectives, right: find the source of the so-called seed capital, find the person or people behind the scam, and pull it down before the innocent investors lost all their money. We didn't achieve any of those objectives. I found that I was having no contact with anyone in the organisation, other than Gresch, and I suspected the guy had been keeping secrets from me.' He drained his glass again, and refilled it.

'I was supposed to be the sales director,' he continued, 'and he, the older man, was supposed to be the CEO; that meant that he, rather than I, received funds from investors, either by cheque or transfer. When I asked him what he was doing with it, he said that I didn't need to know that. I told him that I damn well did, but he said something about having orders from above to share only necessary information as a basic security measure.'

'You didn't believe him?'

'No. I checked with my controller, and she said it was crap. So, next time we received a payment I followed Gresch and, blow me, didn't he go straight to Caballero.'

'What did you do? Confront him? Is that when it all got rough?'

'No, not then.' He grinned. 'I broke into Caballero's house, didn't I? There was a civic do one night and I knew that he and his wife would be there, so I let myself in, as I'd been taught to do . . . imagine, recruiting a guy from prison, then having to train him in burglary . . . and I went through his desk, and his safe. In there I found a file, detailing the money Gresch had passed on, and containing bank slips showing that it had been transferred to a bank in Luxembourg, into the project's company account. I also found a list of the investors, and saw where the seed capital had come from, a French company called Energi, on behalf of something called the Banovsky Corporation.'

'Good for you. Then did you confront Gresch?'

'No. I was due to go to Brussels to meet a potential investor. I left a day early and went to London first, to see my controller. I told her what I'd found and we did some very quick digging into the Banovsky Corporation. We found that it's a dormant company, based in Slovakia. Energi is a coal-mining operation, working in the north of France. A very quick look into it told us nothing about its ultimate owners, the people behind Banovsky, but did reveal that one of its minor shareholders is Emil Caballero.'

'Wow!' That may sound trite, but I really did say it at the time. 'You clever lad! So why's he still walking about?'

'Because I was told to go on to my meeting in Brussels as if nothing had happened, then head on back to Seville and carry on business as usual until I was contacted. My controller said that the piece of the jigsaw they needed was Lidia Bromberg. They'd been trying to find her since that initial contact with Gresch, but with no joy. Hopefully a few days' digging into Energi, and the Banovsky Corporation, would lead us to her, and to the mysterious Canadian.'

'You did all as you were told?'

'Yes, like a good little agent I went back into character, did the deal in Brussels, and took the mug's cheque back to Seville, to number forty-seven. I'd been supposed to visit my mum

before I went back, but my boss said, "No, no time for that."
When I got there, the first thing I saw was Gresch, tied to a
chair and clearly on another planet. The second was the
Canadian. Then another guy came out of the kitchen, someone I'd never seen before. They weren't pleased with me: I
could tell by the size of the knives they were holding.'

'What did you do?'

'Something else I'd been trained to do. I hit them with a
mace spray I carry all the time. It's tricked up to look like an
inhaler. Then I legged it.'

'And all this happened six weeks ago?'

'Yes.'

'So where have you been since then?'

'Keeping as quiet as I could. I have a safe-house; I set it up
as soon as I began to suspect that Gresch was bent, and that the
whole operation might be compromised. It's on nobody's
budget but my own, a rented flat to the north of the city.'

'Couldn't you have got in touch with anyone? Your
controller, for example. Or even, dare I say it, your mother?'

He stared at me. 'And there was me thinking you were
bright,' he said. 'I was shopped, Prim, by my own team, sold
out from within Interpol. I'd suspected Gresch, but he was
innocent. You can tell that now, can't you, because he's
fucking dead. My guess is that they kept him doped up, then
when you started to snoop around, and it all got hairy, they
killed him.'

'You mean Caballero did. I saw him go into the house.'

'So did I. I was watching you, remember.'

'So why didn't you show yourself yesterday?'

'Because I'd probably have got us both killed. They let you stay out there as bait for me. But I didn't bite until I had no choice.'

'So how will it play out in Sevilla?'

Frank shrugged. 'Good question, but this is how I see it. George Macela is dead, exposed as the con-man Hermann Gresch. Lidia Bromberg will limp off and get her arse stitched, telling the hospital she fell and cut it, then she'll vanish. The money has gone, be sure of that; the investors have been done and Energi will post a tax loss. Emil Caballero will scream his outrage at being conned, and may even claim to have invested cash as well as land in the project. The Guardia Civil will launch an investigation that will go precisely nowhere.'

'And you?'

'I'm royally fucked, cuz. I'm totally deniable, and I've been set up by my own team.'

'But why?'

'There has to be a mole, an insider on the payroll of the people behind all this. Maybe it's my controller, maybe somebody above her, but someone's spilled the beans to . . .'

'Alastair Rowland?'

'Why not? Let's call him that. It's as good a name as any other. In any event, he's got my number and my name; now he wants me. And because you're with me, he'll want you too.'

'But how will he find us? You've done, if I may say so, a brilliant job of covering our tracks.'

'He doesn't have to find us.'

'What do you mean?'

He took out his mobile, and held it up. 'I never answer this thing, but it does receive texts. That's why I didn't get rid of it. I haven't checked it today.' As I watched, he hit a couple of buttons, then sighed. 'Ah, shit, the bastard thinks like I do. Take a look.' He handed it across to me.

A text message showed on the tiny screen; it was in proper English, not in shorthand, and it read, 'Either you have three days to live, or your mother has. Involve the police and she'll have no time at all.'

Twenty-one

Somehow that text made me feel like a prisoner again, and I wasn't having that. My mobile had been charging in my room while we were talking. I went in, unplugged it and switched it on.

'You can't use that,' Frank exclaimed. 'They could track us through it, believe me.'

I wasn't sure that I did, but I humoured him. 'It's all right, I'm only going to check my text messages.'

There were three, all from Mark Kravitz, all asking me to get in touch to confirm that I was okay. I picked up the hotel phone to call him, but my cousin vetoed that too. 'You're the paranoid one now,' I told him.

'No, I'm not. If they've been monitoring your phone, they could be tapping the number you're going to dial now, if you've used that to call it before.'

'The man I'm going to call would know if his phone was being tapped.'

'Wouldn't make any difference, if they trace the incoming call back to here. As for me being paranoid, that's no bad thing in a situation like this. Christ, it's almost a requirement.'

'I'll call Susie, in that case, to let her know I'll be out of touch for a while.'

'Did you call her earlier?'

'Yes, to make arrangements for Tom.'

'Then they could be tapping her phone too. These people have someone inside Interpol, Prim. There's nothing they can't do. Do you want to put your son in danger?'

'My son is with Conrad Kent by now; I can't think of anywhere safer.'

'Then be content with that, and let things be.'

There was a line of logic in what he was saying. I put the phone back in its cradle. 'Come on,' I told him. 'Let's get the hell out of here. Let's lose ourselves among the tourists; let's visit the Mezquita.'

Frank frowned. 'I don't know about that.'

Suddenly I was steaming mad. I had volunteered to find the little sod for his mother's sake, and for her sake alone, and here I was, caught up in a mess of his making, my life in constant danger, my aunt God knew where, and my son on the way to a secure location. I snapped. 'Well, I bloody do!' I shouted at him. 'I'm going out, and if the thought of stopping me even crosses your mind, be warned that your Swiss Army knife doesn't have a special tool for retrieving it from up your fundament!'

With a sigh and a shrug, he gave in. 'Okay, if you insist. I'll come with you, though.' He sounded as if he was doing me a favour. I let him carry on believing that.

We left the Hotel Conquistador and crossed the road, passing though an arched gate that led into a rectangular courtyard that was one big orange grove. There was no fruit on the trees, yet it had a distinctive citrus smell. Frank must have caught the twitch of my nose. 'You should see it, here and in Seville, when they're ready to harvest,' he said. 'The trees are thick with fruit; a lot of it falls off before they can pick it, and gets squashed on the ground. The smell is fantastic. They're not very good to eat, though: most get used for marmalade.' I'd known that, but I let him lecture me. He seemed to enjoy it.

We bought tickets at the admissions booth, but declined the audio tour guides, as the attendant wanted us to leave our passports with her as security for the machinery. The Mezquita is vast. I don't know how many football pitches you could fit inside, but I'd guess at more than a couple. It's one of the strangest buildings I've ever been in, having been a grand mosque during the Moorish occupation of Andalusia, until they were driven out and it was reconsecrated by their conquerors as a Christian church. Much of the area was open, encircling a great chapel. We had a look in there: it was full of Japanese tourists and we mingled with their group, until Frank's paranoia kicked in again and he got nervous in case my western face . . . he was okay . . . stood out in the crowd.

We moved across, into a museum section filled with artefacts of the Christian period. We stood for a while, awestruck . . . at least I know I was . . . by a thirteenth-century processional cross fashioned from silver and rock crystal. 'What are we going to do?' I asked quietly.

'I don't know,' my cousin replied.

That gave me no comfort. 'And here was me thinking you had the situation in hand.'

'We've got three days; they've given us that long to turn ourselves in. My guess is that we may need that long to get to wherever they're holding Mum, but we can only find that out if I reply to that message. If I do that they could pinpoint our present location and close in on us.'

'And Adrienne?'

'I don't want to think about that. They want us out of the way because we know the story. She doesn't, but if they've let her see their faces, if she can identify them . . .'

'Are you working up to saying she's a goner anyway, so what's the point of giving ourselves up?'

'Hell, no! I'm going to get her out of this, wherever she is. I just need time to think about how.' His back straightened, and he stood a little taller, as if he had just reached a decision. 'First thing tomorrow,' he declared, 'we take the train to Barcelona, and we recover your car. Wherever they're holding Mum, it won't be far from your place. I don't think they'd risk transporting her any great distance. We'll have the whole of the next day to find her. If we haven't . . . I'll hand myself over, and you do what you were planning, drive to Monaco and get under the protection of this Conrad guy. Once you're there, do what you can, even if it's only recovering our bodies.'

I shivered when he said that. In that ancient church, he'd drawn me back into the reality of the situation, and no mistake. I wanted to stay there, put down roots, cling to the old rugged cross we had been admiring, and hope against hope that everything would be all right after all. Only I couldn't: they'd be closing the place within the next half-hour.

We moved out of the museum area and back into the concourse of the church. As we walked I was looking for the exit sign. I spotted it, in the far right corner of the great building. And, close to it, I spotted something else, or rather someone.

'I know that guy over there,' I said to Frank. 'He sat down at the next table to me in a bar last night, with his gay partner. We had a drink together. His name is Sebastian Loman, his buddy's called Willie Venable, and they're from Kansas.'

He followed the direction of my nod, and stiffened. 'Wherever else they're from,' he whispered, 'it isn't fucking Kansas. That's the Canadian, the guy who interviewed me for this bloody thing, the guy who was waiting for me that day in number forty-seven. You can bet that the other one was good old Willie.'

He pulled me back into the museum. 'How did he get here?' I demanded, as if he should have known more than I did.

'He must have been staking out the station after all. My guess would be that he saw us get on the train and boarded it after us. Then he saw us get off, followed us, watched us and grabbed another taxi.'

'But how would he know to come here?'

'It's the best guess in town . . . no, the only guess. I'm sorry, Prim, I screwed up, bringing us to this place.'

'So what do we do now?'

'Same as we were going to do tomorrow. Come on.'

We backtracked, making sure that we kept ourselves out of sight of the point where Sebastian had been standing. However, that didn't solve the ultimate problem: he was so close to the exit that there was no way we could get past him without being seen.

We were stuck . . . until unexpected help arrived, from the east. The Japanese party, at least fifty in number, poured out of the chapel and headed *en masse* for the exit. 'This way,' I said, grabbing Frank by the arm and pulling him towards the entrance, thanking our lucky stars that he was only a little bugger, as the tourists shielded us from the Canadian. Of course, I was wondering all the time where his boyfriend was. (I was pretty sure they hadn't been faking that.)

The jobsworth on the door tried to stop us, but together we brushed him aside, without difficulty. I could feel him glaring after us as we ran (in my case, hellish painfully) the short distance to the arched gateway, and through it. I made for the hotel, but Frank tugged at my elbow. 'No, we don't have time.'

'But . . .'

'What have you left behind in there?'

'My case, the clothes I changed out of, and the other new stuff.'

'Then leave it: there's every chance the other guy's waiting for us inside. You've got everything you need, and I've got my rucksack.' As he spoke, a taxi drew up, and dropped off an American couple. Frank exchanged thumbs-up signs with the driver and jumped in; I had no choice but to follow him. 'Station, please,' he said.

'Where are we headed?'

'I told you, ultimately Barcelona, but first we're going to the last place they'll look for us, back to Seville.' I looked at him sceptically. 'Trust me.' He grinned. 'Listen, Prim, this is a good move. The Canadian doesn't know we clocked him. If he hasn't done so by now, he and his pal . . . he's here too, I imagine . . . will trawl the hotels around here once they give up on the Mezquita. When they do, they'll find that we're registered at the Conquistador and they'll stake it out. It'll take them a few hours to figure out that we're not coming back. We're gone, it's okay.'

At Córdoba Station, while Frank went to buy tickets, I headed straight for the shops where I bought another top and three more pairs of knickers, since at the time I wasn't wearing any and, no longer having a bloody clue how life was going to turn out, I decided that I didn't really want to die in that state.

We had half an hour to wait for the next AVE, which was due at quarter to eight. We spent it in the club lounge, drinking coffee to keep us sharp, snacking on biscuits and watching the door, never taking our eyes off it. Frank pretended to be reading a newspaper, but he wouldn't have fooled anyone.

He took it with us when we left, and actually did read it on the comfortable, high-speed journey back to Sevilla. At one point I saw his eyebrows rise, and a smile come to his lips, but I was too tired to think of asking him what the hell he found funny in our circumstances.

'Right, Spook,' I challenged him, as the train drew into Santa Justa station. 'Next?'

'How many times do I have to tell you? Barcelona.'

I gave up; I walked away from him and flashed my ticket at the executive-lounge attendant, expecting him to follow me. But he didn't, not right away. As I came out of the ladies' after a thorough freshen-up and after donning a piece of my new underwear, I saw him at the desk, in conversation. He beckoned me, with a degree of urgency. 'Come on,' he called out. 'We only have a few minutes.'

'For what?' I snapped, as I approached.

'To catch the sleeper. I've got us two berths and it's on the platform already.'

I was too gob-smacked, and plain bushed, to argue. Once again I followed in his wake. The berths he had secured were first class; just as well for him. They were also in a double cabin. 'Frank,' I began ominously, as the steward ushered us in.

'It's all I could get,' he protested, as the train pulled out of the station. 'I'll take the top bunk.'

'No, I will,' I told him. 'And I'll pull up the damn ladder after me.'

He winked at me. 'Dunno what you're being so prissy about. I've seen it all before. You went to the toilet yourself when you took me.'

I stared at him. 'You remember that?'

'Absolutely.'

'You little creep. But let me tell you something. There's

much more of me, these days, so you haven't seen it all . . . and you ain't going to.'

He laughed. 'I'll just have to live on memories, then.'

'Hold on to that word, "live",' I cautioned him.

'True,' he conceded.

'Can we eat now?'

'Not until the train's past Córdoba, and we can be sure that these bastards don't get on there.'

'You mean we're heading back there?'

'That's the route.'

'And if they do get on?'

He frowned. 'Then I'll just have to kill them,' he replied, in a quiet tone that I found myself believing, utterly.

Twenty-two

Happily, they didn't get on, so Frank's dangerous little knife stayed in his pocket. We went to the restaurant, for a late dinner, but not before he had gone through every one of the train's carriages, looking, just in case.

As we ate, I asked him about his life in Switzerland. 'If you hadn't got involved with this Interpol thing, do you think it's something you might have done anyway?'

'Maybe. I know I loved it while I was there. It was a really terrific job, and I was more than a little cheesed when I had to chuck it and move on.'

'And Susannah Gilpin: were you cheesed when you had to chuck her?'

'You'd better believe it.'

'What would you have done if she'd agreed to leave her husband? You could hardly drag the poor woman into this life.'

'I'd have walked away from all of it for her. I still would, if she changed her mind.'

'Er, Frank,' I ventured, 'that may be a little academic,

given what's happened. The life seems to have walked away from you.'

He smiled wistfully. 'You have a point there. Maybe I'll still have a chance with her, once I get out of this mess. You spoke to her. What do you think?'

'She sounded to me like the sensible type, very sensible. Ask yourself, honestly. Would a sensible girl take a chance on the likes of you?'

The smile turned into a grimace. 'You never know.' He looked me in the eye, across the table. 'Your late ex-husband was a very sensible type, from what I read of him. He took a chance on you . . . more than once, from what Mum told me.'

God, that one had come from out of the blue. 'As it happens,' I replied icily, 'the chance-taking was mutual. But he dumped me, didn't he, not once but twice?'

'And you've never forgiven him?'

'No, I never have, but not for dumping me. I understood why he did it, both times.'

'So what was his big crime, his unforgivable sin?'

'I'm not going there, Frank. That's something I'm keeping to myself.'

'That's very noble of you, if unnecessary, seeing as the guy's dead. Or are you protecting his memory?'

'It's got sod-all to do with his memory. I don't want Tom to find out, ever.'

'You're properly stuck on that little man, aren't you?'

'So much so that sometimes it surprises even me. I didn't think I could ever be so happy.'

'Too bad Oz isn't around to share it, then.'

'No. Oz was very reserved when it came to sharing.'

He speared his last prawn. 'Suppose he was still around, and suppose the d'Amuseo scam had screwed him for big bucks?'

'No chance, he was way too cynical to get suckered into something like that.'

'But suppose, just suppose. Let's say he'd been taken for five million euros, as a couple of people will have been if the money does vanish. What would he have done? Written it off as loose change?'

I considered the question. 'I can't say for sure, you understand,' I began, 'but my suspicion would be that by now Caballero would be a couple of metres under in his own land, with Lidia Bromberg alongside him, and anyone else Oz's people could find.'

He whistled. 'Are you pulling my chain?'

I shook my head.

'And that's what you don't want Tom to find out about his dad?'

'Along those lines.' I held his gaze. 'Let me tell you something now: if you ever think of using that as a lever against me, you might find out how alike Oz and I were. A couple of his friends are my friends too, and I'd turn them loose in the blink of an eye on anyone who threatened our son, in any way.'

He eyed me up and down: I let the words hang in the air for a few seconds. 'Now,' I continued abruptly, 'change the subject. When you were reading that paper on the AVE, what made you grin like an undersized Cheshire cat?'

'I saw an outside chance for us to get out of this mess, if I can get us close to him. There was a thing called "Agenda" in the political pages, showing forthcoming events, meetings, visits and suchlike. Guess who's due in Barcelona tomorrow, for a consultation on the Olympics in preparation for 2012? None other than the UK junior culture minister, Justin Mayfield, MP. If I can get to see him, and tell him about the bother we're in, and about how we were dropped in it, we could just be in the clear.'

'What could he do?'

'He's a member of the government, for Christ's sake. He's got clout. He could blow the whistle on Interpol, and call for an investigation into how I was set up, by whom, and why. A mole in that organisation has international security implications.'

I had to agree with all of that. 'An investigation would have to start with your controller. What's her name, anyway?'

'I knew her as Charlotte, but I'd be amazed if that's her real name. I agree she's a possibility, but she's not the only one. She has her own line managers.'

'Who are they?'

'Within the Interpol London bureau, I only ever met her. I was a secret even in their world, Primavera. Imagine the consequences if it became known that security services across Europe were recruiting convicted criminals as part of their strategy to combat major international crime.'

'Yes, I can imagine them. And that suggests another way back into the daylight. Why don't you simply phone the *Sun*, or the *Daily Mail*, any bloody tabloid, and sell them the story?'

'Because I'm deniable, all the way along the line. There is no paper trail. The tabloids are interested in stories that shake governments; ours is earthquake proof on this.'

'But somebody must have signed off on it.'

'If they have, those papers will be secret for ever, or until everyone involved is long gone. But I doubt if anyone did. I worked in Westminster, remember. Sometimes ministers just don't want to know about things that might splash mud on their boots.'

'Or blood,' I murmured. 'So how do we get to see your old pal Mayfield?'

'You probably don't. It's an official visit, and he'll probably have a tight timetable, so I'll have to blag my way past his private secretary. That might be more difficult if I had you in tow.'

'Where will you find him?'

'He's going to be in the Hotel Arts, according to the paper. Do you know where that is?'

'Yes, I've been there. It's right down on the sea. It was built as part of the Olympic village, then converted. That may be why he's stopping there. Do you think he'll see you? After all, you did say he distanced himself from you when you went to prison, and he didn't return Auntie Ade's calls.'

Frank nodded. 'I think he will. I know a few things about

him from the old days, like who his cocaine supplier was and how much he and I went through. Plus there was a married lady he was shagging back then, and even now if her name came out it could cost him his job.'

'Okay, so you're going to blackmail your way in to see him?'

'When the devil drives,' he whispered.

I picked up my coffee cup, but it was empty, and there was no waiter around to refill it. 'That's it for me,' I told him. 'I've had it.' As soon as the words passed my lips, I realised just how true they were. I had missed out on several hours' sleep the night before, and since then I'd been running on adrenaline. I really was knackered; plus my foot hurt like hell, and I had no paracetamol.

'Yes, me too,' Frank admitted. 'Let's get along there and lock ourselves in. This train still has a stop to make during the night.'

'I'm too tired to bother about that. If anyone wakens me, I'll rip his throat out with my teeth and that'll be that.'

We walked the short distance back to our compartment, where Frank secured the door and then wedged his rucksack strap around the handle as extra insurance. I climbed into the top bunk, but didn't pull up the ladder; it would have been churlish, after he'd saved my bacon . . . and I didn't really have room for it.

I switched off my reading light, then stretched full out, slipped off my clothing, all of it, folded it as neatly as I could, into the smallest package possible, and put it by my side. Naked, I slipped under the sheet that Renfe had provided.

I waited for Frank's light to go out, but it didn't. I glanced to my left and saw the top of his head, as he faced the basin in the corner. I leaned over for a better look. He was standing, rigid, in his underpants and seemed to be trembling violently, shaking from top to toe. 'Hey,' I whispered. 'What's up?'

'I'm sorry.' His voice was strained. 'You could have died today, we both could, and we're still stuck well in the middle of the fucking forest. I've been in hiding for six weeks, Prim, in hiding from the whole fucking world, including my own mother, and it's done no good because I'm still in danger, you're in danger, and now she's in danger too. It's getting to me, that's all. I need a few moments of weakness to regroup. Don't worry, though: I'll be fine.'

He was still shaking. 'Hey, wee guy,' I found myself saying gently. 'You need a cuddle. Come on up here for a bit.'

He turned and I reached out my hand to him. He climbed the ladder and lay down alongside me. I wrapped my arms around him, as I had done with Tom when he was younger; he felt cold, even though the train's air-con was only a partial barrier against the heat of the night, and he was still shivering. I held him tight, until his tremors began to subside, until he felt warmer, and calmer, and the pounding of his heart had slowed. I realised that my chest was damp, and that he had been crying.

'Here now,' I murmured. 'It's all right. It's all right. Let me show you.' I wrapped the sheet around us both. With the movement, my right nipple pressed against his parted lips: I felt him suck it, very gently, not voraciously, as Tom used to do. I was sure it was involuntary, rather than erotic. It didn't excite me, yet I found it touching. What happened after that was probably inevitable, given all that we'd been through that day, and the state he was in. I slid my arm down his back as he lay there, motionless, found his underpants, eased them past his buttocks, and took them off with my left foot. I reached for him, and found him still shrivelled and flaccid, for all our proximity. I massaged him, gently at first, and then more firmly, as he began to stir. It took a little while, but eventually he was as ready as I reckoned he was going to get. I drew him on to me; he seemed to weigh hardly anything. His head was on my shoulder as I guided him to the entrance, and took him inside me, into my moistness. I ran my fingers through his hair, and began to move, slowly. I wrapped my legs around him, pulling him deeper, until finally he responded, thrusting, and we were in rhythm.

It didn't last long, and I didn't have anything approaching an orgasm, not even after those years of total abstinence, but he did, or at least he came, for I'm told that's not always one and the same thing for a guy. It wasn't great sex, in fact it didn't even approach good, but somehow it left me feeling at peace with myself, realising as he finished that until then, until that very moment, I hadn't thought of the Algonquin, not once.

'I'm sorry.' He breathed the words in my ear.

I smiled. 'Less of the sorry, okay? We're going to get through this, and if we don't, well, what the hell? We've eaten, we've drunk, and we've made merry.'

I slid out from under him and down the ladder. I filled the

basin, washed myself thoroughly with one of the cloths and a small bar of soap, then dried myself with a hand-towel. When I climbed up again, he was on his back, sleeping like a baby, with a look on his face that would have become an angel. I reached over him, retrieved my small parcel of clothes, and took the bottom bunk.

Twenty-three

I still felt okay about it in the morning, when I woke just before seven, to the gentle rocking of the train as it pulled out of a station, Tarragona, I guessed, recalling the destination list I had seen as we got on.

I got out of my bunk and did some stretching exercises, as far as I could in the limited space. I washed the rest of myself, smeared my roll-on antiperspirant under my arms and on the inside of my thighs, then dressed.

By the time I was finished, and looking acceptable, Frank had begun to stir. He propped himself up on an elbow and looked down at me. 'Morning.' He yawned.

'And to you. How do you feel?'

'Fine. The tiger's back, I promise.' He paused. 'Prim, about last night, I'm sorry.'

'Listen,' I replied, 'I'm not going to shag you every time you say you're sorry so give it up.'

He laughed. 'Damn it,' he said. 'No, I didn't mean that; it was lovely. What I meant was I'm sorry you saw me like that, but the truth is, all that stuff yesterday, it scared me shitless.'

'And what's wrong with that? How do you think I felt when I walked into that hotel room and saw Caballero holding a gun on me, or when you told me the truth about the Canadian and his mate?'

'I meant to ask you about them,' he told me. 'When you met them in that restaurant, did you tell them why you were in Seville?'

'Hell, no. I told them I was a single mum playing the tourist for a few days, while my aunt minded my child.' The implication of that dawned on me as I spoke. 'Oh, shit! I told them where they could find your mother. Frank, I'm so sorry.'

'Now you're at it,' he exclaimed. 'Prim, you weren't to know. Don't give it another thought, please.'

'That'll be difficult; shooting my mouth off to two strangers. What was I thinking of?'

'Nothing, forget it.' He swung his legs over the edge of the bunk, and sat there, looking down at me. He had a small erection . . . not that he could ever have a large one, to tell you the truth . . . and in the full light of day, that made me feel a little awkward, and want to get out of there.

'I'll make room for you to get washed and dressed,' I volunteered. 'I'm off to the restaurant car for breakfast. I'll order for you. Coffee and croissants enough?'

'That'll be fine.'

I left him to it and made my way along the train. As I sat down at a table for two, I realised I wasn't sure whether I should be feeling like a whore or a social worker. I settled for the latter, and gave my double order to the waiter.

I had finished mine and was contemplating scoffing Frank's croissant when he arrived. He must have been carrying a razor in his rucksack . . . or maybe the Swiss Army knife did that job too . . . for the slight stubble he had been sporting was gone. He had changed into a white T-shirt, so new it almost gleamed: I could see creases, as if to confirm that it had just come out of its wrapping. His hair was perfectly groomed and he smelled of something I thought I recognised as Aramis.

'I wonder where we'll be having breakfast tomorrow,' he said, as he sat.

'With respect, Frank,' I told him, 'I hope I'll be having breakfast in Monaco with my son and his half-siblings, and that you'll be safely reunited with Auntie Ade.' It had occurred to me that maybe the smartest thing for me to do when the train pulled into Barcelona was to jump into the first available taxi, head for the airport, reclaim my Jeep and drive as fast as I could out of the Dodge Goddamned City that my life was threatening to become.

The croissant stopped halfway to his gob, as if he had read my mind. 'I hope so too, love, but I need you with me when I go to see Justin.'

I frowned at him. 'First, please don't call me "love". For the avoidance of doubt, what happened last night happened mainly because I felt sorry for you, and partly, I suppose, because I haven't had sex for going on three years. Second, why is it so important that I go with you?'

'Corroboration,' he replied. 'What the security services and Interpol tried to do through me and Gresch, and the way we were sold out from within the organisation, has massive implications. Governments have fallen for less, and Justin's a member of the bloody government. But he's a highly moral guy, not the sort to let a wrong go uncorrected. I can persuade him to take this to the highest level, but he'll need both of us to tell our stories. If heads are to roll over this . . . and they bloody well will, or my name's not Frances with an "e" . . . it'll take your evidence as well as mine to convict them.'

I couldn't argue with his reasoning; also, I thought of the weakness he'd revealed the night before. It was more than a possibility that whatever inner strength had sustained him though six weeks in hiding had been exhausted, and that he needed to draw on any resources I had in that department. 'Right,' I said, 'I'll come with you. Hopefully, he'll arrange protection for us, and organise a proper search for Auntie Ade.'

'Thanks. I appreciate it.'

I asked our waiter for more coffee, and for some toast and jam. As the train moved north, we finished breakfast, looking out of the window at the rugged skyline, through the slight haze that rose from the ground as the sun evaporated the dew that had settled through the night.

Before long the countryside began to change as we reached the outskirts of the urban sprawl that is Barcelona. The place has become a tourist Mecca since the 1992 Olympics helped to bring Gaudí's wonderful architecture to the world's attention, but all of that is to be found at its heart. Like virtually every city I can bring to mind, it ain't very pretty on the outside.

The platforms in Sants Station aren't architect designed either. They used to be darker than the London Underground, until new construction let some daylight in. As the train pulled in, we went back to our cabin and packed, if that's what you could call it. For all my good intentions, I had become a bag-lady, alongside Boy Scout Frank with his rucksack. We took our time over it, waiting until no more passengers seemed to be leaving the train; only when the cleaners began to move in did we step down on to the platform.

He led the way up the escalator, ever cautious, in case our enemies had got ahead of us once more, a possibility if they had a car and had driven like hell through the night. But there was no sign of the Canadian or his mate. I was going to head for the taxi rank, as usual, but Frank vetoed that. Instead we left the station by a side entrance, went into a shop on the edge of the square, and mingled with the early-morning shoppers for a while, before leaving by a different door, into another street, further away from the station. My guide and protector seemed to be back on form.

We walked briskly along the shaded pavement until we saw a taxi available for hire. I flagged it and climbed in as Frank took one last look around, to be sure. 'Hotel Arts, please,' I told the driver. The courtesies are always observed in Spain. I don't know another nation where 'please' and 'thank you' are used as often.

He nodded. 'You've been to Córdoba?' he asked, as he drove off.

'How did you know that?' I asked suspiciously; paranoia had me in its grip, good and proper.

'Your bag,' he replied. 'I recognised it. My sister lives in Córdoba; I go there a couple of times a year, and sometimes I shop with her. Did you visit the Mezquita?'

'Yes. Everyone does, don't they?'

'All the tourists, yes. Are you tourists?'

'What do you think?'

I saw him smile in the rear-view. 'You, I'm not certain, but your friend, he's not Spanish.' I glanced at Frank, sitting silently beside me, looking inscrutably Asiatic.

'No, that's for sure. Actually, I'm Scottish, and so's he . . . well, half of him.'

'That explains it. Scottish people speak good Spanish; better than the English. They cannot make our sounds.' It hadn't occurred to me before, but he was right: the ability to pronounce 'loch' properly does help a hell of a lot when speaking Castellano.

The morning traffic was at its peak, and so it took a while to reach the hotel. Our driver apologised for the delay, but said that it would have been worse if he had gone on to the throughway, the Ronda Litoral. Frank frowned doubtfully, but I knew that he was speaking the truth.

We pulled up in the covered driveway that is the entrance to Hotel Arts. A doorman came forward to greet us, but backed off when he saw how we were dressed and noted our lack of luggage. We walked up to Reception. 'Has Mr Justin Mayfield checked in yet?' Frank asked.

'He arrived last night, sir,' the clerk replied.

'Is he still here?'

'I believe so, sir.'

'Could you page his room for me, please? Tell him that Frank McGowan is downstairs and needs to speak with him on a matter of great urgency.'

'Certainly, sir.' As we looked on, she lifted a handset and dialled. There must have been an answer for she turned her back towards us abruptly, as if to make it difficult for us to hear what she was saying. As I watched her back, she nodded, then swung round to face us once again and handed the phone to Frank. He took it from her, picking up the base as well. 'Yes, Justin,' I heard him say, 'it's me. No joke. I'm not alone either. My cousin's here with me. She and I are in a bit of a crisis and we need your help.' He was silent for a while. 'Listen,' he said eventually, 'I didn't come all this way to be brushed off. I'll say two words to you, okay? Gretchen Roberts.' I saw a smile cross his face and then he nodded. 'Much better. Yes, we can do it that way if you want; she won't mind.' He recradled the instrument, and handed it back to the clerk. 'We're in,' he told me. 'At least, I am for now. He wants to see me first. When he's one hundred per cent happy, he'll call you up. You okay with that?'

I shrugged. 'And if I wasn't?'

'Thanks, Prim. I'm sure it won't be long.'

He headed for the lift: I found a big, soft chair in the lobby and sank into it. I was still carrying my handbag inside my shopping bag from Córdoba. It had some spare capacity; I rolled the remaining knickers inside the still-wrapped top and transferred them, then folded the redundant container, and slipped it under my seat.

The handbag was unzipped; inside my mobile, recharged, stared up at me. Bugger it, I thought. We were in a place of safety, more or less. If the clever people who were after us could triangulate my position, or whatever the hell it is they do, let them. I called Susie.

'Prim,' she exclaimed, before I had a chance to say a word. 'Are you all right?'

'We're safe,' I told her. 'How's Tom? He got to you, didn't he?'

'Tom's fine. As we speak, he's trying to teach the other two Spanish. And Charlie's gone down a treat. I fear Janet and wee Jonathan won't rest until they've got a four-legged pal of their own. But you: what's been happening to you? I've had Mark Kravitz on the phone, wondering if I'd heard from you.'

'I've had an interesting twenty-four hours. I'm with Cousin Frank; he's in a bit of bother, and as a result so am I, but he's sorting it out now.'

'Given his past, are we talking about go-to-jail bother here?'

'No, nothing like that.' I seized on what she had said. 'How did you know about his past?'

'Oz told me, a few years ago.' *Of course he did*, I thought. *After he'd had Mark spell things out for him.* 'What about your aunt?' Susie asked.

I confess that I hadn't thought about Adrienne for a little while. The question brought the three-days threat back to mind. We only had two left, and yet I'd been thinking about cutting and running for Monaco. 'No word,' I replied, a little economically, truth-wise. 'There are people after us, Susie. They have her, and they're using her to force us to give ourselves up. Frank's with someone now who can help, but it'll have to be discreet, no high-profile police searches.'

'Jesus. Is there anything I can do?'

'Look after my boy. Call Kravitz and tell him that I'm not able to get in touch with him, but that I'm okay. Thank him for his help over the last couple of days.'

'Couldn't he do more? Mark's got all sorts of connections.'

'True, but there's a chance that he might approach the wrong people. You sit tight, Susie.'

'I will. But let me know as soon as everything's sorted.'

'As soon as it is, I'll come straight to you.'

We said our farewells, and I called Alex Guinart. 'Primavera, at last,' he exclaimed. 'Where have you been?'

'Phone problem. Any sign of my aunt?'

'We haven't found her, if that's what you mean. I told my boss what had happened and we have a search under way, but low-key. The lady is over seventy; sometimes older people wander off, get lost in the countryside, in the woods. Occasionally, someone vanishes and we never see them again. We've been asking questions, without scaring the tourists. That's the standing order these days: be nice to the visitors.'

'So there's been nothing? No news of her?'

'Not quite. One of my officers spoke to a French couple who were in St Martí yesterday morning. He was a retired policeman, bossy type, the sort who sees everything, knows everything. He said that he saw a woman and a man walk down through the village. She was quite tall for a woman, he told us, with dark but shiny hair, whatever that's supposed to mean; not young, but not ancient either, in her sixties maybe. That sounds like your aunt, yes?'

'That's Adrienne . . . or at least it's a good description of her. What about him?'

'Much younger: he was about one metre eighty, slim, with bleached-blond hair and a little moustache. The Frenchman said he was a homosexual, and probably American, but I have no idea how he came to either of those conclusions.'

Maybe not, I thought, but if he was describing the guy I knew as Willie Venable, and I was damn certain that he was, he was spot on with the first, and close to the mark, at the very least, with the second. 'Did he say anything else about them?' I asked Alex. 'St Martí's usually thronged. How did he come to remember that couple?'

'He said they were walking very close together, as if he was helping her, holding her by the elbow. And they didn't speak. When the Frenchman said, "*Bonjour*", they both ignored him. What do you think, Primavera? Could it have been her?'

'I'm damn certain of it. I think I know the guy. If you can, you might organise a search of non-EU-citizen airport landing cards, looking for the name Venable, Willie Venable, possibly American, but just as likely Canadian. It's a long shot, though.'

'I'll make a call to the immigration office, in Madrid, to see if they have that name logged in their computer. When will you be back here?'

'As soon as I can, but my first priority will be to get to Tom. My second,' I told him, 'will be to catch up with my goddaughter. How is she?'

'She's lovely, and growing by the day. You get back as soon as you can. I'll keep an eye on your house till you do.'

I felt better after those calls, more in touch with reality, somehow. And for some strange reason, I felt better about Adrienne. If she was being held captive by 'Willie Venable', at least she was in the hands of someone I'd met, someone I'd spoken to, and someone who had a streak of kindness in him, unless my judgement of my fellow humans had gone completely out of the window. I wasn't nearly as confident about 'Sebastian Loman'. There had been a certain air of toughness about him. But the other one, even if he was an abductor, was capable, I hoped, of treating my aunt properly, and with respect.

I was still thinking positively when the receptionist called across to me: 'Excuse me, madam, you may join your friend. Take the lift to Reception on the thirty-third floor, where you'll be met.'

I thanked her and walked across to the bank of lifts; there was one waiting, and it zipped me up to thirty-three in around a quarter of that number in seconds. The doors opened, to reveal a man waiting on the other side. He was in his thirties, tall, a bit over six feet, immaculately dressed in pale green linen trousers and a crisp white shirt, with short sleeves and a button-down collar; I was sure that the lot was straight out of Marks & Spencer. His dark hair was perfectly cut, and a gold Rolex gleamed on his wrist as he held out his hand in greeting. His face was vaguely familiar, from *Sky News* coverage, and from the British newspapers that I buy occasionally.

'Mrs Blackstone,' Justin Mayfield exclaimed, with a politician's enveloping bonhomie, 'how good to see you. I had the pleasure of meeting your late husband on a couple of occasions through my ministerial office. A fine man, a great British achiever and a very sad loss.'

'My late ex-husband,' I felt obliged to point out. 'Many people share your views,' I chose my words carefully, 'and that pleases me, for my son's sake most of all.'

'Come and join us,' said the junior culture minister. 'My friend Frank has been filling me in on your remarkable adventures over the last day or so, and on his over the last few weeks.' He led me into a room that occupied an entire side of the great steel-and-glass tower, offering panoramic views of the Port Olympic and the Mediterranean. There was a waiter on duty, but nobody else in sight, other than Frank; he was sitting on a sofa at the far end of the room, with plates and cups on the table before him. 'Coffee for the lady,' Mayfield said to the waiter as we passed him, 'and a selection of sandwiches.' He ushered me to the sofa, then took a seat facing us.

'Where's your meeting?' I asked him.

'Downstairs,' he replied, 'at midday. I'm seeing the former mayor of Barcelona, from 1992, and my opposite number in the government.'

'National or Catalan?' The question seemed to take him by surprise. I guessed that he might be one of those Westminster types who look down their noses at devolved parliaments.

'Oh, national, of course.' I interpreted his superior smile as confirmation of my suspicion. He waited as coffee and some very fancy sandwiches were placed before me, and as the waiter withdrew to a distance. 'Now,' he continued quietly, looking at me, 'from what Frank has told me, this is a very serious situation. He's says he's been set up by an informer in the security service, or Interpol. Now your lives are in danger, and that of your aunt. Does that sum it up?'

'Succinctly. They've already murdered one man, two days ago, in Sevilla. I saw his body being taken out of the house where he was held. Yesterday the man I believe killed him tried to kidnap me, together with a female accomplice. If Frank hadn't been there to intervene, I . . . I might have gone the same way, maybe found on a park bench, dead, with a needle stuck in my arm and my prints on the syringe.'

'Then let's thank God he was there,' said the minister, 'and as resourceful as he's proved.' He grinned at him. 'You've changed since we worked together, chum. That spell inside must have done you good after all.'

'I don't recommend it,' my little cousin retorted. There was something childlike about his expression. I couldn't help it: I thought of him sucking my breast, and felt my cheeks go hot under my tan.

'Maybe not.'

'Can you help us?' I asked Mayfield, point-blank.

He turned towards me, leaning closer to both of us. 'I've heard whispers of these black operations,' he said, his voice lower. 'They're a European initiative, and I've also heard that not everyone in our security service approves of them. So Frank's story hasn't taken me completely by surprise.' He looked me in the eye. 'Yes, Primavera, I can help you. But I have to do it very carefully, or I could put you in even bigger danger. Before I can initiate action, I have to get back to London. My programme here is informal, but it's fixed, so I can't cancel any of it. However, I'll be back in Westminster tomorrow; as soon as I get there, I'll ask for a private meeting with the security minister. I know her well, and I expect that she'll go ape-shit when she hears what's happened. Meantime, I need you to lie low for twenty-four hours. As soon as I've briefed the minister, we'll try to bring you in, and we'll round up the people who are chasing you.'

'And Frank's mum?' I demanded. 'My aunt? What about her?'

'I gather that you still have two days of this deadline to give yourselves up. She'll be safe until then.'

'Or as safe as she can be,' Frank muttered gloomily. 'We can't even be certain she's still alive now, or if she is, that they'll let her go.'

'So why don't we offer to turn ourselves in,' I suggested, 'at the end of the deadline? Your people could close in then, and round them up.'

Mayfield frowned. 'There would be an unacceptable risk of something going wrong. If we did that and any of you was killed, the government would be seen to have sanctioned using two civilians as bait. None of my colleagues could ever be seen to go along with that.'

'Unofficially?'

'Not even. You take that course of action and you'll be on your own.'

'So what you're saying is that you can save us, but that Adrienne's probably had it. Am I correct?'

'I'm trying desperately not to say that,' the minister admitted. 'Do what I say: lie low and wait. We'll do all we can to rescue Ms McGowan.'

Frank jumped to his feet, taking me completely by surprise. 'Fuck off, Justin,' he exclaimed. 'That's not good enough. If push comes to shove, we can look after ourselves. I'm going to do all I can to rescue my mother. Come on, Prim.'

I could have stayed there. I could have let him go on his own and taken a room in the Hotel Arts for as long as proved necessary, or I could have gone back to my earlier plan, pick up the car and leave at full speed. But I didn't. I owed the little guy, didn't I? Someone had to watch his back. So I stood up and limped after him, still favouring my cracked toe as we headed for the door.

'You'll be on your own,' Mayfield called after us.

'So what's new?' Frank yelled back at him, holding up his right middle finger as a parting gesture of friendship.

Twenty-four

A s the lift descended I had a fleeting concern that Mayfield might have us stopped and held for our own protection, but either the thought didn't occur to him, or he didn't have the clout in Spain, for the lobby was clear as we stepped out.

As we crossed it, a large white Mercedes pulled up at the doorway and a middle-aged guy got out. His face was familiar: *The ex-mayor*, I thought. It looked as if the minister's meeting was about to begin, getting in the way of any further concern about us.

We didn't wait for a taxi. There's a metro station adjacent to the Hotel Arts. I led us to it. We bought tickets and boarded the first train. By this time I was thinking clearly, if not too far ahead. We changed lines after two stops and surfaced again in Plaça Catalunya. I pointed to El Corte Inglés. 'In there,' I said.

As always, the place was busy. If a pandemic hit the city, wiping out most of the population, Corte Inglés would still be full of shoppers. I found the lifts and we rode to the top-floor cafeteria, where I found a window table. I ordered two American coffees with a little milk on the side, and a sticky bun for me (I hadn't touched anything in the Hotel Arts clubroom), and we sat in silence until they arrived, and for a while after that.

'I'm out of ideas,' Frank confessed, at last. 'I've just told Justin that I'd save my mum without his help, but I don't know how to do it. We don't even know where she is.'

'No, but I do know who she's with,' I told him, then related Alex Guinart's story about the inquisitive, homophobic French ex-cop. My cousin's face fell. I reached across the table and squeezed his hand. 'Frank,' I said briskly, to convince myself as much as him, 'for the last twenty-four hours we've been fearing the worst and acting accordingly. It's time we changed that, and assumed the best. You reckon these people might have technical and other resources behind them, and that they could be tracking us. If that's so they know we're in Barcelona, for I used my mobile to call Alex and Susie.'

'Aw, Prim,' he protested.

'Bugger it. Let them follow us here if they can. This may not be the vindictive enemy you reckon.' (I wasn't sure where that phrase had come from. I didn't work it out until much later.) 'Who do we know that's against us, for sure? There's Caballero, who was in a lot of difficulty when we left him. There's Lidia Bromberg, who won't have sat down since yesterday. There's your Canadian chum, Sebastian Loman, whom we avoided in Córdoba, and there's his chum Willie.'

'Alastair Rowland?'

'I'm not sure that he exists.'

'Oh, he does, although I've never had a sniff of him. He's

somebody who's only wheeled out to tie up the biggest investors, someone with real clout.'

'But would he be involved in the nasty side of things?'

'Personally? No.' Frank nodded. 'Your timetable fits, I admit. Those two guys quizzed you on Monday night, with their friendly-Yanks act, you told them where Mum was, and we haven't seen the Willie character since. I'll grant you, he'd have had enough time to drive north and be in your village by yesterday morning, to snatch her.'

'Exactly.'

'But would she have gone without a struggle?' he mused. 'That wouldn't be like her.'

'I don't believe she had any choice. From the Frenchman's description he could have had a hidden gun on her, but he might not have needed that. Or . . . Tom was on the beach with Charlie the dog when she was taken. She may have decided to go quietly before he got back and was caught up in it. Or Venable could have pulled the reverse of what they're doing with us, "You come or they die." Any of those scenarios, plus the fact that she is seventy-two years old, would have pretty much forced her to co-operate. Whatever, Willie has her. So what's he done with her? He could hardly dump her in a hotel and tell her to behave herself till he got back, could he?'

'Granted, no.' He glanced out of the window, across the square. 'Maybe he's killed her already,' he whispered, 'to save himself any trouble.'

'We're not even going to imagine that possibility,' I told him.

'You're right.' He nodded vigorously. 'Maybe he has her in a safe-house, like I had in Seville.'

'There's plenty of property for holiday rental in and around St Martí,' I conceded. 'But . . . mostly it's apartments or villas all stuck cheek by jowl, and just now, nearly all of them are occupied.'

'Maybe he's hiding out in a gay club,' Frank said bitterly.

I was about to scold him for being flippant, but stopped myself. 'That's not as crazy as it sounds. There are plenty of gay-friendly hotels in Barcelona, and just down the coast there's Sitges; that has the most famous gay community in Spain.' I paused. 'Hey, Sebastian and Willie told me they were heading north for a spell, to a place they'd heard of near Girona; a retreat, was what they called it. Could it be that they let a bit of the truth slip out?'

'It's worth checking out, I suppose. But how?'

'Leave that to me. We're in my territory now.'

I reached for my phone. 'Hey!' Frank exclaimed.

I held up a hand to cut him off. 'I've used it already this morning, and I don't see any bad guys around. Besides, we're in the middle of a big city and we'll be on the move soon. When we do, we need somewhere to go. I'm going to try to take care of that. You want to do something useful, check your phone for messages.'

Among my circle of friends in St Martí is a lady named Shirley Gash. She and I go back at least ten years, to my first visit to the area with Oz. You either hit it off with her or forget it, but Shirl and I clicked. Her life hasn't been plain sailing since then; she had family and business trouble all at the same time, but she's back in calm waters now, and in virtual retirement. She adores Tom and Charlie, so I see quite a lot of her. Mind you, there's quite a lot of her to see: she's a large and elegant lady, tall, blonde and buxom. I called her home number. It rang a few times, and I was about to give up when she answered. 'Hello.' She's lived in Spain, mostly, for decades now, but she still speaks English when she picks up the phone.

'Shirley, it's Prim.'

'Hi, gal,' she said breezily. 'What you up to? You at home? I was just heading up to St Martí, for coffee in Can Coll. You and your small tribe want to join me?'

'Love to, but we're not at home. Tom and the dog are in Monaco, with the other family . . .'

'Fuckin' little tart,' she growled. Shirley does not approve of Susie for the way she and Oz got together, and for all I tell her we're fine now, she never will.

I let it pass, as I always do. 'I'm out of town too,' I told her, 'but I'm planning to head back today. Thing is, there's a small problem with my place just now. I was wondering, have you got anybody in your summer-house just now?'

'No, it's empty. Do you want to stop there?'

'Please. And I've got someone with me, my cousin, Frank McGowan.'

'What? The one you told me about, the Japanese sailor's spawn, the one who was in the nick?'

'Yes. You don't mind, do you?'

'Hell, no. I'd love to meet him. I'll do you one of my

'champagne risottos . . . bread-and-butter pudding too, if you fancy.'

'Stop it! I'm getting fat just thinking about it.' A little extra and unexpected sunshine had come into my day: that's her special-friends supper, and it's memorable. 'Shirley,' I continued, 'it's pick-your-brains time. Am I getting this right, when I recall you mentioning to me a place for gays that's opened up somewhere near us, in an old country house?'

'Masia Josanto, it's called,' she replied. 'It's on the other side of Gualta. Turn off the main road just past the golf course and go through the village. Got me?'

'Yes.'

'It's run by a couple of blokes, and that's where the name comes from. Lovely boys. José's from Mexico City and Antonio's from Málaga. Gay-friendly, they prefer to call themselves. That means they don't turn straight people away, but they don't pitch for their business either. I've eaten there. Damn good. The place is beautiful, very old: José's wealthy and he spent a lot of his fortune doing it up. They showed me round. It's all suites and such, very comfortable.'

'They would take a man-woman couple, though? Mother and son?'

She laughed. 'You thinking about taking your Frank there?'

'Less of it.' I chuckled. 'He's not that much younger. No, I was thinking of his mum.'

'No problem there. Here,' her tone changed, became suddenly mischievous, 'how many beds will I make up in the summer-house?'

'Shirley!'

'Do I take that as one, or two?'

'Two,' I said, maybe a little too defensively.

'Whatever you say, but it's a long time since you've had your bones jumped, and I won't be telling anyone.'

'Two,' I repeated.

She laughed again. 'See you later. What time?'

'Some time after six. So long for now.'

I turned to Frank. He was staring at his phone. He held it out to me. 'Take a look,' he whispered. I did, and saw a frozen image of Auntie Ade, sitting in a chair, in a well-furnished room. 'Press the green button.'

I did, and she began to move; it was a video clip, taken by a mobile. 'Son,' she said, in an unwavering voice, 'I imagine you know what this is all about. This man seems to be serious, so . . .' her eyes blazed '. . . don't do what he wants. Save yourselves and let them kill me if they've got the balls to do it.' A muffled sound came from off-screen. She glared at the holder of the phone. 'Fuck you!' she shouted. 'I'll say what I . . .' And there the clip ended.

I found myself smiling. 'She's a tough old bird, isn't she just? I hope he tied her up good and tight before he went to sleep, otherwise he'd be likely to wake up with a pair of nail scissors in his throat.'

'It's ironic, Prim,' Frank moaned. 'She's saying the same as Justin: accept the inevitable.' His eyes misted over.

'Which we won't,' I promised him. 'We've got a possible lead to her, and a definite bolt-hole for ourselves.' I told him about my call to Shirley. He looked less excited than I'd hoped. 'Come on,' I said. 'It's a long shot, but worth a try.'

'And it's all we've got.' He sighed.

'Hey,' I laughed, although his mood worried me, 'I thought you said the tiger was back.'

He squared his shoulders and seemed to perk up. 'You're right. I'm sorry; I'm still disappointed by Justin, that's all. How do we get there?'

'I'll show you.' I led the way downstairs and back to the metro, stopping on the way to draw cash with my Caixa de Girona card. Frank didn't protest that I was being reckless: he knew it would have been a waste of time. We took the underground to Gràcia, then caught the first train for the airport. I headed straight for the multi-storey car park and paid the charges in the ticket machine. There was nobody lying in wait for us; not that I expected company, not there. It took me a little while to find the Jeep in the chock-a-block level two . . . I really should note down the row number every time . . . but I did, eventually. It was intact. Frank wanted to check underneath for a bomb, but I pointed out that it would have been impossible to fix anything without leaving tell-tale marks in the dust that, I am ashamed to say, usually cakes the vehicle.

I fired it up and we headed out, into the daylight and into the stock-car-like traffic, air-con going full blast, and Del Amitri . . . a great, but underrated, Scottish band . . . full blast too, on the Boston Acoustics sound system. It felt great to be back behind the wheel, so great that I started to sing along. To my huge surprise Frank joined in; he liked the band too. I've got a decent voice, and he turned out to be not half bad either; I reckon we must have sounded pretty good, singing harmony with Justin Currie on 'Don't Come Home Too Soon', which is, incidentally, in my humble, if biased, opinion, the best World Cup anthem ever written.

We were still winding down the chorus when I took the Ronda Litoral through Barcelona . . . As we passed Hotel Arts I wondered if Mayfield's meetings were still going on.

By the time we hit the other side of the city, we were on to Graham Parker, more good road music, but not sing-along stuff. Soon we were past the Grand Prix racing circuit and picking up our *autopista* ticket. As I pulled it from the machine, it occurred to me that I had fulfilled my promise to Auntie Ade. I had gone to Sevilla and brought back her son. Now I had to find her for him.

Twenty-five

I didn't put the hammer down, but the A7 is a three-lane highway up to the Palamós exit, and so we made decent time, even though it was busy. It was ten past two as we reached the next turn-off. 'We'll jump off here,' I told Frank.

'Are we there?' he asked.

'No, but we need to discuss what we do next, and there's a good restaurant half a kilometre away.'

La Roca Petita is all that: it's near the airport, but unknown to the travelling punters. Most of its clients are business people from Girona. We didn't need or want much, just a selection . . . *escalivada*, anchovies, Jabugo ham and toasted bread, some Vichy Catalan to wash it down . . . and they were happy to provide it, with no sales pitch for the full menu.

As we ate, Frank was fidgety, all the way through. I could understand why: indeed, I was as anxious as him to be getting Auntie Ade out of her captors' hands. But I knew that we couldn't just go charging into Masia Josanto like a SWAT team. If Willie was holding her there, and we spooked him, there was no telling what he might do. Our approach required just a little subtlety, and it was best made at a time when, on a hot Spanish day in July, even elderly ladies and their kidnappers were likely to be having a siesta. I persuaded my cousin of the sense in this, but that didn't stop him squirming around in his chair as if his arse was hoaching with red ants.

'What about the money?' I asked, to distract him as much as anything else.

'What money?' He looked at me blankly.

'The investors' money, you idiot. A little over seventy-seven million euros at the last count.'

He blinked. 'Where did you get that figure?'

'I told you. I did some research before I set off in search of you.'

'What, all on your own, from St Martí?'

'No, I had help, from one of those people I told you about, Oz's people. So what about the money? Will it still be accessible in the Luxembourg bank, or will it have been transferred by now?'

'If it hasn't been,' he told me soberly, 'I suspect that'll happen very soon. And that will make it all the more important that they get us out of the way, so they can disappear, free and clear.'

I recalled something that Mark Kravitz had told me. 'Alastair Rowland: he'll have to surface.'

'Come again?'

'Funds can only be transferred out of the company's account on the written instruction of the chairman, signed over the company's seal. So he'll have to surface in Luxembourg.' A blinding possibility occurred. 'Maybe we should be there. Adrienne's going to be all right for another day at least. If we can intercept him, we could blow the whole operation.'

As swiftly as the flame had arisen, Frank extinguished it. 'Sorry,' he said. 'He doesn't: the chairman can send a signed authority to the bank from anywhere in the world. The company seal is held by one of the directors, as an insurance against Rowland, or anyone else, bolting with all the swag. Gresch had it; no prizes for guessing who's got it now.'

'Bromberg,' I concluded. 'Yet she would still have to get it to him. And yesterday, if you remember, she was planning to meet me with a view to taking my money. Okay, now they're cutting and running, but she's had precious little time to get the seal to Rowland.' I stopped, as the obvious dawned. 'Unless . . .' I whispered.

'What?'

'Unless, all along, Alastair Rowland and Emil Caballero have been one and the same person. You said yourself you've never met Rowland. Is it possible?'

He nodded reluctantly. 'It's possible,' he said. 'In fact, now I think about it, it might even be likely.' He looked at me. 'But with respect, Prim, you're taking your eye off the ball here. Fuck the money, all seventy-seven million of it. I'm not having my mum in that guy's hands for a moment longer than necessary. That's my only objective.'

I felt guilty. 'I'm sorry, Frank. You're quite right. So let's get on up the road and follow our only lead.'

He paid the bill, from his roll of cash, and was waiting for me outside after I'd fitted in a pit stop. 'Is it much further?' he asked, as I popped the locks on the Jeep.

'No,' I replied. 'We can stay off the motorway from here.'

The car park led almost immediately on to a roundabout, which fed on to the N11, heading north. We stayed on it as it passed to the east of Girona, then into a complicated junction, which set us on course for Palafrugell and Palamós. We didn't go that far, though. Just past Púbol, where Dalí created a castle for his Gala, we took a turn that set us on a long, straight road. I guessed that we were about twenty kilometres from our objective.

As we crested a hill a broad horizon was revealed; I knew it well, but it always impresses first-time viewers. 'What are those islands?' Frank asked.

'Isles Medes; they're a marine conservation zone, and a haven for divers.'

'And that building?' He pointed to a structure that from that distance showed as not much more than a dot on top of a perfectly rounded summit.

'Castell del Montgri. The English ex-pats call it Tit Hill. I imagine that the Belgians and the Germans call it something similar. It's an impressive landmark, and no mistake.'

'I can see where the name comes from,' he conceded. 'Speaking of such things,' he murmured, suddenly hesitant, 'yours are very impressive too. I should have told you that last night. I'm sorry I wasn't more gallant.'

'Frank,' I snapped. (I was pleased though: at forty-plus such comments are rare, and so all the more welcome.)

'I'm sorry I wasn't more impressive too.'

'Frank,' I said, more quietly, 'let's not talk about it any more. It shouldn't have happened, but it did; my fault, not yours. You were fine, you were tender, and that impresses me more than anything else, so don't worry about it. But it's history now, and it stays between us. Okay?'

'Okay,' he agreed, and I was satisfied with that.

'By the way,' I added, 'that means that if and when I meet Susannah, I certainly don't breathe a word to her.'

He smiled ruefully. 'Thanks. I hope you get the chance to say nothing.'

That sensitive subject dealt with, we drove on. Tit Hill grew larger and larger on our left, and the Isles Medes before us, until finally I spotted a sign advising me that Gualta Golf Course was coming up, but before it, the village itself. I turned right, drove the few hundred metres that led to it, then carried on through until I found myself on a road I didn't know. It was a dirt track, literally, but that is still not unusual in Spain. I slipped the Jeep into four-by-four mode . . . it's a politically correct SUV, using the facility only when necessary . . . and drove on through fields on either side.

'What are those?' Frank asked.

I risked a glance. 'Rice paddies, I think.'

'Rice?'

Newcomers always react that way. 'It's a big crop around here. Think paella; then think of its basic ingredient.'

I had very little warning of the sign that read 'Masia Josanto': I took a curve and I was upon it, so close that I overshot and had to reverse. We found ourselves on an even narrower track, with room for nothing bigger than a single tractor but with passing places every so often. We couldn't have gone more than half a klick, although it felt more, before it opened out and we found ourselves facing a high, wide gate. It was set in a formidable wall, between two stone pillars, on the right of which there was a sign confirming that we had reached our destination, and a box, with a buzzer, a speaker and a glass insert that I took to be a camera.

The sun was as high as it was going to get, and it was baking hot outside, but there was no way I could manoeuvre the Jeep close enough to push the button. I'd have sent Frank, but I reckoned I'd a better chance of getting that gate opened. I always keep a folding umbrella in the driver's door pocket: I took it with me as I stepped out of the car and used it as a parasol.

I pressed the buzzer, stood back to allow the camera a proper view, and waited. Just as I began to reckon that I'd have to sound the car horn as well, a male voice came from the speaker asking if its owner could help me.

'My companion and I are looking for a place to stay for a couple of nights. Not necessarily right now, but soon. We need a little solitude.'

'That might be possible,' the disembodied man said cautiously. 'But do you know we're gay-friendly?'

'Yes, I know that. Actually, I'm travelling with my half-brother.' Since I was busking it, including the 'half-' was a stroke of genius. One look at Frank, and he'll never pass for my full sibling. 'He's gay, and just coming off a failed relationship.' I added what I hoped would be the clincher: 'Shirley Gash told me about you.'

It worked. 'Ah,' the voice exclaimed. 'The lady Shirley. In that case, drive in and up to the house. Honk a couple of times when you're inside. The car park's at the side. My name's Antonio; I'll be waiting for you.'

He was a middle-aged man of medium height, wearing cream cargo pants and a T-shirt with a Gaudíesque illustration of a lizard on the front. As I introduced us . . . real names, having played the Shirley card . . . there was nothing about him that said, 'I'm gay,' as he shook my hand, although his fingers may have lingered just a little longer with Frank, and he may have looked into his eyes a little more deeply. 'I'm on my own today,' he told us. 'José, my partner, is in Figueras taking care of some legal business, but things are quiet after lunch, so I have time to show you round.'

'Thanks,' I said. 'I mentioned Shirley just now, but we know someone else who's a client of yours. His name's Willie; he's American.'

Antonio gasped, then laughed. 'American, yes, but with an English mother. Coincidence is such a devil, isn't it? You've just missed the two of them.'

My heart fell, but I gave what I hoped was an appropriate response. 'No!' I exclaimed. 'You're kidding. What a bitch! We'd have loved to catch him unawares.'

'Too bad.' Our host shrugged. 'I may as well show you the

suite they had on the way round. It would suit your purposes, I'm sure.'

We agreed and he set off. 'Let's start with the pool. There's a covered walkway leading to it; on days like this it's worth every cent it cost to build.'

We had no interest in seeing his pool but we had to smile and go along with it. It was surrounded by decking and by a dozen sun-beds, eight of them occupied by slumbering same-sex couples, half of them holding hands, and one bold pair holding something else. Happily Antonio didn't linger in the heat, but led us back to the shelter of the hotel's controlled climate, to the dining room, to the guest lounge and to the spa, which he described as 'the pampering centre'.

We had been there for around three quarters of an hour before he led us upstairs and into the suite that Willie and his 'mother' had occupied. It was lavish, no mistake, with one bedroom, a very private terrace, overlooked by nothing save the sky, and a convertible couch in the sitting room that could have slept a family of four. Nearby, there was a single chair; I knew who had occupied it, not that long before, and what she had done there.

I took out my mobile. 'Mind if I take a picture?' I asked.

'Not at all.' Antonio laughed. 'Can I be in it?'

'Of course, sit in the chair.' He did. I snapped him and stored the image.

'I've never met Willie's mother,' said Frank. 'Is she nice?'

'Very grand. She looks early sixties, so she must have been over thirty when she had him, but she carries it well. She had very little to say for herself, though. Nor did he, for that matter, unusually for him. Maybe he was missing Sebastian. They stayed here throughout their visit, and had all their meals room service.'

'How long did they stay?'

'Just one day. They checked in for lunch yesterday, then out again mid-morning.'

'They didn't happen to say where they were going, did they?' I quizzed him. 'It would be nice if we could bump into them, as a surprise.'

'No, I'm afraid not; they didn't mention it.' He ushered us out, back into the corridor and downstairs to Reception. 'So,' he asked, 'were you impressed enough to come and stay with us? I think you'll find our atmosphere restful, whatever your sexual orientation.' I had the fleeting impression that maybe he hadn't bought our cover story, but that maybe he didn't care either.

'Absolutely,' I assured him. 'Give me a card and we'll be in touch as soon as we can define our available days.'

He seemed happy with that, and gave me not only a card, but a glossy brochure. He waved us off as I drove out of the car park. I'd found some Shirley Bassey to play on the stereo. He seemed to like that. 'Remember,' he called out, 'honk again when you're clear of the gate.'

I honked. And then I stopped. 'The video of Adrienne,' I said. 'Do you have the number it came from?'

Frank slid his phone open. 'Yes.' He called it up and handed it to me. I recovered the image of Antonio in the chair, selected 'send in message', keyed in the number and gave the transmit command.

'What the hell are you doing?' my companion exclaimed.

I looked at him, right eyebrow raised. 'As my late former husband would have said,' I announced, 'I'm rattling our Willie's bloody cage.'

Twenty-six

There was no chance that Sebastian, or anyone else, was on our tail . . . the terrain was such that we'd have seen them a kilometre off . . . and so, instead of hiding out, I drove back the way we had come, turned into the Gualta Pitch and Putt course, and parked the Jeep.

'Where are we going now?' Frank asked, a little irritably. I think he sensed that I was taking control of the operation. He was right too. I was on ground I knew, and I reckoned that gave me an advantage.

'I feel the need of a beer,' I told him, 'or a glass of white wine.' I led the way into the club house and to the bar. We found a table outside, in the shade, and I ordered drinks. 'Tom's having golf lessons,' I volunteered. 'I bring him here.'

'I'll bet he's good,' Frank muttered. He sounded a little jealous. Would you believe it?

'He is,' I admitted cheerfully. 'Lovely swing for a seven year old, the pro says. His dad was a good player; his grandpa Blackstone still is, and so's his cousin Jonny. In the autumn he's going to college in Arizona, on a golf scholarship.'

'Lucky lad,' he growled.

'Listen to you,' I retorted. 'You had a Cambridge education, then chucked it all away trying to prove you were the cleverest lad on the block.'

'Bloody well am, too. I got away with the three hundred thou I've stashed in Switzerland.'

'You got away with it? You did five and a half years inside for it. And will it support you for the rest of your life?'

'It might, if the Canadian catches up with us,' he pointed out.

'To hell with Sebastian. I told you, we think positive from now on.'

He shot me a wry smile. 'So, Detective Blackstone, what do we do next? We had a lead, and now we don't.'

'We wait. It's their move.'

'What if they don't make it?' He was deadly serious again. 'What if they go ahead and kill my mum?'

'What would they have to gain by that,' I put to him, 'even in two days, when the so-called deadline expires? You'd be an even bigger danger to them if they killed her. She's a bargaining chip; they need her to get you. Why did Willie send that video? Not to prove they have her; we know that. He did it to prove she's alive.'

'What if they send me her ear through the post?'

'How? Through your old Sevilla post-office box number? I don't think they'll expect you to be emptying that any time soon. Trust me, the next step is theirs.'

We sat there and watched the day wear on, until it was well

past six, and until I would not have been driving anywhere else with just one more beer. I went to the ladies', put some of it back into the system, then called to Frank from the terrace doorway: 'Come on. Time we were going.'

'Where?'

'To our bolt-hole. It's only ten minutes away.'

In fact it took longer. The traffic into Torroella de Montgri was screwed up, thanks to punters going home from the beach at Pals, then we found ourselves behind the inevitable tractor, and so half an hour had passed by the time we arrived in L'Escala, and at Shirley's. I phoned her as we turned into her street, and she opened her massive sliding gate so that I could drive straight in. Her garden wall is even higher than the one round Masia Josanto. The place is a fortress, complete with a look-out tower on top that reminds me of Oz's old loft in Edinburgh, where he and I first . . .

She was waiting for us at the top of the staircase that leads to her door, wearing the usual swimsuit but with a sarong wrapped round it. She hugged Frank, almost enveloping him, as I introduced him. 'Come on through, the pair of you. You look bushed. Go on out to the pool while I get some drinks.'

'Just water for me!' I called after her. I know the way, so I led Frank through to the garden and to Shirley's enormous pool, one of the biggest in any house in L'Escala. I was unbuttoning my top before he closed the glass-panelled door behind me. I peeled it off, unfastened my skirt and let it fall, stepped out of my pants, and dived straight in. Maybe I'd have been a little more modest if I hadn't had the beers, but he'd seen the territory, even if he wasn't getting close to it again.

'That's our Primavera.' Shirley laughed as she carried a tray from the kitchen. 'She always prefers skinny-dipping,' she revealed to Frank. 'There's a nudie beach along the coast. She and I go there sometimes, when Tom's in school. Don't mind me if you want to join her in there. If you're shy, go and have a rummage in that box outside the summer-house. There's all sorts in there; you're bound to find something to fit.'

He took her at her word, and re-emerged after a couple of minutes, wearing a pair of red shorts. I hadn't seen Frank's body before, in a proper light. For all that he was lightly built, his muscles were well defined, and he looked fit, in the way a runner does, or a featherweight boxer.

By that time Shirley had joined me in the pool: I caught her eyeing him up as well. 'Trim little chap, your cousin,' she whispered. 'I've made up those two beds like you asked, but if you're really not wanting, you can always send him across to the big house.' She was joking, of course, although with her, you can never be a hundred per cent sure.

We swam for a while, until I felt parched again. I climbed the steps that led out of the pool, feeling the day's fading heat on my body as I walked over to the place where Shirley had dumped some big white towels, and feeling Frank's eyes as well. There were two robes there, also. I slipped one on, gathered up my clothes, and headed for the summer-house. 'I might have a nap, Shirl,' I said. 'When's supper?'

'Half nine okay?'

'Fine by me.' I looked in the big box as I passed by, and found a bikini inside, one of mine that I'd left there after a pool party. I took it with me.

By the time Frank came to join me, I was wearing it, and my hair was towelled dry. He looked around the bungalow's living area, and at the murals that decorate it. 'These are fantastic,' he exclaimed. 'Who did them?'

'An old artist friend of Shirley's. His name was Davidoff. He lived here for a while and he painted them for her. There are more, in the bedrooms.'

He whistled. 'If you'd said it was Dalí, I'd have believed you. Is he still around?'

I shook my head, hoping he couldn't see my eyes as I remembered him. 'No,' I replied. 'He died ten years back.'

'Did you meet him?'

'Yes, but that's another story, for another time.'

'Speaking of bedrooms . . .' he began.

'Yours is the far-away one; mine's next door. Bathroom's in between. I'm off for a kip.'

I left him to whatever he had in mind, set my mobile to wake me at nine fifteen, and lay down on the bed. In little or no time, I was asleep and dreaming, of an ancient artist, and a strong, reckless, much younger man.

When I awoke, my pillow was damp, and not with sweat. The bathroom was empty, and so I took a quick shower, arranged my hair in a more or less presentable form, slipped my bikini back on, and went outside.

Frank and Shirley were there already, lolling in white garden chairs set around a low table, drinking cava and eating crisps. They were laughing, and both looked up, sharply, as I approached, making me wonder briefly if they had been talking about me. 'He's some kiddie, your cousin,' she said. 'He's been telling me about his time in the nick, and about the perils of dropping the soap.'

'The guy we saw this afternoon had no trouble believing that he picked it up often enough.' I chuckled. For a fraction of a second Frank frowned. That's all it was, and then it was gone, but I wasn't mistaken. I wondered if I'd been close to the mark. I hadn't considered it before, but he's a pretty guy, and we all know the jail stories.

Luckily, Shirley didn't hit on that. Instead she asked, 'What's the problem with the house?'

'The water's polluted,' I told her. I hated lying to my best girlfriend, but no way was I going to involve her in what we were up to. 'Something got into the tank. It happened just when Tom was due to leave for Monaco, and I was heading south to meet Frank in Sevilla.'

'Nasty; that happened to me once. Stop here for as long as it takes.' She poured me a glass of bubbly. 'Get into that and talk among yourselves while I finish the risotto.'

I disobeyed, as I often do with Shirley. I picked up my glass and followed her into the kitchen, watching her as she transferred rice from a pot into the big wok that she uses for the purpose, then added peas, prawns, diced squid and a liberal amount of cava.

'You sure you're not shaggin' him?' she asked abruptly. 'You had it all on show for him this afternoon.'

'He's family,' I said, to fend her off.

'Not that close,' she pointed out. 'From what he tells me, he'd only ever met you about three times before this, and it's not as if he's your brother or anything. Your aunt screwed a sailor on holiday and he popped out, according to the story you told me.'

'And it's true,' I confirmed.

'He thinks you're a goddess, you know.'

'Gerroff.'

'No kidding. That's what he says. He says that now he's really got to know you, he sees you as twice the woman your sister is, and he's besotted with her. But he thinks that underneath it all, you're sad, and lonely.'

'Cheeky little bastard!' I exclaimed, but I couldn't help thinking about what Tom had said to me, a few days before.

'Is he wrong?'

'I'm neither of those things. I've got Tom. What he sees just now is me missing him.'

'Prim, Tom's a little boy. What Frank sees, like we all do, is you missing his dad.'

I looked at her as she mixed the rice, helping it absorb the liquid. 'Is that really what you think?'

'It's what we all know, me, Alex, all your friends.' She paused, to give the pot a vigorous stir. 'Frank told me,' she went on, 'that when he needed it most, you helped him.'

'Did he say how?'

'No, he just said that he wishes he could do the same for you. Maybe you should let him.'

'But why must I need help? Maybe sad and lonely suits me best.'

'Then that really would be sad, girl.'

I was pondering that comment as she finished. I carried the plates, cutlery and glasses out to the garden table, the cook following with the risotto wok, ready to dish up.

It was fabulous, as always, and afterwards, the bread-and-butter pudding was just as good, although I didn't have much. With my lifestyle, it's too easy to put on weight, so I tend to eat small portions. I laid off the wine too: I reckoned I'd had enough alcohol for the day, given that I might need to be as sharp as possible over the next twenty-four hours. Frank didn't, though: he tucked in good-style. It's amazing, the way little guys can stow the grub away. He and Shirley killed a bottle of Esmeralda between them, and had a couple of Bailey's over coffee. As he drained his glass, he looked around the garden, which seemed to shimmer and sparkle under the effect of the pool's underwater lights. 'Lovely place, Shirley,' he said.

'It suits me,' she replied quietly. It's too big for her, of course. Sometimes I think she'd really like to move, only she has too much of her life tied up in it to pass it on to someone else.

'Must be worth a fortune.'

'Probably, but to me it's priceless. So's Prim's house, for that matter.'

'Which I've never seen.'

'You will tomorrow,' I told him. His eyes widened, but he

said nothing. 'I have to check it out, and pick up some stuff,' I added, in explanation.

'Tomorrow's nearly here,' Shirley pointed out, rising from her chair, and gathering up the plates. Frank helped her pile them into the wok, then followed her into the house, carrying the glasses, cups and bottles on a tray. 'Night, Prim,' my friend called to me. 'Think on what I said.'

I watched them go, then slipped off my bikini and walked slowly to the far end of her damn great pool: as she said, I really do prefer to swim unencumbered. I stood for a few moments, naked under the moon, then dived in. When I surfaced, Frank was back, standing on the edge, looking down at me, at my brown body, in the ever-shifting light.

'Don't,' I told him. 'Either come in or piss off and let me swim.'

'Since you put it like that . . .' he turned and started to walk towards the summer-house . . . then stopped and turned back, kicking off his shoes and reaching for his belt. It was my turn to watch as he undressed. I rolled on to my back and paddled away from him, back towards the deep end. He had very little body hair, I noticed idly, as he stepped out of his briefs. He ran towards the pool and dived in, expertly, barely making a splash. He came up for air, thinking he was alongside me, but I had moved away, into shallower water once more.

'Don't get any ideas,' I told him. 'We're swimming, and that's it.'

'I'm not about to.' He laughed. 'Anyway, the water's too cold.'

I made a choice. I don't know why. Maybe what Shirley said had got to me, or maybe not; maybe I simply wanted to see if I could do better than the night before. Whatever, I made a choice and, to this day, I can say honestly I've never regretted it. 'That's pretty defeatist talk,' I murmured, 'if you don't mind me saying so.' I swam closer, and reached for him. 'It's also a lie.'

He followed me as I swam across to the side of the pool, and spread my arms wide along the concrete edging, supporting myself. He dived, and I felt him lick me, then fondle me, then slide easily into me as he surfaced. 'Wow,' he whispered in my ear, as he reached out, put his arms around my neck, drew his legs up to part mine a little more, and . . .

We took our time over it, as long as we could make it last, but when he could hold back no longer, he came, and I did too, crying, 'Yes!' loud enough to make me hope that Shirley was asleep, or I'd never hear the end of it. I held him inside until he began to subside, kissing him, nuzzling him. 'Okay,' I whispered, as I felt him leave me. 'Now can I swim?'

He laughed. 'For as long as you like; but I think if I tried now, I'd drown. I've never had it under water before. It takes it out of the legs. I'm off to bed.'

I didn't join him, not in his, at any rate. I thought about it as I swam lengths of the big pool, ridiculously pleased with myself, but I decided that any more intimacy might suggest an attachment. Instead I resolved to treat him as Auntie Ade had probably treated his dad thirty-five years before; strictly 'so long, and thanks for the memory'. The consequences of

Adrienne's encounter with the doomed Kotaro crossed my mind briefly, since I've been off the pill for years, but I was only a couple of days past my period, so I decided, rightly as it turned out, that there was no risk, without ever considering the possible contraceptive effects of submarine copulation.

I was lost in my thoughts as I walked up the steps and out of the water, and as I dried myself with one of Shirley's big white towels, until a sound to my left broke through. I glanced at the glazed garden door and saw her framed in it, smiling. She winked at me, then disappeared into her fortress.

The door of Frank's bedroom was open, an invitation, I had no doubt. I could see him in the light from the corridor, lying naked, on his back, asleep. I confess that I almost did settle down beside him, but my resolution held and I walked on, closing my own door behind me.

Twenty-seven

I had no more crying dreams. I did have a bad one, though, one that involved Frank, Sebastian and Willie, Lidia, Auntie Ade, Emil Caballero and his gun. We were all in the burned-out barn, at the site of the so-called casino, and it didn't have a happy ending, not for Frank and Adrienne, at any rate. I woke up before they got round to me.

He was in the bathroom when I stepped out of my room. I had a towel wrapped around me, but he was in the buff, his back to the open door as he shaved. 'Put some clothes on,' I told him, for all that I noticed how pert his bum was. 'We're not a couple, so don't act like it.' Maybe that was a little harsh, since I'd made the running the night before, but he got the message.

'Sorry,' he said, frowning in the mirror.

I couldn't help it; I laughed, out loud. 'And what did I tell you yesterday about saying "Sorry"? It won't work.'

I grabbed a bar of soap, left him to finish in the bathroom, and had a shower outside in the garden, by the pool. The water was cold, but that was what I needed, something to waken me properly. I was still under the spray when Frank came out of the bungalow. 'What was that you were saying?' he called across to me, making me feel just a little guilty. I went inside to dry myself. By the time I was dressed and presentable, Shirley was in the garden, back at the table with her standard breakfast, melon, pineapple and coffee, this time for three.

'You know,' she remarked, deadpan, as she poured a cup for me, 'my pool man was saying the other day that I should stop putting chlorine in and use bromide instead. What do you think, Prim?'

I returned her question with another. 'Is it a softening agent?'

'So I've heard.'

Frank looked at us as if we were daft. I think he was puzzled, genuinely.

'In that case, I wouldn't, if I were you,' I concluded. 'One never knows the moment.'

We finished breakfast, and sat around for a while, talking about nothing much. I still felt slightly unreal as I contemplated my nocturnal behaviour. It had been good, full-bore sex, far different from the sympathy shag on the train, and the whore within me wanted to rip his clothes off and start all over again. It wasn't that easy, though. One difficulty was that the rest of me, my sensible, discreet, proper majority, didn't even fancy him. Another was that in the aftermath, my old ghosts hadn't been laid as I'd hoped. The opposite in fact: they were starting to haunt me; I was starting to think of New York.

'So,' Shirley asked, bringing me back to the present, 'what's your game plan for the day?'

'Check the house, I suppose,' I replied. 'Pick up some stuff, and after that maybe show Frank some of the scenery.'

She nodded. 'Sounds good. But steer clear of L'Escala. I went down there yesterday, to the bank, and it was crawling with people.' She turned to my cousin. 'I never asked you, Frank. How long are you staying?'

'That depends,' he told her, 'on how long Primavera will put up with me.'

'Play your cards right with her and you could be okay for a while yet.'

'That would be nice,' he said, 'but it also depends on my mother. We're expecting her to show up soon. Once she does, I'll have some business to sort out in London.'

'What is your business?'

'I'm in property these days: sales. Recently I've been in Seville, where Prim and I met up.'

She grimaced. 'Don't plan on settling down here, in that case.' I found myself shuddering at the thought. 'There are too many estate agents here as it is.'

'I don't intend to,' he said, to my private relief. 'I'll be moving to another part of Europe soon.' He looked at me. 'We should get going. I'll go across and tidy up.'

'You're staying tonight, aren't you?' Shirley asked him, hopefully.

'If that's okay, and if Mum doesn't turn up out of the blue.'

'Bring her if she does. I've got plenty of room, and I enjoy company.'

'We'll see.'

She gazed after him as he walked away, then turned to me. 'Well, then?'

'Well then what?'

'You know. Well, then?'

'Were you watching us all that time?'

'Give me credit for having more class than that. No, I came down to switch the pool lights off, and got to the door just as you were hitting high C. You took my advice, then? It sounded like more than a hug between friends.'

'It was.'

'And?'

'It was nice. I should do it more often.'

'With the right bloke, yes. Nice, you said. It sounded more than nice.'

'Okay, more than nice.'

'Scale out of ten?'

'Six.'

'Six!'

'Okay, seven.'

'And bonus points or artistic impression, in that case. Gonna try for a higher score?'

'No. That's as good as it's going to get.'

'Don't be daft. Enjoy it while he's around. Who knows? It might be another three years to the next time.'

'Cheers.' I chuckled. 'You do wonders for a girl's self-esteem.'

'You know what I meant.'

'Yes, but he's so much younger than me. I've never had a younger bloke in my life.'

'Was it so bad?'

'No.'

'There you are, then; a whole new world's opened up for you.'

'When all I want is the old one back?'

She frowned, and I was instantly sorry I'd said that. 'You think I don't want Clive back?' she asked. 'Course I do, but I gave up fantasising about it a long time ago.'

'I'll try, Shirley. But I can only move on when I'm ready inside. I'd better go now.' I rose and walked across to the summer-house.

Frank was in the living area, waiting for me, ready to go, with his rucksack slung over his shoulder. 'Are you sure about going to your house?' he began. 'It's the one place they're likely to be watching.'

'And it's the place where we'll be safest, once we're inside. My policeman friend Alex has been keeping an eye on it for me.'

'No cops!' he exclaimed. 'You saw the message. I won't let you take chances with my mother's life.'

'He's looking out for me,' I told him, slightly inaccurately, seeing no point in mentioning that he was also on the alert for sightings of Auntie Ade with a young man. 'But relax. With very little luck, we can get in without being seen by anybody, not even him.'

'How? We can't make ourselves invisible.'

'Damn near it.' He stood, still looking anxious. I put my hands on his shoulders, and kissed him. 'Easy now,' I whispered. 'It's going to be all right, I promise you.'

He slipped his arms around my waist, and put his forehead against mine. It felt a little moist. I leaned back, and stroked it. 'Promise?' he said.

'Take it to the bank.' Our eyes met, neither of us blinking. I felt him hardening against me. 'Do you want to go to bed for a while?' I found myself asking.

He shook his head. 'I couldn't concentrate. Tonight, if we're back here. Once we've found Mum and got her away from that bastard, but not now.'

'I'm still not going to tell Susannah,' I murmured, smiling.

'Maybe you should. Might make her jealous enough to leave her husband.'

'Is that what I am?' I asked. 'A weapon to be used against her?'

He hugged me tight. 'No!' he replied earnestly. 'You're much more than that.'

'Tonight, then.' What the hell? Shirley was right, as usual. 'But first, speaking of weapons, what do you have, apart from your clever wee knife?'

'Nothing. I used up my mace spray getting away from those two guys. Why?'

'When we catch up with friend Willie, he's unlikely to put his hands up and say, "It's a fair cop," is he? We're going to need to take him down, then hand him over to the police, once Adrienne's safe.'

'I could take him.' He stepped back from me. 'I've been trained, remember.'

'So have I, but that doesn't make me bullet-proof.'

'*Touché*,' he conceded. 'Let's buy a replica gun. They're on sale in all the tourist shops in Seville, so I guess we'll find one somewhere.'

'Let's go to mine,' I decreed, 'before we get round to that.'

I picked up my bag and headed for the door. We went into the big house to say farewell to Shirley. She wished us luck with the water repair, and tossed me one of her remotes, to open and close the gate, so that we could get out and in later, whether she was there or not.

A few minutes later we were back on the move. Rather than go through L'Escala, we took the ring road, built to take some of the traffic away from the busiest spots. The Brits have been calling it the M25 for so long that now some Spanish people have adopted the name, without having a clue why. Even that was busy, but most of the traffic was headed in the other direction, towards the beach. Soon we were past the football ground and bound for St Martí.

There's a roundabout with a junction that accesses the 'M25', a couple of supermarkets, and the road to Figueras and beyond. As we approached it I saw that the Mossos d'Esquadra had set up a roadblock, as they sometimes do, to give the appearance of being ever-vigilant. I swore softly, for they can be a pain at times, until I recognised Sub-inspector Alex Guinart. He recognised the Jeep at the same time, and flagged me down. 'Hey, Primavera,' he greeted me. 'You never told me you were home.'

'I was going to, though. We got back last night, went to Shirley's and stayed there.' I leaned back, so that he could see inside the car. 'This is my cousin, Frank McGowan. It's his mother who's missing.'

Alex frowned. 'My regrets, sir,' he said, in English, then switched back into Catalan. 'I'm sorry, Prim. There have been no more sightings. We're no nearer finding her.' I thought about telling him that we'd just missed her at Masia Josanto, but decided against it, since I know that Alex doesn't approve of free enterprise. If he'd had an inkling we were tracking her ourselves, he'd probably have detained us, although he'd have insisted it was for our own safety. 'You go home?' he asked.

'Yes.'

'House is fine: I checked it this morning. I couldn't go inside, because Tom took the keys with him when his escort picked him up, but it looks fine from the outside.'

'Good. Thanks, Alex. How's Marte?'

His sudden smile was distinctly uncopperlike. 'A little lovelier than she was yesterday. You know, when she grows up I have plans to marry her to your Tom.'

'He may be a bit too old for her,' I pointed out.

'Seven years? What's seven years?'

I laughed, although he had a point. 'Let's allow them their childhood first,' I said. One of the drivers in a growing queue behind us risked a brief toot on his horn. Alex's smile vanished, and I decided to leave the guy to his fate. 'See you,' I called out as I drove off.

It was only just gone eleven, but there were cars parked along much of the road to St Martí, taking a chance, as they've started clamping. We took a curve and Frank had his first view of the village, of its ancient wall and the dominating church within. 'Is that where you live?' he asked.

'Yup.'

He whistled. 'How would you feel about me moving in for a while?' he asked.

I wasn't sure he was kidding. 'How I felt wouldn't decide the issue,' I told him. 'Even if we do get free and clear of all danger, and if we rescue your mum, I'd have to put the matter to the vote.'

'You have a democratic household?'

'Not exactly. Even if Charlie and I voted in favour, Tom would still have a veto.'

'So that's why you don't have a man.'

I looked at him sharply. 'No, it's bloody not. You know, Frank, underneath it all, you're a typical bloke. You can't get your head round the idea of a woman choosing to be a single mother, and liking it that way.'

He held his hands up in surrender. '*Pax*,' he exclaimed. 'Bad joke; I take it back. Young Tom must be some guy.'

'He is.'

'What does he look like?'

'A lot like his dad and a bit like his mum. Tall for his age: give him another seven years and he'll be bigger than you and me. He's bright, he's inquisitive in a good way, by which I mean he's eager to learn. His Spanish and Catalan are better than mine, because he picked up all the playground stuff from his mates, and his French is on a par. Last summer, he met some German kids whose folks rented here for a month. By the time they left he was starting to speak to them in their own language.'

'Does he speak English?'

'Don't be bloody silly! Of course he does, and I'm making damn sure that he's literate in it as well.'

'You hire a tutor?'

'I am his tutor, you idiot.'

I slowed down as I reached the roundabout in front of the village. I saw another police presence there, Guardia Civil this time, but they recognised me and waved me through. The car park on the right was almost full, and the other would be heading that way, even though it was bigger; as usual, there would be thousands of people on the beach.

All of a sudden I felt in danger once again, as I realised that it was a hell of a lot easier for Sebastian to hide from us in those crowds than it was for us to hide from him in my tank, for all its tinted windows. And I realised something else. My bravura gesture in sending Adrienne's captor that photograph of Antonio, in the same chair from which she had given her message, hadn't been clever at all. It had told Willie that we were in the area; now it was more likely than not that his pal was staking out my home, waiting for us to come to him.

'Look out for him,' I told Frank, as I eased my way through the people emerging from the parks, laden down with parasols, plastic seats and cool boxes, taking special care near the many who were pushing push chairs or shepherding youngsters. I took a turn to the right, into a road that few cars use, then forked off up the track that leads to my garage.

As I approached, I slowed to a crawl, scanning the surrounding trees for watchers, for if Sebastian had really done his homework, that was where he would be waiting. But I saw no one. I found my remote in the storage bin where I had left it, pressed it, then counted to ten to give the garage time to open. I gunned the motor, shot forward and swung the Jeep in a blind turn. Frank was almost standing upright in shock, until he saw the opening, relaxing as I swept through it. We both sighed with relief as I hit the closer button and as the darkness descended.

My headlamps came on automatically as I opened the driver's door, allowing me to switch on the garage lights. I stepped across to the keypad, to deactivate the alarm, until I realised there was no sound. The warning tone that gave me thirty seconds to enter the code was conspicuous by its absence; the system had not been activated. 'That's funny,' I said aloud.

'What?' asked Frank.

'The alarm's not set.'

'Should it have been?'

'Standing operating procedure.'

'Who was the last person in the house?'

'It must have been Tom, or Conrad Kent, but no, Conrad doesn't know the code.'

'There you are.'

'But Tom does. He knows to set it, always.'

'Would they have left through the garage?'

'They didn't have to. The system has twin control pads. This one, and one at the front door.'

'In that case, I'm afraid, the likeliest explanation is that young Tom has slipped up.' I wasn't certain, but I suspected there was a hint of satisfaction in his voice.

I beat back my indignation, and focused on what should have been our primary concern. 'The real question is,' I said, 'is there someone here now?'

I'm not a DIY woman, but I do keep a big wrench in the garage, for emergencies. I picked it up and went to the fire- and smokeproof door that opens on to the stairway to the house. I was about to lead the way up, when Frank stopped me. 'Let me,' he murmured. He took the make-shift bludgeon from me. 'Shut that door after me, bolt it, open the garage, and unless you hear three knocks on the other side, or if I'm not back in five minutes, get the fuck out of here.' I didn't have time to argue. He thrust his rucksack into my arms and headed for the stair, pulling the door closed after him.

There was nothing for it but to do as he had said. I secured the exit with the two big bolts I had installed, top and bottom. When it came to opening the garage, I had second thoughts. That would make me vulnerable from behind, and if the need did arise, I could get the Jeep out of there whether it was closed or not.

There's a big white Timex on my garage wall. My dad gave us a hand-made cuckoo clock as a housewarming present: it went into the kitchen and the one it replaced went downstairs. I watched it, counting off the minutes, listening all the time, in vain, for sounds from above. No noise was good noise, I decided, until four minutes had gone by, and I found myself watching the second hand as it swept round in a final countdown.

Nothing happened. Not a single knock did I hear, far less three. I gave him a sixth minute, then a seventh . . . it's a big house, after all . . . but still there was no action, no knocks, no movement from the handle being tried. After eight minutes, I reckoned it was time to follow Frank's instruction. I got behind the wheel: the key was still in the ignition. I reached for the remote control . . . and then I said, 'Oh, shit!'

I couldn't leave the little bloke. I'll never know why, for sure; maybe it was because we had a date for that night, but I just couldn't.

My garage is big. When Tom's older, it'll hold his car as well, there will still be room for a third and for our bikes. Right now, I keep a lot of stuff down there. One night not long after we moved in, once Tom had gone to bed, I watched a Jodie Foster movie called *Panic Room*, the one where she and her kid are under siege in a secure room in their house. I'd decided that the garage would be ours. That's why I had the bolts fitted. That's why I have a small fridge down there, and a freezer and a microwave; all spares, I tell Tom, but the fridge and the freezer are always stocked and the microwave is tested regularly. I call them 'garage barbies' and he thinks it's a joke. I also have a safe; it's built into the wall, at my head height, it has a combination and it's one of the very few things in the place that my son is not allowed to touch. In it, I keep my most valuable jewellery, some cash, our birth certificates, a certified copy of my will, in Spanish (my sister, who witnessed it in Scotland, has the other), and the deeds to the house. I got out of the car, went across to it and spun the dials until I heard the click and it opened. Oh, yes, and I keep something else in there.

Domestic firearms are pretty much illegal in Spain, and that's fine, because I wouldn't have one. However, I do own an air taser: I bought it over the Internet without any questions being asked. It weighs next to nothing, it works off eight AA batteries, and it looks like a conventional gun, but instead of firing bullets it shoots two little darts on wires over up to fifteen feet. They hit your attacker, then fifty thousand volts paralyse his central nervous system and he falls down. He isn't dead, but for the short term he's pretty well goosed.

I took it out, closed the safe again, spun the dials, and then I headed for the door. I slid the bolts as quietly as I could, and opened it. Happily its hinges are just about the only ones in the house that don't ever squeak. I crept upstairs towards the light that came from the basement utility room at the top. Reaching it I peered into the space, ready for instant action, but there was nobody lying in wait for me, no recumbent Frank, nothing. I pressed on, checking the boiler room and the basement store, before steeling myself to climb the next flight of steps up to street level.

This time there was no door at the top: I would be exposed as soon as I set foot on the first rung. I stepped out, the taser trained on the space before me, knowing that there were more than fifteen feet between me and the top of the stairs. Again I saw nobody; I climbed quickly and silently, until I was in the entrance hall.

The front door was ajar. I gazed at it, then spun round, holding the gun on the living-room door. It was open; just inside on the floor, I saw the wrench, and the blood. There wasn't a lot, but it was fresh and I realised that the spots led towards me. I followed the trail; it seemed to end just short of the door. I stepped into the living room, hoping against hope that I'd find brave little Frank recovering from a fight, stunned but victorious, having seen off his opponent.

But I didn't. He was gone.

Twenty-eight

I almost ran out into the village brandishing the taser, but stopped myself just in time. Instead, I checked the rest of the house, thoroughly, in case I'd interrupted the intruder and he was holding Frank somewhere within.

It was clean. There was no sign of anyone, or that anyone had ever been there, apart from the blood. I did go out into the square then, just as the first of the holiday-makers were making their way up from the beach to grab open-air lunch tables at the cafés before they all filled up, as they do every day in the high season. It was busy already: I scanned the faces seated under the big waterproof umbrellas, deployed against the sun and against the odd shower, which can sometimes sneak down from the Pyrenees when no one is looking in that direction. Not that I expected to see Frank there, tucking into a beer with the Canadian: it was a reflex, that was all, born of the need to be doing something. I looked at Esculapi, Can Coll, Mesón del Conde, Can Roura, drawing waves at all of them from their friendly staff, but no chat, since everyone was busy.

I headed down the slope, out of Plaça Major, towards El

Celler Petit, the local wine shop. Its owner, who was English before he settled in Catalunya and went native, was standing in the doorway, talking to a Belgian who lives nearby. They greeted me as I approached, turning serious as they saw from my face that something was wrong. 'Has either of you seen two men?' I asked them. 'One about my height, slim dark hair, Asiatic, the other taller, blond maybe. They'd have been heading out of the village.'

The Belgian nodded. 'I saw them,' he said, 'about fifteen minutes ago. They were moving quite fast, too fast for the heat of the day; that's why I noticed them. The little guy, he was in front. He had a mark on his face. Why, Primavera? What's up?'

'They've been in my house,' I told him. 'They came to the door, asking for directions to L'Escala. I went inside for a second to get them one of the maps I keep in the kitchen. When I came back, they were gone, and so was the cash I keep in a drawer by the door.'

'Bastards!' He frowned. 'I thought you'd have known by now, though.'

'Don't say any more. I'm usually very careful about opening the door to strangers, but Tom's away just now, and . . . if he'd been there, I wouldn't have.'

The ex-Englishman chuckled. 'If he'd been there he'd have chased after them, him and Charlie.'

'Where did they go?' I asked his pal.

'To the car park, I think. I'll go and ask if they're still there, but like I said, it's been fifteen minutes.'

'Yeah, they'll be gone. I'll have to put it down to experience,

I reckon.' To make myself seem otherwise normal, I ordered a case of cava, and another of Riogenc, my favourite *rosado*, then headed back to the house.

Inside, I went through to the kitchen, picking up the taser as I passed the hall table. Realising that my mouth was horribly parched, I took an isotonic drink from the fridge and drained it in one go. Then I sat down on a bench, and began to think.

Frank was gone. They had him. They had been waiting inside for us, all along. So why not take me as well? Because Sebastian, the Canadian, must have been on his own and couldn't handle both of us. I gripped the butt of my weapon. *I wish he'd tried*, I thought. But he hadn't. Would they come back for me? That was the question uppermost in my mind. My guess was that they wouldn't. They had the guy they were really after, the other Interpol plant in the organisation. I was nothing to them, really, once they were free and clear.

But they had Adrienne too.

Their messages had been very specific about the danger of police involvement, but in the changed situation, what I had to ask myself was, which posed the greater threat to her? Telling the police all I knew, or keeping quiet and hoping that, now they had her son, they'd cut her loose?

I couldn't decide. As I wrestled with the options, I went back down to the garage, to recover my bag, and the key from the Jeep. As I drew it from the ignition, I saw Frank's rucksack, lying on the passenger seat where I'd chucked it as I prepared to escape. I slung it over my shoulder and carried it back up to the kitchen with the rest, noticing idly that it didn't seem as heavy as it had in Sevilla.

Seated at the kitchen table, I opened it, the mystery luggage, and looked inside. It had two compartments. The larger, at the rear, was full of clothes; the used items were in a polythene bag, to keep them from the little fresh stuff he had left, a new black T-shirt, a pair of white socks and a pair of pants. There was also a travel pack containing toothbrush, toothpaste, comb, razor, shaving foam and a small deodorant spray, the brand, guys, that's supposed to make women rip your clothes off.

I opened the front compartment. All it held was his mobile phone (no signal), his passport, a UK driving licence (photographic version), a leather Gucci billfold with a couple of fifties inside and four bank cards in slots, and a roll of notes secured by an elastic band. I counted them (he was down to his last thirteen hundred euros), then took out the plastic and studied it. There were MBNA cards, Visa and MasterCard, in his name, a debit card from an Andalucían savings bank in the name Roy Urquhart, and an Amex gold card, bearing the holder name, Jason Lee. I tapped it with my index finger. 'Frank's hoard, I'll bet,' I whispered. I was in the process of putting everything back, when I found something I'd missed, in the rear pocket: the Swiss Army knife.

I took it out, opened the main blade and tested it, carefully, on my thumb. The point had been sharpened, and indeed he could have shaved with the cutting edge. But there, in my hand, it was of absolutely no use to him. The poor little sod really was on his own.

Twenty-nine

That was when I made my decision. My thinking came together, and I reckoned that even if the police found him, they have no record of subtlety and would certainly turn up noisily and mob handed, thereby getting Adrienne killed, and Frank, although I really did fear that the worst might have happened to him, even then.

So I decided against involving Alex. Instead, I secured the doors, put the alarm on night setting and went into the sleep zone, which includes our bedrooms, mine, Tom's and the one Ade had been using, and my east-facing terrace. I took with me my bag, Frank's stuff and a litre of fizzy water. In my room, my bed looked so inviting I almost got in, but instead I stripped off, sprayed myself with Piz Buin, and went outside to lie on my sun-bed. That may sound uncaring to you, given all that had just happened, but I do some of my best thinking out there.

The question that was troubling me as I closed my eyes was how Sebastian, the Canadian, had got into the house, and past the alarm. I could have called Tom to confirm that he had set it, but that would have upset him, for the certain answer would have been 'Yes, Mum', with unspoken resentment because apparently I didn't trust him to do so.

My eyes had barely closed against the sun, when the simple answer came to me. I'd given Adrienne the third key when she had taken Tom to the ruins and got herself into dehydration trouble, and I'd told her what the alarm code was: I'd even done what I'd never done before, and written it down for her on a slip of paper from the phone pad. When she'd been abducted both must have been in her pocket. Sebastian and Willie's lucky day: they'd found the key and they hadn't even had to torture her to extract the number.

I propped myself up on my elbows, and was contemplating what a total arse I'd made of everything when a ring-tone broke the silence, a strange ring-tone, not one of mine. It came from Frank's rucksack, which I'd tossed, with my stuff, into the shade offered by the terrace table. I leaned across and grabbed it, then fished out his phone, just as the sound stopped.

There's an odd fact about St Martí. It has so many solid stone walls that mobile signals are practically non-existent within buildings and hard to pick up even on the square. But on my terrace, facing L'Escala and its forest of masts, there's no problem. My missing cousin's phone had come back on-line.

I peered at the screen, but the sun was too bright for me to make it out, so I jumped up and stepped just inside the door, not too far to kill reception, drawing the curtains behind me so that I couldn't be seen from the top of the nearby slope.

It told me there was one message waiting, and an option below invited me to 'read'; I accepted.

The message was another video of Adrienne, sent, according to the screen, around the time that Frank and I were leaving Shirley's place. I hit the view button. This time, my aunt's face was in close-up, giving no clue to where it had been shot. She spoke quickly, as if she knew that the time limit on these things was only around twenty seconds.

'I've been moved,' she began. 'We've come to the crossroads of this affair. I've to tell you that time is drawing short and they will kill me tomorrow morning at eleven o'clock. You know what I want you to do, son. I'm praying you make the right choice.' Her face froze on screen as the video clip ended.

I played it again, then a third time. There was something about her expression, something in her eyes, something imploring. The more I played it, the more I looked at her, the more I was convinced she was telling me something, giving me a message she'd intended for Frank.

But what the hell was it? When I was in my teens I won a pen from the *Scotsman* prize crossword, but I couldn't begin to crack that clue. Nor had I any idea of how to go about solving it. Life and bloody death, Auntie Ade was trying to tell me something, and I didn't get it. I stood there behind the curtains, my face screwed up in concentration, thinking, thinking, thinking, achieving nothing, nothing, nothing, until I felt tears of frustration run down my face.

And then the church bell rang. As I've told you, my son and I live next door to the medieval church; a few years back, the parishioners raised money for a new set of bells, and they've been active ever since, striking the quarters and the hours, then striking the hour again at two minutes past, in case you lost count the first time . . . a quaint but useful local custom. They are loud, yet Tom and I no longer notice them. Like farmyard smells, they have become our norm, and while others may feel their teeth jar with the sound, we sleep through them.

That one, though, it smashed its way right into my consciousness. It rang once signalling the hour, but then began to peal again, not just the big bell but all its brothers and sisters, calling the faithful to Mass.

I'm not one of those faithful, but I know the parish priest. I threw an ankle-length day-dress over my head, and ran downstairs, holding the mobile. On the way out of the door, I grabbed a sun-hat, in case a bare-headed woman in church upset any traditionalists.

I felt myself beam when I saw he was there, in the doorway. Tall, black robed, handsome: it's a bugger but the few men I do fancy in my village are either happily married or celibate. Still, he and I enjoy the odd drink together. I looked inside; there were so few worshippers that I reckoned he'd better ring the bells again. 'Father Gerard,' I said.

He smiled. 'Come to seek absolution, my child?' he asked.

'First of all,' I told him, 'I'm older than you, so "my child" sounds a bit silly. Second, I doubt that you'd want to hear my sins.'

'I never turn away a sinner, Prim.'

'In that case, I want you to listen to something. When you've heard it, you might be alarmed, but I need to know what she's trying to say. At the moment, it's beyond me.'

'I'll try,' he replied. 'Come back here a little nearer the altar.'

I followed him; we stood to the side of the church, our backs to the tiny congregation, and I played him the video. I saw his face darken as he listened. I played it again. 'Primavera,' he hissed, 'the police. Tell Alex Guinart.'

'They've promised to kill her at the first sight of a police car or uniform. I've got no time left for specialists. Things have moved on since that was sent. They have my cousin too. Gerard, can you help? What does she mean?'

'Yes, I think I know.' I sighed with relief. He leaned closer to me. 'Across Spain there are many old pilgrim trails. People still walk them today. In the old times, where these trails crossed, it was the custom to set up a shrine, for the travellers to pray and to make offerings. Many of them still exist. For example, there's one near Camallera. You can see it from the road. There's another near St Jordi des Vallès. But the nearest, it's close to Bellcaire. You turn left at the crossroads, go along until you see a sign that says "Santa Caterina". Follow that track and it will take you there. If she's around here, and I read her right, that's the one you want.'

'Why are you so sure she's there, not near one of the others?'

'Because there's an old building up there. It used to be a retreat, used by nuns mostly, but it's been deserted for many years.'

I kissed him on the cheek, in front of his small flock. 'Thanks, Gerard.'

He held my arm as I made to leave. 'Wait,' he said. 'If you

won't call the police, wait until after the service and I'll come with you.'

'No time,' I told him. 'But you're a love for offering. You could pray for me, though. Every little helps.'

He smiled. 'That's not a little. Often it's everything you need.'

'You're a wise man, Father Gerard.'

'Me? No, I'm only a priest. You'll find wisdom, and courage too, where you least expect it.'

Thirty

I went back to the house, excited, then took some mental deep breaths at the thought of what I was about to do. I was right, I knew . . . at least I knew then. It was a matter of risk management. Significantly, to me, Gerard had accepted my view that a police assault would lead, probably, to Adrienne being killed. I was her best chance. (By that time, subconsciously, I had abandoned Frank to his fate.)

I picked up the phone without even thinking about it, and dialled the land-line number in Monaco. Audrey Kent picked up. She told me that Susie was working and had asked not to be disturbed, but that Ethel Reid, the nanny, was looking after the children.

Soon, Tom was on the line. 'Hi, Mum,' he said breezily. 'Charlie and I are having a great time. I've been to the motor museum; they've got some new cars in.'

'You mean new old cars?'

'*Oui*.' He chuckled. 'I mean yes. You know what I mean, Mum.'

'Have you and Janet been speaking French?'

'Yes. We were at one of her friends' birthday party yesterday so we had to. Jonathan too. Not Charlie, though. He only speaks dog. How's Auntie Adrienne?' he asked suddenly. 'Has she come home yet?'

'I'm on my way to collect her now,' I told him, thinking on my feet. 'She had to go away with someone, someone Frank knew. He turned up out of the blue.'

'And she went away and left Charlie and me? He must be important.'

That's the closest I'd ever heard Tom come to criticising an adult, but I let it pass. The little guy was entitled. 'What are you doing?' I asked him.

'We're having lunch. Then Ethel says we can have an hour on the PlayStation, and after that we're going to swim with Mum.' Tom calls both Susie and me 'Mum'; I've never worked out how he manages it, but when he uses the word, he never leaves anyone in doubt about which one of us he's talking about. 'Did you find Frank?'

'Yes, but he's gone away again.'

'What's he like?'

I had to think about that. I wanted to reply, 'More complex than you could ever imagine. A sheep in wolf's clothing. A lovely little guy that I've let get to me in spite of myself.' But he wouldn't have understood any of that so all I said was 'He's nice.'

That was okay by Tom. I told him to be a good boy, and to be sure to let wee Jonathan win every so often on the PlayStation, then let him rejoin his lunch.

The church bell struck one thirty. Time, precious time, was moving on, I realised, and I had things to do. First I had to dress properly for my task, and that did not mean a long flowery day-dress. I went back upstairs, had a very quick shower, then dug out a pair of jeans I had discarded for the summer. I put them on, with a thick black belt, and added a checked cotton shirt and a light, sleeveless jacket. Too much in the heat, I knew, but I needed the pockets. Finally, I put on a pair of thick-soled sandals with heavy toe protectors. My right foot was still painful when I moved the wrong way, but if the need arose to kick someone where it hurt the most, they would do the job.

When I was ready I went down to the garage with the taser, reopened the safe and took out the half-dozen replacement cartridges I'd included with my order, then spent ten minutes practising reloading the weapon. The on-line sales pitch had claimed it could be done in four seconds, but the best I could manage was six. I hoped that would be enough, for I knew Sebastian and Willie would be reunited, and that I'd have to be ready to drop them both.

I was almost ready to go. I took a bottle of water from the stock in the garage fridge, and a couple of isotonics, just in case Adrienne needed rehydrating once she was free. She'd looked well cared for in those videos, but I couldn't be sure. Almost as an afterthought I ran upstairs and fetched Frank's rucksack. I'm not certain now, but I reckon my reasoning at the time was that, *if* he was still alive, and *if* I could spring both him and his mother, he might want to disappear before the police arrived.

Since Interpol had disowned him over the Sevilla affair, there might be a danger of him being caught up in any aftermath.

'Have I everything I might need?' I asked myself. Not quite. The taser would knock them down, but for how long? I took Frank's knife from his bag and cut four lengths from an old blue towrope that hangs on the garage wall, a relic from our former, less reliable vehicle.

I heard two o'clock ring, or maybe even two minutes past, if I'd missed it the first time, since the sound was muffled by the bulk of the great stone house above me. I slid the taser into its holster, safety off, clipped it on to the front left of my belt, so I could reach it quickly, opened the garage door, set the alarm and backed out. I didn't even wait to be sure that the door had closed behind me, but put the Jeep straight into drive.

Not much was in my favour at the start of the journey. The first hazard was a fat, half-naked middle-aged slob, plodding along in the centre of the track, heading the same way as I was, and refusing obdurately to budge. Eventually I lost patience and blasted him with the horn. He stopped, turned round, glared at me, then stepped sideways when he saw the look in my eyes. As I passed he took a half-hearted kick at the Jeep, a stupid thing to do when you're barefoot, especially if you connect. I took some satisfaction, as I drove on, from the sight of him in the rear-view mirror, hopping on his left foot, and clutching the toes of the other.

It didn't get much better when I rejoined the main road: the day was so hot that families were deciding to abandon the beach before they and their kids melted. The car parks were emptying and the traffic was queued back a quarter of a kilometre from the L'Escala–Figueras junction. There was nothing for me to do but grimace and bear it.

Normally, on a clear road, it takes me five minutes, tops, to drive from my house to Bellcaire, the village beyond L'Escala. That afternoon it took thirty-five, and I had made a dent in my water supply by the time I reached the crossroads. I did as the priest had said, and took a left, then drove slowly, looking out for the sign. It was hand painted, but clearly visible. I turned in, left again, stopped alongside it and drew breath.

A dirt track lay before me leading upwards, up a hillside, not directly towards the summit that we Brits all call Tit Hill but to a lower crest alongside it. I had taken Tom up to Castell del Montgri a few months before, on a fine day during the school's winter holiday, but we had climbed by the path that starts from Torroella. I recalled the view from the old citadel walls, and realised that the building I had seen below, on the edge of a clearing, must have been the abandoned retreat of Santa Caterina. From what I could recall of the terrain, I knew I would be wise to stop short of the place and approach on foot.

Was I nervous? Too damn right I was; I could feel my heart thumping in my chest at a rate well above the normal seventy beats per minute. But also I felt the holstered taser against my side. That, and the sure knowledge that I wouldn't even think once about pulling the trigger of the lightweight but super-efficient weapon, gave me comfort. I slid the Jeep into drive once more, engaged four-wheel mode, and moved forward.

At first, the track ran parallel to the road alongside, but then it veered off and curved, rising more steeply. I climbed, steadily, up the bumpy road. I had probably driven for a kilometre, when I saw, through a gap in the trees, the spire of the retreat. I hit the brake. There were trees on either side of the road. This was no plantation: they had taken root naturally, and were thickly packed in places, but a short distance ahead, I spotted a small circular area, possibly cut as a passing place. I drove past it, then reversed in, ready for a quick getaway.

I did a spot-check. The cartridges were in the pockets of my jacket. Ropes? I picked them up, stuffed them into Frank's rucksack, together with the drinks I'd brought for Adrienne, slung it over my left shoulder and stepped out of the Jeep, leaving the key in the lock and closing the door quietly behind me.

The sun was blazing above me as I stepped out on to the track, and its force hit me like a blast from a giant hair-dryer. The road was steeper than I'd realised while I was driving. I pushed myself as hard uphill as my injured toe would let me. Soon I felt my breath quicken, and my shirt wet against my skin. I could see Santa Caterina more clearly, and something else, a pathway off the track, through the woods, that led up behind it. I headed for it.

And Sebastian Loman stepped out from behind a tree, about twenty feet before me. He wore a grey linen suit and white shirt, tie-less, with a little maple-leaf pin in the left lapel; there was a smile on his face. 'You took your time, Primavera,' he said.

He was unarmed. I could not believe it, but he had no gun,

in his hand or anywhere else that I could see. But I had. I stepped towards him, closing the distance between us, and reaching for the taser. He was still smiling, but I didn't have time to consider that. I cleared my pacifier of its holster, and sighted it on his chest.

That was when I felt the pressure on the small of my back, against my spine, of something hard and circular. I didn't need to be told what it was.

'Best drop that,' Willie Venable murmured in my ear.

I didn't have much choice, did I? I sighed and let my insurance slip from my fingers. As it fell, Frank's rucksack was yanked from my shoulder.

'And raise your hands.' I did that too.

Still smiling, Sebastian stepped forward and reached down to pick up the discarded taser. As he did so, I thought about kicking him in the nuts, but decided that if I did I might not be alive for long enough even to hear him moan. He stood up, admiring the weapon. 'I've never seen one of these. Impressive.' He removed the holster from my belt, his hand brushing the inside of my pocket in the process, and bumping against my spare cartridges. He took them too, and my mobile, then turned and headed up the way through the woods, beckoning me to follow. Willie jabbed me with his gun, to give force to the command. I walked between them, silently, until we reached the old retreat, and its main entrance. As we reached it, I looked across the clearing, and saw, parked on the other side, a big green vehicle, a Land Rover, perhaps.

The doors of the building were secured. As Sebastian

produced a key from his jacket, unlocked the padlock that held them and swung them open, Willie stepped alongside me, and I saw him for the first time since Sevilla. He didn't look as kind and considerate any more.

Light flooded into a big room, a million dust motes swirling in its rays. Through them I saw my aunt, and my cousin, their arms and legs tied as they sat in high-backed wooden chairs. They were gagged. A hand, Willie's, I think, shoved me inside.

'So, we have it,' Sebastian announced, as he closed the entrance, plunging us into gloom, 'the family reunion.'

'Yes,' I snapped, 'you have it. Now show some decency and let my aunt go.'

'Honey,' Willie drawled, 'this ain't about decency, this is about money, and you know how it has to play out.'

I looked around the room, and saw that it was lit only by slivers of light coming from four windows, two above the doors and the others in the walls on either side. All of them had been boarded up.

'This is how it will happen.' Sebastian had become formal. 'One by one. The McGowan family first, I think.' He stepped behind Adrienne's chair, untied her and helped her to her feet. It was the first time I'd ever seen her looking her age, but still her eyes blazed above her gag as she glared at him. 'If you'd come with us, Mother,' said Loman.

Willie handed the gun to his partner, then manhandled me across to the empty chair, and shoved me down on to it. He ripped off my jacket and tried to use it as a gag, but it was too big, and so he took my shirt instead. That served the purpose;

it felt clammy as he jammed it across my mouth, parting my teeth and hurting me as he tightened it. I heard a sound from beside me, and realised that it was Frank, trying to say something that escaped only as a snarl. Willie ignored him as he tied me tightly to the chair with the cloth bindings he had taken from my aunt.

Sebastian nodded towards the door. Willie opened it, stuck his head outside to check for intruders, then signalled the all-clear with an upraised thumb. As they took her out, Adrienne looked back at Frank; I could see real fear in her eyes, until the door closed again, we were in the virtual darkness and they were gone.

I shifted my chair round so that I could see more of my cousin. His left cheek and the side of his nose were red and swollen, and he was slumped in his chair. I wondered if they'd given him a going-over once they'd got him secure. I tried to work the gag out of my mouth, but Willie had done too good a job. I looked at the chairs, and wondered if we could move them together and untie each other but, again, our bonds had been very efficiently fastened.

Frank's gag was their only slip-up. As I watched, I saw him work away at it, until finally, although he hadn't rid himself of it entirely, he had moved it enough to be able to speak, after a fashion.

'You shouldn't have come,' he mumbled. 'Prim, I'm so sorry it's come to this. My mess, but it's caught you too.' He was looking me in the eye. 'Shouldn't say sorry, though, should I?' I'll swear he was trying to smile.

And then the pair came back.

'Time's up, Frank,' said Willie, dispassionately.

He didn't bother to untie him; he simply cut him loose, with Frank's own wee knife, I noticed, taken from his rucksack, and hauled him towards the doorway.

I lost it then: I went crazy, filled with fury. I'm sure that if I'd been loose and they'd been unarmed I'd have destroyed the pair of them, but I was tied up tight and all I could do was shuffle my chair towards them, screaming obscenities through my gag, as they took my little cousin out of my sight for the last time.

I made one final lurch towards Sebastian, as he stood facing me, framed in the doorway. And that's when the bastard shot me with my own taser.

Thirty-one

I tell you now, those damn weapons do exactly what it says on the tin, as the wood-preservative ads insist. I saw those probes coming at me, and when they hit, and the fifty thousand volts followed, I was completely helpless. I was pitched backwards, overturning the chair, my limbs convulsing and twitching within their restraints. I was barely aware of it, though: along with loss of physical control there was a feeling of total confusion. As we say in Scotland, I was completely wandered. I had no idea where I was, or what I was supposed to be doing there. If I had been asked what my name was, and I'd been able to speak, I'd have replied, 'Uh?'

I have no idea how long I was out of it, but gradually my bewilderment began to dissipate; I returned, slowly, to my senses, and felt the paralysis wearing off too. Of course, that didn't mean I could move: I was still tethered to that very solid chair, on my back and, as all of it came back to me, acutely aware that at any moment I could expect a return visit from Sebastian and Willie. If there really is a Shit Creek, I was well and truly up it. Yet as I turned my head to look around I caught a glimpse of something that might just be a paddle.

Frank's clever little Swiss Army knife lay only a few feet away, where Willie had discarded it after cutting him loose, and the razor-sharp blade was open. If I could get to it . . .

I thought about rolling over, but realised that even if I could manage it once, I'd never have the leverage to do it a second time, as I'd need to if I was going to reach it. So, rather than try that, I began to shuffle sideways, using my hips to generate the movement, and my palms to help. My hands weren't tied together behind my back; instead, my arms were lashed to the sides of the chair, giving me a little flexibility.

It took me more time than I believed I had to get to it, but I managed to pull myself the few feet that I needed. I felt sideways, blindly, for the knife, until my fingertips touched its plastic casing, and I was able to grip it, and manoeuvre it in my hand until I reckoned I knew where the blade was in relation to everything else. Something told me that I might only have one shot at what I was going to attempt. The same prescience told me that there was a fair chance I'd slice my wrist open in the process and maybe bleed to death. I closed my eyes and thrust the blade upwards . . . straight into my binding, cutting through it far enough for me to rip my arm free.

The rest took seconds, that was all, and then I was out of the chair and on unsteady legs, unfastening the gag that had once been a serviceable shirt. My eyes had grown accustomed to the light, or lack of it. I could see two small red dots on my belly where the darts had hit. My arms were filthy from the dust on the floor, and my jeans felt damp. I hoped it was only sweat, and that I hadn't wet myself under the grip of the non-lethal but, by Jesus, bloody powerful current. I sniffed, and was reassured.

As I stood there, I heard a noise and saw movement in the handle of one of the double doors, the one on my right. I went cold inside, knowing what I had to do. There was no time for subtlety. Sebastian or Willie, whoever would draw the short straw and come first into that room, was getting the blade in the throat, and then, broken toe or not, the other one was getting the benefit of everything I'd ever learned in those *tae kwon do* classes, until he wasn't moving, or breathing either, if I could manage that. I took a couple of steps to my left and waited as the handle turned fully, and as the door creaked open.

'Primavera?' The voice was anxious, but it was strong.

I only realised that I had been holding my breath when it escaped from me in a great gasp of relief. 'Gerard,' I yelled, and then my sense of danger kicked back in. 'Be careful. They're out there.' I reached out to pull him inside, but he held my wrist.

'There's nobody out here,' he said gently, drawing me into the daylight. He had changed out of his priest suit into a grey shirt and camouflage shorts, the sort of gear he often wears when he's not ministering. He stood there, built like a good-sized brick outhouse, and I felt safe. I felt even safer when I looked around. The Land Rover was gone.

'I followed you as soon as the service was over,' he told me.

'It took longer than I thought, as some more worshippers came in from the beach.' He smiled. 'That can happen when it's really hot. I've come to regard it as one of God's mysterious ways. Now tell me, what's happened, and where are your aunt and your cousin?'

Suddenly my legs felt weak again. A couple of metres away, I saw the remnants of a small stone wall. I tottered across and sat on it. 'They're gone,' I told him. 'Sebastian and Willie, the men who were holding them, took them away, one by one, to be killed. I thought I was going to be next; they tied me to a chair and shot me with a stun gun. When you opened the door, Father Gerard, I thought you were them. If you'd stepped inside . . .' I was still holding the knife. I smiled at him weakly. 'Going to give me absolution?' I asked, and then I burst into tears.

He sat beside me and held me until I'd cried myself out. 'There's nothing to absolve, little sister,' he whispered. 'You have no sin in your heart.' He stood, and I did also; I looked down at my sweaty, begrimed body and felt embarrassed by my state of undress. I walked back to the retreat and looked inside. My shirt was useless, but my jacket was still there, on the floor. I put it on and fastened it. Not pretty, but it did the job.

'We must call the police,' said Gerard, taking out his mobile.

'Yes,' I agreed. 'But I'm going to look around. Frank and Adrienne, their bodies . . .' My words tailed off.

'You should leave that for the Mossos.'

'Yes? And what if one of them's still alive?'

If they were there, I guessed that they'd be in the open. There couldn't have been time to bury them, surely. I headed across the clearing to where the vehicle had been. The ground was hard and dry. There were no tyre marks, but crushed twigs and leaves showed where it had stood. All around, the bushes were thick. If two bodies had been dragged in there, I'd have seen the evidence. I was about to look in another area when something dark caught my eye, on the ground, a few metres distant. I approached it, carefully, and knelt when I reached it.

'What is it?' Gerard called to me. 'I'm speaking to Alex Guinart.'

'Blood,' I replied. 'Tell him I've found blood.' There were two of them, side by side, big pools of dark blood. I'd seen things like that before, in Africa, and the people involved hadn't walked away. I didn't want to touch them, but I could see that they were fresh, still not quite dry, for all the force of the sun. 'Tell him it looks as if they were killed here, and their bodies taken away.'

Thirty-two

Alex was there within half an hour. He was first on the scene, with the same cop who'd been with him earlier at the roundabout. He took me back to the stone wall and sat beside me, with Father Gerard on my other flank, listening quietly and patiently as I told him about the clue Adrienne had given me, and how it had led me there.

When I was finished, he looked past me at the priest, accusingly. 'She could have been killed, Father.'

'I should have stopped her physically from coming up here, are you saying?'

Alex shook his head. 'No, but you could have called me.'

'And you would have done what? As Primavera supposed, you would have come storming up here with your guns at the ready, and there would have been a battle. Frank and his mother would have died anyway, and maybe, friend, so would you. She didn't want to risk you, and neither did I.'

'But that's my job.'

'Your job is to die? I don't think so.'

'My job is to protect.'

'I believe that these people were beyond protection.'

'Then now my job is to apprehend. Primavera, what can you tell me about these two men?'

'I've told you some of it already. Their names are Sebastian Loman . . . he's Canadian, I believe . . . and Willie Venable. I told you about him yesterday, remember?'

'Yes, and I checked with Immigration. There's no record of anyone with that name, but that doesn't prove anything. He could have come into Spain by road, from France or Portugal, or through Andorra. How did you come to know him?'

'I met them both on Monday evening, in Sevilla, in a restaurant. I thought it was a casual encounter, but I know now that it wasn't: they'd set out to look for me. They were friendly; in conversation, I told them I was having a break and that my aunt was here, in St Martí, minding my son. Next morning, Willie Venable kidnapped her. I'm sure if Tom had been there . . .'

'But he wasn't,' said Alex, calmly, 'so be cool. Go on.'

'Next day in Sevilla, two people from the fraud that Frank was sent to infiltrate tried to abduct me from my hotel. Their names are Emil Caballero, a city councillor, and Lidia Bromberg. But Frank had been watching me, without me knowing. He intervened and we escaped. We made it to Córdoba, but saw Sebastian Loman in the Mezquita, searching for us. We evaded him and went to Barcelona, on the night train, then yesterday we came here. The rest you know.'

'What can you tell me about the Land Rover you saw here?'

I frowned as I considered the question. 'Alex,' I answered, 'given the state I was in, I'm not even sure it was a Land Rover, or what colour it was. It was a big vehicle, that's all. I didn't see the number.'

'I understand.'

'What do we do now?' I asked.

'We wait for my bosses to get here from Girona. I fear the day isn't over for you yet, Primavera.'

I was sure he wasn't kidding. 'One thing I don't get,' I told him. 'They didn't come back for me after they killed Frank and Adrienne. Why not? Did Father Gerard interrupt them?'

He shook his head. 'They didn't drive past him, and that road back there is the only one out of here. Okay, if you take a chance you might get off another way in a four-by-four, but you'd need to know the lie of the land. No, I'd say, my dear friend, that they left you because you're high profile, Mrs Oz Blackstone, the mother of his son. If you'd died, it would have made news internationally . . . as it did before, if I may remind you.'

He frowned. 'Your cousin, on the other hand, is a former criminal, if I remember correctly what you told me about him before. Nobody will care that he's wound up dead. Your aunt, that's unfortunate, but she's not famous either. Her murder will be forgotten in a couple of weeks in England, and will barely make the front page here in Spain.'

I thought about what he'd said, and realised that it was all true: sad, but inescapably true.

Alex's middle-aged and higher-ranking colleagues, an

intendant whom he introduced as Gomez, and an inspector, whose chest badge identified him as J. Garcia, arrived from Girona not long afterwards, with a support team who went to work at once on the drying blood. I wanted to give them a statement, then go home, but they insisted on taking me to the Mossos station in L'Escala, for interrogation, as they put it bluntly. Father Gerard did some insisting too, that he would accompany me. The unsmiling coppers tried to put him off, but he wasn't having any.

In fact, they didn't take me straight to the station. Instead I was driven to the adjacent emergency medical centre, where I was given a thorough physical examination by the receiving doctor while they and Gerard waited outside. I could hear the medic through the half-open door as she briefed them. She said I hadn't been raped . . . I'd never claimed to have been raped, as my friend the priest was quick to point out . . . but I had suffered some form of trauma, in the aftermath of which I was in a confused and highly excitable state.

'You mean she could be delusional?' I heard Intendant Gomez ask.

'That is possible,' she replied.

'I'm not delusional!' I shouted, proving beyond reasonable doubt that at the very least she'd been right about my excitability.

I didn't contribute to the improvement of relations between us by refusing to get dressed. 'I want fresh clothes,' I demanded, from under a sheet on the examination table. 'I don't have a proper shirt and those jeans are filthy.'

Garcia scowled at me. 'We need those anyway,' he said, 'for forensic testing. What you're going to wear, that's your problem.'

'No,' Gerard told him, in a quiet tone that might have been threatening if it hadn't come from a man in holy orders, 'it's yours.'

Gomez stepped between them; he sent the inspector to the police station to fetch a T-shirt and shorts as close to my size as he could find. 'What did he mean by forensic testing?' I asked, as the door closed on him.

'We need to check your garments,' the *intendant* replied coolly, 'for blood splashes. There was a lot of it up there.'

'You're wasting your time,' I told him. 'I knelt beside it but I was careful not to touch it.'

'You don't understand me.'

'No, I don't.' The doctor had been right about my confusion too.

'We need to check them for blood splashes,' he repeated patiently.

'For Christ's sake!' I shouted, as finally I grasped what he was saying, lapsing into English and drawing a frown. 'Listen to me,' I continued, in Spanish once more. 'My cousin and my aunt have just been murdered, almost before my eyes, and their bodies taken God knows where. I've just been shot with the sort of weapon they use to subdue bears, and you're implying that I might have had something to do with their deaths. Someone in this room is delusional, as the doctor said, and it's you.'

'Madam,' he said stiffly, 'I am implying nothing. But I must eliminate. That's why I need to test your clothing; to answer questions that I will be asked myself. Now, are you calm? Would you like me to ask the doctor to give you a mild sedative?'

I was on the point of laughing in his face, but I stopped myself. Instead I paused for breath, a deep breath. 'I am calm, Intendant,' I told him, once I was sure that was so. 'I appreciate that you have to interview me, and I would rather not be under the influence of drugs when that happens.' I asked him to leave me with Gerard until his colleague returned, and he did.

'There's something I haven't done,' the priest murmured, once he had gone, 'for which my bishop would reprove me.' He took my hand and began to pray, for the souls of Frank and Adrienne, that their bodies would be found so that they could be properly committed, and for me, that I would be able to put behind me all the things that had happened to me over the previous three days.

'I think that, maybe, I should join your team,' I said, when he was finished.

He smiled. 'You're a member already, whether you know it or not.'

The replacement clothing that Garcia brought was adequate, even if the T-shirt was a little tight and the shorts were knee-length. I walked the short distance to the Mossos station with the two officers and Gerard, suspecting that I looked like a Girl Guide leader, but grateful that I felt cool for the first time since . . . since the first hour of that day, in Shirley's pool.

I thought of what I'd promised Frank. *Tonight.* No more tonights for him; no more days. The enormity of what had happened was beginning to sink in. I knew that I had to keep it at bay, to deal sensibly with the police.

As we turned the corner, I was distracted by the sight of my Jeep in the station's secure park. I had forgotten about it, completely; the key left in the lock, too. I guessed that Alex had driven it back, and felt a surge of gratitude.

My interrogation lasted for three hours, and Father Gerard stayed with me for all that time. Gomez and Garcia were solemn but polite, never threatening as I related my story, from start to finish, although I could sense the inspector's scepticism on more than one occasion. They took me through it for a second time, asking questions this time, and for a third. By that time I had been told that my clothes had come up negative, and so the heat was off, to an extent. Still, I felt that I was reaching the end of my physical and emotional resources when the *intendant* called in a clerk and dictated a statement on my behalf, summarising everything I'd told them. It was typed and put in front of me for checking; it was a formal denunciation accusing Sebastian Loman and Willie Venable of the murders of my aunt, Adrienne McGowan, and her son, Frances Ulverscroft McGowan. I noticed that it contained no mention of the Hotel Casino d'Amuseo fraud, confining itself to the events surrounding the killings, but I accepted that as reasonable, and signed it.

It was almost ten, and darkness had fallen when Gomez showed me to the waiting Jeep. 'I'm sure you're safe now,' he said, smiling for the first time since we'd met, 'but I'll put a guard on your house, front and back, to be sure.'

'Thanks, but no thanks,' I replied. 'My alarm will be security enough.'

'As you wish. You'll be kept informed of the progress of the investigation.'

Father Gerard drove me back to St Martí, and took the car right into the garage. The system was still active, and that was a good sign. Nevertheless my friend insisted on going through every room in the house to ensure that no intruders were lurking, anywhere. Then he made me change the entry code, his back to me as I did it, and extracted a promise that next day I would have the locks changed. After all that, the least I could do was feed him, once I'd changed out of my police-issue clothes and into something comfortingly familiar.

The humidity was pretty high so we chose the air conditioning of Esculapi rather than take a table outside in the square. Gerard is a typical Catalan carnivore, and had a steak, but I couldn't manage more than a pizza, and even then, I cut off the crust. However, I could and did manage the best part of a bottle of Torres Coronas.

When we were finished he saw me home yet again . . . I had a moment of panic when I thought I'd forgotten my new code . . . then went off into the night. It was only later that I discovered he'd left his trail bike up on the track to Santa Caterina, and had to walk to the parochial residence in L'Escala.

That was it. Finally I was on my own, at the end of the day I had thought, for a time, wouldn't have one. I sat on my bedroom terrace, safe within the cocoon of my alarm, half sloshed but cuddling a bottle of Coronita, and tried not to think of what had happened. Instead, I tried to think of the next morning and the things I had to do: check with Alex for overnight developments, call on Shirley to tell her what had happened, then fuel up the Jeep and drive to Monaco, to be with the only person in the world I wanted to see, no, needed to see, my lovely boy Tom who'd never get to know that he might have lost his reckless, stupid mother.

I really did try not to think of what had gone down, but it was impossible. My hand crept under my shirt, of its own volition, found the two puncture marks on my belly, and a second later, I had given in to my memories of Auntie Ade, of her crazy little half-Japanese son, and to more salty, unstoppable tears.

Thirty-three

Honestly, I'm not the hysterical type: I can recall every occasion when I've shed tears as an adult. I can recall all of my good times and all of my sad times. The best? Giving birth to Tom. The saddest? Being alone when Tom was born, without family in the delivery room, friends or the man who'd made him.

Not the killings of Frank and Ade? No, I've never thought of them in terms of sadness, but of shock, the kind for which nothing can prepare a person.

As I had begun to say, I don't cry a lot, but when I let myself go, it usually does me good, and so it was when I was awakened next morning by the rising sun, as I sat slumped in my terrace chair, my hair and clothes damp with the dew, my mouth like the slops tray of a beer tap. I sat for a while longer as the awful memories returned, one by one, dimming the bright glory of the new day. I contemplated going inside, closing the shutters and chasing more sleep, but I knew that would be a pointless exercise. Instead, I put on trainers and a swimsuit, let myself out through the garage, clipped on my bum-bag, with my keys and a bottle of water stuffed inside, and started to run.

I headed along the walkway that leads to L'Escala, past the ruins, past the hotel and the beach bar outside, until I reached the road. I stopped at the Olympic statue. I had run harder than usual, and my breathing was heavy, so I waited until it had eased, then turned and jogged back the way I had come.

When I reached the beach bar once again, the guy who runs it was opening up for early breakfast customers. I know him, so I asked him to look after my bag and shoes, then plunged into the sea. I swam for about ten minutes, walked along the water's edge for a bit, until I began to dry off, then went back to the bar, retrieved my bag, and had a chorizo and cheese mini, with a double-espresso chaser.

I walked the rest of the way home barefoot, since I didn't want to get sand in my trainers. As I let myself in through the front door, remembering the new code without difficulty, I felt renewed, back in control. I thought about what Father Gerard had said about finding courage where you least expect it, smiling as I wondered whether that included a chorizo and cheese sandwich.

I showered and dressed for the morning, in not very much since it was going to be another hot one. Remarkably I still felt hungry, so I took some sliced bread from my freezer stock and toasted it, eating it hot with butter and jam, the way you shouldn't, but the way I've always liked it.

I thought of calling Alex, but it was still early, and I feared

I might disturb Gloria and Marte. Instead I went on-line, and found the electronic edition of the Costa Brava newspaper. I searched the latest stories, and found the one I was after. It reported that the Mossos d'Esquadra were looking for two unnamed English visitors, mother and son, who were missing, last seen at Santa Caterina, near Bellcaire, on the edge of a heavily wooded area. Short, succinct, no hint of murder, no hint of violence, no hint of anything beyond a couple of careless punters lost in the woods, where wild boar are rumoured to roam. 'No, we mustn't upset the tourists,' I whispered.

I decided I had to see Shirley; a phone call wouldn't do. I didn't head for the house, though. It had just gone nine, and on most mornings at that time she's to be found having breakfast at a pavement table outside Café del Mar.

'Hi,' she called out, as I approached from the car park. I took a seat beside her, and asked the waiter for coffee, with milk. 'I guess your water's fixed,' she said, 'since you didn't come back last night. Where's Frank, then? Have you exhausted the poor little bugger?'

There was an abandoned newspaper at a nearby table, the print edition of the one I'd looked at on the computer. I fetched it, found the story, on page three, and showed it to her, watching her eyes widen as she read. 'Prim,' she gasped, 'what the fuck is all this about?'

I gave her a very potted version, speaking English to lessen the chances of being overheard, although often we use Spanish, even when it's just the two of us. 'Frank got involved with some bad people in Sevilla. They snatched his mum to get to him.'

'How bad are they?' she asked quietly.

'Lethal, I fear.'

'Seriously?' I nodded. 'You're not involved, are you?'

'No. They got who they were after.'

'And your aunt?'

'Innocent victim. Caught in the crossfire. Collateral damage. Choose your favourite cliché.' I took her gate opener from my bag and handed it to her. 'I owe you an apology, Shirl. It was wrong of me to impose on you without telling you the whole story. I could have put you in danger as well.'

She gave me back the device. 'Keep it,' she said. 'For the next time you're in bother. You're my pal, remember.' She paused as the waiter brought my coffee. 'You'll miss him, won't you? Just when you and he were getting close.'

'That was just something that happened on the road.'

'No, it wasn't. For all I might kid you about it, I know you don't do casual sex.'

'Well, from now on,' I told her, 'that's going to be the only kind for me. Seems that if I get too close to a bloke, he dies.'

'In that case, I'll bet Father Gerard's relieved he's a priest.'

I blinked. 'Whatever do you mean?'

'You know bloody well what I mean, but let's leave it at that. Is there any chance that they'll be found safe?'

'You never can tell, but I don't see it. There was blood; a lot of it.'

'Oh dear.' Shirley's eyes misted over. She had liked Frank too. 'What are you going to do now?'

'Go and get Tom,' I replied. 'I sent him to Monaco for safety when all this started to happen. After that, I'm not sure. At some point I'll need to tell my dad what's happened, and my sister; we're all the family Adrienne and Frank had. But I'm not up to that yet.'

'When are you off?'

'Now. I'll call you when I get back.' I slid a five-euro note for the waiter under my empty cup, stood up and headed back towards the car park.

Thirty-four

I had packed a small case before I left, with clothes for a couple of days, and slipped my passport into my bag, with my cash and my cards. With no need to go back home, I headed straight for the *autopista*, and France.

As I passed Camallera, noticing the shrine by the roadside that Gerard had mentioned, I switched on the CD player. Del Amitri filled the Jeep with sound. I selected another disc, pronto, knowing that I'd never hear that band again without thinking of Frank. Texas took over, but the Scottish connection was too close, and Faith Hill was too maudlin. In the end I settled for a French pop radio station that I knew would be in range as far as Montpellier.

By the time I'd crossed the border, the music was in the background and I was thinking again, about Sebastian and Willie mostly, hoping I'd given Gomez and Garcia enough information to track them down, but without, I found, too much optimism. Those guys had been pros; it was improbable that they were still in Spain.

Yes, they were pros all right. They'd never made a wrong

move from the time they'd sat at my table in Sevilla. They'd been on the look-out for me. But how had they known I was coming? Adrienne's first phone call, in search of Frank, had probably been enough to sound the alarm. My Scots accent when I'd set up my date with Lidia probably hadn't been too clever either. But when I'd gone marching up to the door of number forty-seven, then quizzed that wee twerp of a shopkeeper, well, that had more or less hung out a sign. 'Trouble in town, she's blonde and she's a Jockess.' How much more stupid could I have been? I'd got in trouble, Frank had had to leave his safe-house to rescue me and, in the process, got himself and his mother killed. Unless . . .

I searched for straws to grasp. Maybe he'd put up a fight and they'd had to subdue him. Maybe all that blood was his. I thought back to Africa and remembered that once or twice I had seen wounds that bled as much but turned out to be more or less superficial. Maybe . . . I persuaded myself there was a little hope.

I clung to it as I drove east, through the morning, past Narbonne, Montpellier and to Nîmes. I stopped near Marseille for petrol and water. Before getting back on the road, I called Susie to let her know that I was on the way and should be with them in less than two hours. She sounded a little underwhelmed, but I put that down to her being busy, and to the unnecessarily short notice I was giving her.

When I got there, just after two thirty, to the secure villa on the hilltop overlooking the harbour of Monte Carlo, I decided I had been kidding myself about that. She was her usual effusive self, when she and Charlie greeted me, welcoming me in, then taking me through to the playroom where the kids were amusing themselves, out of the heat of the day. 'Mum!' Tom called out, jumped up and ran towards me, into my arms. He's not usually so demonstrative; I guessed he must have been far more worried than he was letting on.

Of course the first thing he asked me was 'Did you collect Auntie Adrienne?'

'Yes, love,' I told him. 'She and Frank have moved on now.'

'That's a shame. I liked her.'

'Perhaps you'll see her again some time.'

'And meet Frank?'

'Perhaps.'

I stayed with him for a while, making a fuss of wee Jonathan, and of Janet, as far as that growing young woman would let me (I know she's only eight, but try telling her that). Then, when it was swim time, Susie and I joined the three of them in the pool. (Charlie was barred from the terrace, I discovered, after an earlier incident in which he had tried to life-save wee Jonathan, who's probably a better swimmer than the bloody dog is.)

It wasn't until Ethel came in to call time up . . . she's in charge of the children's activities; that's her absolute rule . . . that us two mums had the chance of some time alone. 'Well?' Susie demanded, as soon as wee Jonathan, always the laggard, was out of earshot, and we were settled on two couches, under an awning.

'It's not good,' I said. 'Frank's associates caught up with him.

He and Adrienne are missing, believed dead.' I didn't see the need to tell her any more than that.

'Believed? What are their chances?'

I looked at her, and shrugged.

'God, Prim, I'm so sorry.' She glanced at the ground between us. 'I have to confess that when you called me on Tuesday the words "drama" and "queen" came to mind, given that you've got a track record in that area. I was expecting your aunt to be found wrestling with a trolley in the local supermarket. But this; it's shocking. How did your cousin get mixed up with these people?'

'He was working undercover for Interpol, to break a major international fraud, but he was betrayed by someone on the inside. He might have got away in one piece, until I went crashing in there after him, like a cow in a bloody china factory.'

'That's why they took your aunt? To get to him?'

'Yes.'

'Oh dear.' She looked at me. 'I see now why you wanted Tom out of it. How about you? Are you okay?'

'Apart from being knackered, I'm fine.'

'Would you like to stay here for a while?'

'A couple of days, if that's all right with you, and then my boy and I will get back down the road.'

Susie frowned, her red hair glinting in the sun. 'Actually,' she ventured, 'I was going to talk to you about that. We'd agreed that Tom would come here for a couple of weeks in August, yes?'

I nodded.

'Well . . .' she hesitated before continuing '. . . I've pretty much decided to sell the Loch Lomond estate. It would suit my book to go back there in August, to get the process under way. There would be no point in now. You know what Glasgow's like: you can barely sell chips in July. So, seeing as Tom's here now, can we bring his stay forward to . . . well, to now?'

I thought about it. Tom and I had no firm plans for the rest of the month. That said, I always missed him while he was gone, and after the past few days, did I need to be brooding on my own? On the other hand . . .

'Sure,' I said. 'The rest of this week and next.'

'Thanks. You can stay too, if you like.'

'That's good of you, but it's best if I don't. Let's stick to our normal practice.' It's not just two women in one kitchen, as I'd told Adrienne. While Susie and I do get on fine now, we both know that if we were together for a couple of weeks we'd wind up either going out on the batter every night, or arguing over the past or, probably, both.

'Why are you selling Loch Lomond?' I asked her. 'It's a palace.'

She glanced at me, then looked away again. 'Janet thinks it's haunted.' She tried to chuckle, but failed.

'It's a big old house,' I pointed out. 'It's not unnatural for a kid to imagine things, especially one with the enquiring mind she's got.'

'It's not just the house, Prim, it's the whole damn place. There are some woods that she just won't go in. To tell you the truth, I find it really spooky myself now. No, it's going, and that's an end of it. I'll buy a smaller house, with an ordinary garden, not something the size of a bloody farm.'

'Do you ever feel haunted here?' I asked.

'No.' This time she did manage to laugh. 'Did you think the bugger was stalking me from beyond the grave?'

'I wouldn't put it past him.'

'Are you still afraid of him,' she asked bluntly, 'even though he's dead? For he is, believe me. I saw the body.'

'No, but I never really was. When I disappeared after the crash, I was confused, but I reckoned that was what he'd want me to do.'

Her brow furrowed as she realised what I'd said. 'Wait a minute. Are you implying that you thought he wanted you dead? That he arranged that plane crash?'

'I'm not implying it; I've never told anyone straight out, but that's what I believe. We knew him better than anyone else, Susie. Can you put your hand on your heart and deny that he was capable of it?'

She had to think about that for a while. 'No,' she confessed. 'I can't. But I don't believe he'd have harmed you. He loved you, Prim, for all you spent half your time at each other's throats. My secret fear, even after Jonathan was born, was that one day he'd leave me and go back to you. If one of us fixed that aircraft it would more likely have been me.'

'Now that I can't accept,' I protested. 'You are definitely not capable of such a thing. Honest, I wish I didn't believe what I do, but that's the way the evidence points.'

'Fuck the evidence. Take my word for it: Oz didn't do it.'

One day, I may be able to accept that. There, on her terrace, I told her I'd try, but I'm still a way short of succeeding.

Thirty-five

I stayed with Susie and the family for two days, until Sunday. Both mornings, I went on-line and checked for developments in the search, but there were none reported. I studied the London media too. The story hadn't gone unnoticed: I found it on the BBC website, and in the *Telegraph* and the *Guardian*, but without names to go on it wasn't front-page news.

Tom was fine about the idea of extending his visit, especially when I promised to take him to America in August, to see his aunt Dawn and his cousins, Bruce and Eilidh. He hadn't asked me any more questions about Adrienne or Frank; I was pleased about that.

I headed off after breakfast, but I didn't drive home. Instead, I went to Nice Airport, where I parked the Jeep and caught a flight that I'd booked the day before, to Edinburgh, via London. My dad was waiting for me at Arrivals, as arranged. I could have hired a car, but as usual he wouldn't hear of it. Since Mum went, he's seized every excuse to get out of the great big house in which he still lives, having refused to sell it, despite suggestions, entreaties and downright bullying from my sister and me.

I spent a lovely, peaceful evening with him, and later, in my old bed, managed a night's sleep that was, as far as I can recall, free of dreams of any sort. I didn't raise the subject of Adrienne's visit, but he did, over breakfast. 'I had your aunt on the phone,' he said casually. 'Has she been in touch?'

'Yes,' I told him. 'She invited herself, stayed for a couple of days, then buggered off without as much as a thank-you.'

His eyebrows rose; that's about as dramatic as he gets. 'That's fairly typical of her, I'm afraid. Adrienne always was a law unto herself. She has the odd beliefs that flamboyance entitles you to be rude, and that unacceptable behaviour can be explained as eccentricity. The arrival of her son was a classic example of that.'

'She isn't all bad.'

'Nobody is, my dear. She was a damned good agent for your mother when she started to write her children's stories.' He smiled. 'The trouble is, the woman still sends me a copy of every book published by every one of her clients. They're filling up my damn shelves. Take some of them when you leave, please, Primavera, for Tom, and yourself.'

I promised that I would. We finished breakfast, and I did the dishes, while he went off to work. He's a craftsman carpenter, designing, carving and painting chess sets, and other pieces, like the cuckoo clock he gave to Tom and me.

When I was done . . . Dad doesn't have a dish-washer

because it never occurred to Mum and him to buy one . . . I called Fanette, in Adrienne's office. She became a bit stand-offish when she realised it was me, not having forgiven me for ripping strips off her in our previous discussion, but eventually she told me that, no, she hadn't heard from Adrienne and, yes, she had been expecting her back in the office that morning. Of course, without her, she was terribly busy, so if I'd excuse her . . . I did, with a private vow that I would sort her out when I had time.

I'd brought my aunt's mobile with me from Spain, as a temporary replacement for my own. I used it to send texts to my number and to Frank's, a pointless gesture, as I neither expected nor received replies, but one that I felt I had to make.

Dad doesn't have a computer either, but he does have the *Courier*, the *Herald* and the *Scotsman* delivered every morning. I read through their news pages, but none of them was keeping tabs on the story of two missing English tourists. (If they had been from Dundee, Glasgow, or Edinburgh, that would have been another matter.)

I felt helpless after that, frustrated that there was nothing more I could do. I kept it from Dad, though, as I devoted myself to looking after him, not that he needs much. My mother was a formidable cook, and after her death, I'd had recurring visions of poor old widowed David living on a diet of Tesco ready-meals and Wall's ice-cream. Those notions were banished in the spell when Tom and I lived with him, before moving to Spain. I discovered that he had taken over

Mum's mantle: the vegetable garden and the fruit bushes were as well tended and productive as ever, and in fact he was cooking so damn much that every so often he'd have to deplete the stock in the freezer by catering for a church evening function.

The main way in which I cared for him was simply by listening to him as we sat together over meals, or in the garden, providing a ready ear, and an alternative viewpoint when I disagreed with him. That was how he and Mum had lived out their lives, and that was what he missed most of all. As we talked, I discovered he was not as solitary a figure as I had thought. He and Mac Blackstone, Oz's retired dentist father and Tom's other granddad, kept in touch, and visited each other frequently. It didn't surprise me when he told me, for Mac's a good man, but I was delighted to hear it.

It wasn't until the third day of my visit that I thought about Mark Kravitz, and realised I owed him a call. I rang his landline. As always he was brisk and business-like when he answered.

'Mark, it's Primavera. I'm in Scotland, at my dad's.'

'You're safe?' he exclaimed. 'Thank Christ for that.'

'Didn't Susie tell you I was?'

'Yes, but it didn't stop me worrying, especially when I saw a report in the *Telegraph* on Saturday morning about a missing English couple. Them?'

'Yes.'

'Is it as bad as it read?'

'Yes. They haven't found any bodies yet, but I'm having

trouble looking on the bright side.' I paused. 'Mark, are you still up for checking a couple of things for me?'

'Of course.'

'Then would you please look into a French mining company called Energi, and find out what you can about its ultimate ownership, and its finances, especially about a twenty-million-euro investment in Hotel Casino d'Amuseo. Also, find out, if you can, whether there is any money still held in the company bank account in Luxembourg.'

'Will do.'

'Thanks. Hey,' I added, 'remember Lidia Bromberg?'

'Yes. You didn't go to meet her, did you?'

'I didn't have to. The bitch tried to kidnap me in Sevilla, her and Councillor Caballero.'

'I'm not going to say I told you so,' he murmured, after a few seconds' silence. 'Oh, hell, I am. How did you get away?'

'Frank rescued me.'

'Frank?'

'Yes. He and Hermann Gresch were planted in the operation by Interpol. He was recruited in prison by MI5.'

'You what?' he gasped.

'Does that surprise you?'

'Prim, nothing about those people surprises me. Mind you . . .'

'In that case here's another for you: someone on the inside sold them out. Frank reported back to his controller and he was betrayed.'

'With seventy-seven million euros in the pot that doesn't

stun me either. Leave all that with me, Prim. I'll make those checks.' He paused. 'But tell me: what are you going to do with this information when you get it?'

'I don't know for sure, but one way or another it's going to help me get even with whoever did this to my aunt and my cousin.'

Thirty-six

$\mathbf{M}$ark called me back next morning, just as Dad and I were about to head off on a shopping expedition to Perth. I still have a few items of clothing at his place, but I'd exhausted the summer stock.

'I've done your digging,' he began. 'First and foremost, the money's been moved out of Luxembourg. Pintore and Company, the lawyers, weren't for telling me anything, so I had my London solicitor call them and imply that they were representing an investor in the project who was getting worried about his cash. They admitted that the funds had been transferred to a new account, in the Cayman Islands, outside their control. It was done legally and above board, on the basis of a written instruction signed by the chairman, Alastair Rowland, over the company seal. It was delivered to their offices by courier last Thursday, and the money was transferred the same day.'

'More or less as I thought. What about Energi?'

'As you said; they stand to lose twenty million euros if the project collapses. But don't read too much into the transfer:

there may have been a legitimate reason for it. The test is what happens to the money next.'

'Come on, it's a scam. Frank told me as much.'

'Maybe, but I haven't found any proof of that, not yet at any rate.'

'Why did Energi make the investment in the first place?'

'On the instructions of the nominal owners of the company, the Banovsky Corporation.'

'That fits with what Frank told me he found when he broke into Emil Caballero's house.'

'He broke in? Your cousin was full of surprises, wasn't he?'

'Much good were they to him. What have you found out about Banovsky?'

'At the moment, not a hell of a lot. It's based in Bratislava, but as a corporate entity it doesn't really exist any more. It's an old family business going back several generations. That's all I know for now, but I'm going to do some more research to build up the complete picture.'

'Who runs Energi?'

'Hired hands. There's a CEO, a director of mining operations, and an accountant, none of them shareholders. I've spoken to a French mining-sector specialist. He told me that Energi is highly geared; currently it has over seventy-five million in bank debt, and that's just about its turnover. That borrowing is supported by the book value of its assets, but the cost of servicing it has pushed it into the red for the last few years. The time-bomb, though, is that its mines are approaching exhaustion, and they don't have any reserves to tap, so those assets are actually significantly overvalued. Its future is tied to the success of Hotel Casino d'Amuseo.'

'Won't they be able to write off the twenty million against tax? Wouldn't that help?'

'No. If the owners of the company, the Banovsky Corporation, could come up with seventy-five million euros to eliminate bank debt, that would help. Otherwise the plug will be pulled.'

I frowned. 'Seventy-five million,' I repeated. 'More or less the sum that's just been moved out of the Hotel Casino d'Amuseo account.'

'Yes, but again, let's not get ahead of ourselves.'

'Come on,' I said. 'Whoever owns Energi, whoever owns the Banovsky Corporation, they could have set up the scam themselves, to keep the business afloat. Couldn't they?'

'They could,' Mark conceded, 'if it is a scam. If it's not, it's a corporate gambler's last throw. Even if it is bent, it can be presented that way.'

'So,' I asked, the seventy-five-million-euro question, 'who does own the damn thing?'

'Not "who", Primavera, "what". This much I do know: the owner of Banovsky is a private numbered trust established through a Swiss bank, and it would take an order from a judge to reveal who the beneficiary is. To make that order the judge would have to see strong evidence of likely criminal involvement.'

'Well?'

'How often do I have to say this? There is no such evidence.

303

Energi will say that it made the investment in d'Amuseo as a step towards securing its future by diversifying into other sectors.'

'How do you know that?'

'Because my contact has already asked the CEO, and that was his reply. Energi is just another investor. If this does turn out to be a fraud, and the owner of Energi is behind it, we have a perfect circle, pretty much a perfect crime.'

I sighed. 'So that's it?'

'That's it.'

'How about Lidia Bromberg? Does she have a past?'

'Not one that I can uncover.'

'And Sebastian and Willie, where do they fit in?'

'Who the hell are they?'

I'd forgotten he didn't know; I explained.

'Hired heavies,' he declared, at once. 'Hit-men, bought and paid for. You'll never find them either. Nor,' he continued, 'will you ever find a trace of Frank and his mother, if they've been as efficient with that end of the operation as they seem to have been with the rest.' He must have heard my reaction. 'Sorry, Prim. They're your family. I shouldn't have been so blunt, but it's the truth, I'm afraid.'

'It's a truth I've been trying not to face,' I admitted. 'But I can't avoid it any longer. They're gone, and the door's closed on the affair. I suppose all I can do now is thank my lucky stars that they didn't kill me too when they had the chance.'

'What do you mean?' Mark asked sharply. I filled him in on the only relevant piece of the story that he didn't know (I'll never give him all the detail; not the personal stuff), and added Alex's view of the reason I'd been spared.

'You are undoubtedly crazy,' he told me, when I'd finished. 'You are also very lucky, for I don't buy your pal's theory. Suppose you had disappeared along with the others? Yes, it would have made news, but given your history, when no bodies turned up, it would have been written up as Primavera buggering off again. A lot of money was spent searching for you once before, remember. I don't believe that would have happened twice.' I could almost hear him shake his head. 'A taser,' he murmured. 'Jesus.'

'Hey,' I retorted. 'I was shot with the fucking thing. Now I know for myself how effective they are, I'll be getting another one.'

'Not in Britain, please. They're illegal.'

'Why should the bad people have all the advantages?' I protested.

'Because that's the way real life is,' Mark replied seriously. 'Look at the thing we've just been investigating. We think it's a crime, but it isn't, not yet at any rate. We're no further forward.'

As I thought about that, I realised he was wrong. 'We are,' I countered. 'We might not know who Alastair Rowland is, but we've got a sample of his handwriting, in that law office in Luxembourg.'

'You know,' he said, 'sometimes you can be smarter than you usually act. Leave that one with me. I'll call you if I make progress.'

'Okay. If it's more than a couple of days, you'd better use my temporary mobile. I'm heading home on Thursday.' I gave him Adrienne's number.

'Thanks, but . . . there's something else. When you go back, could you do it via London?'

'That's what I am doing. I could rearrange my flights, I suppose, and stop over.'

'Do that. Come to my place, but let me know when you'll be arriving.' He gave me an address, and said it was near Paddington.

'I'll do it,' I promised, 'but what's this about?'

'Someone wants to meet you, that's all.' If I hadn't known him as well as I did, I might have thought he was being evasive.

Thirty-seven

Although I couldn't help wondering what my mystery meeting in London was about, I put it to the back of my mind during the rest of my stay with Dad, trying to concentrate on him and on him alone. The night before I left, my sister rang from California, as she does at least twice a week. She was surprised to find me there, but pleased too. She's never said so, but I suspect that she'd hoped I'd raise my son in Auchterarder, and look after our father at the same time.

We had a chat and she agreed that Tom and I should visit her the following month. I said nothing about the situation, deciding to leave that until I saw her. Dawn's excitable: she deals with things better when she hears them face to face.

When Thursday came around, I found myself regretting that I was leaving so soon. Being back in Scotland had done me good, and I had no valid reason for rushing back to Spain, but my arrangements were made and by that time I couldn't cancel them. Dad and I were up at six and on the road half an hour later so that I could catch an early flight to London. Before we left, I humoured my father by taking some of his unwanted gifts from Adrienne: half a dozen children's books for Tom and a small adult selection for myself.

I'd told Mark to expect me at eleven, but the Heathrow Express ran more frequently than I'd thought and I found myself with time to kill at Paddington, before I could pick up a taxi at the rank and head for the address he had given me. It turned out to be a block of art-deco apartments, not unlike the place where Poirot lives in the television series. I was impressed: having been a Londoner myself, when Tom was very young, I know how much such a place, in such a location, is likely to cost. There was a concierge on duty. I told him who I was visiting and he directed me to the lift. 'Ninth floor,' he said. 'I'll call Mr Kravitz. He asked me to let him know when you arrived.'

If I wasn't surprised by the style in which Mark lives, I was when he opened the door. In truth, I was shocked. He was in a wheelchair, his hair was mostly grey, and he seemed to have lost about twenty pounds in weight. The last time I'd seen him, he'd been a strong, athletic, dark-haired guy. My thoughts must have been written on my face, for as he reached up to shake my hand, he murmured, 'Tell you later. Come on through. And be serious, please.'

I wondered about his remark as I followed him into a big reception room. There was no carpeting anywhere that I could see, not even a rug. The floors were polished wood, streaked in places by the rubber wheels of the chair. The space was brightly lit, by two windows, and by the french doors they framed. They were open, and a light, cooling breeze fluttered the curtains. There was a massive plasma screen on the wall to my left, above a desk, its surface lower than normal, upon which sat a computer and every electronic toy imaginable. *Heaven for Tom*, I thought.

There was a third person present; a woman, blonde (not real; I am, and I can tell the dye jobs), power dressed, maybe ten years younger than me. She wasn't pretty, she had rat-like features that made me think of a plague carrier: I didn't take to her. She sat on a black-leather sofa, stiffly upright; I read her posture as a sign that this was not an informal gathering. Mark wheeled himself over to a table, poured me coffee from a cafetière, added a little milk and brought it to me. 'This is Moira,' he said, as I took it from him, 'the person who wants to talk to you.'

'Fine,' I replied. 'Nice to meet you, Moira, but it had better be interesting, given the cost of changing my plans.'

'Frankly,' she drawled coolly, in a crusty accent that made me remember how much I dislike Trinny and what's-her-name, 'I don't care whether what I have to say interests you or not, as long as you get the message and act appropriately thereafter.'

All of a sudden those two fashion gurus weren't so bad after all. 'Better try me,' I told her. 'But first, maybe you'll begin by telling me who the hell you are.'

'That's not important. What you need to know is that I have the authority to be here. Word has reached the ears of my service that you have been telling a story about us.' As she spoke, I had a flashback, to Frank, in the Conquistador. I thought of him telling me of his recruitment to MI5 by an unnamed woman. Moira fitted his description pretty well.

'And how has it reached your shell-likes?' I murmured.

'Through one of Mark's friends, who's a junior colleague of mine.'

'And the story was?'

'That convicted felons are being recruited and trained to infiltrate organised crime.'

'Are you saying that's not true?'

'I'm not authorised to discuss the methods of my service, or give you any operational information. All I'm here to do is to tell you to stop; no, to order you.'

I almost pitched my coffee at her, but it would have made a mess of Mark's pricey sofa. 'Hold on a minute, sister,' I snapped. 'You will give me no damn orders.'

'I just did. You will not repeat the story you told Mr Kravitz, or there will be consequences.'

'Such as? Will I be found in the Thames?'

'Nothing so extreme; that won't be necessary. Instead, you'll be treated as a security risk. Let me assure you the consequences of that might make you want to jump into the Thames. I'll give you a small example. You have a criminal conviction, Mrs Blackstone. At the moment, you are able to enter the United States unhindered only because your well-connected brother-in-law, Miles Grayson, vouched for you and obtained you an entry visa. That can and will be cancelled at once, and your visit to California next month, with your son, will be off.'

For the first time, apprehension overcame my anger. 'How did you know about that?' I asked.

'We tapped your father's telephone,' she said bluntly. 'Call it a small demonstration of our power. When you go back to Spain, we can arrange for yours to be tapped also. We can monitor your mobile communications and your email. We can arrange for your residency in Spain to be brought into question. We can even arrange for your custody of your son to be reviewed.'

'Enough,' Mark shouted, taking both of us by surprise. 'You've made your point, and I'll make sure that Primavera takes it. Now get the fuck out of here!'

She smiled. 'Mark, calm down. You know that we have enough on you to close down your business, and even to put you away, if we choose, so cut the histrionics.' She turned back to me. 'Do you get the point, Mrs Blackstone?'

I wanted to punch her lights out, but I suspected that her martial-arts skills were better than mine. Also, her last threat had really scared me. 'Yes,' I admitted quietly. 'For what it's worth, the story's lost its relevance as far as I'm concerned, but you probably know that too.'

'As it happens, I don't. But we understand each other, yes?'

'Yes,' I repeated, like a good girl.

Moira, although I doubt that was her name (my world had become filled with aliases), stood to leave. 'Once thing I can tell you,' she said. 'I've never heard of Frank McGowan. Not that anything should be read into that, of course. I'll let myself out, Mr Kravitz.'

We watched her leave. When she was gone, Mark spun his chair round to face me. 'Primavera, I'm sorry. I couldn't warn you in advance. She wasn't kidding when she said that about me. I do need their goodwill or I'm out of business.'

'Who was she? Interpol? Frank said his controller was a woman.'

'No. She's MI5, but they do overlap and my guess is that when I tried to check your story about Frank it touched a very raw nerve somewhere.'

'Because he was set up? Because they have a mole?'

'Quite possibly. Whatever, do what they say. Don't cross them.'

'I won't. I may be crazy, but not that much.' I paused. 'Mark, the chair?'

'Multiple sclerosis. I've had it for a year and a half, and it's been pretty aggressive. I can still get around on sticks, just about, but this way is easier.' I felt hugely sorry for him, and told him so, but he brushed it off. 'Listen,' he said, 'I'm lucky to be alive, given the life I've had, in the army and afterwards, and the things I've done. They say it may well stabilise, and that I could have years with this much mobility. I can handle that.'

'That's some consolation.'

'That's good, because this won't be. Two nights ago, there was a break-in at the offices of Pintore, in Luxembourg, where the d'Amuseo company was registered. All of its records were stolen, every single piece of paper, including all of Alastair Rowland's signatures.'

'Shit.'

'That's what the investors will be saying. Yesterday there was a formal complaint to the Luxembourg police, and guess who made it? Emil Caballero. He's asked for a full investigation of the company. Looks like it's crunch time.'

'What? That man held me up with a gun. Mark, I'm feeling crazy again. I'm going to face him up. Will that get your friend Moira excited?'

'No, their interest is very specific.' He sighed. 'But, Primavera, please . . .'

Thirty-eight

Thirty-eight

I had to do something, or at least make myself believe I was doing something. That was the thought in my mind all through my return journey, including the five-hour drive back from Nice Airport to St Martí, which got me home just after one a.m. next day. I could have spent the night at Susie's, I know, but I didn't want to disrupt Tom's routine by popping in and out of his life.

I slept late after the trip, until eight thirty; that's mid-morning for me. It was too late for me to run, so I contented myself with a swim from the beach below St Martí, made myself breakfast with the little that I had at my disposal . . . scrambled eggs, toast and orange juice . . . and took it upstairs to eat on the front terrace, overlooking the square, watching the cafés get ready to open for the day.

I enjoyed being back in my own house, even if it was silent, even if it did feel empty. It made me think again about what Susie had told me, that Janet was no longer comfortable in the Loch Lomond place because she felt a presence there. It didn't surprise me too much. Oz once confessed to me that he had

315

had similar experiences, involving Jan; if such gifts exist I suppose that it's natural for them to be inherited. It made me wonder how she'd get on in my place on her next visit. It's so old that it's bound to have a few spirits hanging about, if you have the right antennae to pick up their signals.

I was on my first coffee of the day when I saw a Mossos d'Esquadra car cruise in front of my house. I watched as it parked and as Alex Guinart got out. I waved at him from the terrace, then trotted downstairs to let him in.

'You okay?' he asked. 'I thought you'd have been back with Tom before now.' He didn't say as much, but I could tell from his tone that he was a little miffed.

'*Mea culpa,*' I confessed. 'Tom's staying with Susie until the end of next week, and I've been in Scotland. I should have let you know what I was up to. Apologies, Alex.'

He grinned. 'That's okay. But you'd better make up with the priest too. He's been worried about you as well.' He eyed me up and down. 'You look well, a lot better than the last time I saw you.'

'Thanks, I feel it too. I had to get out of this place for a while, after last week's excitement.'

'Excitement, you call it? That's an understatement.'

'Any developments while I've been away?' I asked.

'I'm not meant to know, Prim. Intendant Gomez has kept me out of the picture, more or less from the start of the investigation. He feels that I'm too close to you to be involved in any way, so I've had no information. I can't argue with that: professionally, he's right.' He paused. 'However, I have friends and they drop hints. There's something.' He kissed me on the cheek. 'Now I must go: I'm on patrol.'

'See you, Alex,' I called after him as I closed the door. I went straight to the phone and called Father Gerard at the residence. He was visiting a sick parishioner, so I left a message saying that his neighbour in St Martí was back and in good health. As I replaced the handset the digital read-out told me I had messages waiting. There were eight in all. Six were from friends including Shirley and Gerard, leaving polite, stumbling messages, wondering where I was and when I'd be back, as if the machine could tell them. The other two were from Intendant Gomez, inviting me to call him on my return, at a Girona number.

I dialled it; a switchboard operator answered. At first he wasn't sure if he could put me through to the *intendant* . . . *Important man,* I thought . . . and tried to fob me off with Garcia, but eventually I persuaded him that as I was returning his messages, he should take a chance.

'Thank you for getting in touch, Mrs Blackstone,' he said, as he came on the line. 'I tried to call you on Sunday, and again on Monday, until Sub-inspector Guinart advised me that you were out of town.'

'You have some news for me?' I asked bluntly.

'I have, but I'm afraid it isn't good.'

'Fire away.'

'An unfortunate choice of words,' he murmured. 'Last Thursday night there was an outbreak of fire in the hills behind Cadaques, in the forest. It took a long time to put out, and at one point it even threatened the town.' This wasn't news to me: Shirley and I had seen the smoke from Café del Mar. 'It wasn't until Saturday that investigators could begin to determine the cause. They did this very quickly. At the seat of the fire, they found remains that have proved to be human. They had been reduced to ashes, and it was clear that an accelerant had been used.'

'How many bodies?' I asked; my mouth had gone dry, and my voice was hoarse.

'There was very little that was identifiably human, but our pathologist has determined there were two. This is borne out by the fact that my forensic team discovered two bullets among the residue. They also found fragments that they believe were parts of two mobile phones, and a larger piece of a polymer-based substance that we have now determined is what's left of your taser weapon.'

'Anything else?'

'A few scraps, bits of metal, more melted plastic, which may have been the remains of credit cards, ashes that weren't human, but were probably fabric and paper.'

'DNA?' I suggested.

'Not a chance. Everything was consumed beyond the point of discovery. It's like a cremation. I'm sorry, Mrs Blackstone, but as far as I'm concerned, it's conclusive. Your aunt and your cousin are indeed dead.'

I felt my last, lingering hope disappear. 'Thank you for letting me know,' I murmured.

'I have to ask you,' Gomez continued, 'who is the next of kin?'

I hadn't thought about that. 'I suppose I am,' I told him. 'My grandparents . . . Adrienne's parents . . . died long ago. My mother was her only sibling, and she passed away a couple of years ago. Adrienne never married and Frank's father died at sea before he was born. I'm older than my sister so, yes, it has to be me.'

'In that case, I will need you to come to Girona. At my request the judge has issued the certificates of death, but they need to be registered. There is a form and it requires family information that only you will have. You do have it, yes?' he added.

'Yes, I do.'

Among her many interests, my mum included genealogy. She had compiled the entire Phillips-McGowan-Blackstone-Grayson family tree, in considerable detail. It's on my computer now, updated to include her own death.

I printed the pages I'd need and took them with me to Girona that afternoon. Gomez helped me through the registration process, which is pretty simple, and obtained for me six copies of each death certificate. (This is not the same as the certificate of death, but that's Spain for you.)

'What about a funeral?' he asked, when it was all done. 'Normally, it would have to happen within twenty-four hours from now, but this situation is unique in my experience. Effectively, it has taken place already.'

'What happened to the remains?' I asked him.

'We have them. I can return them to you, in one or two caskets, whichever you prefer, if you wish that they be scattered or buried in Britain.'

'Can I have some time to think about that? I should consult my father; he may wish the ashes interred beside my mother.'

'Of course. Take as long as you like. They're not going to be a health hazard, not any more.'

As I drove home, it occurred to me that another trip to London might be necessary. I hoped that Adrienne had left a will. If not, with no obvious heir, the settlement of her estate could be hellish difficult. I made it home in time to catch Fanette, who was able to give me the name of my aunt's legal adviser, a man called Harold Liddell, a specialist in copyright and contract law. I called him, and told him what had happened. He was shocked, but he composed himself quickly. What he told me took a weight off my mind.

'I drew up Ms McGowan's will; it names me as her executor. It leaves everything to her son, with the proviso that if he should pre-decease her, it's divided between you and your sister, Mrs Dawn Grayson.'

'But who did die first? How can anyone say for sure?'

'English law will decree that she did,' Mr Liddell replied, 'on the simple basis that she was older: crude but practical. If your cousin also left a will, that overrides your interests, but there is no evidence that he did. However, I must explore that possibility.'

'How?'

'Public advertisement. I'll need to consult an inheritance lawyer about where and for what period, but it won't be too long.'

'What about the agency? What happens there?'

'That dies with Ms McGowan. Her relationships with her author clients were direct; in other words, she was personally entitled to commission. In law there was no agency; she was a sole trader. As her executor, I'll be required to write to all her clients and their publishers and advise that future royalties should be paid direct. If I remember rightly, that includes your father, as beneficiary of your mother's literary estate.'

I hadn't thought of that. Mum's books still sell to children across Britain and the Commonwealth, in decent numbers. 'Left to himself,' I told him, 'Dad will stick the letter in a drawer and forget about it. I'll see that doesn't happen. What about Fanette?' I added, as an afterthought. 'Adrienne hinted to me that she was backing out of the business and handing it over to her.'

'She couldn't,' Liddell replied instantly, 'without the clients' agreement to the new arrangement. It's tough on Fanette, but she's out of a job.'

I didn't feel too much sympathy, I'm afraid. 'What do you need from me?' I asked him.

'The Spanish death certificates, both of them: give me your address and phone number and I'll instruct a courier to pick them up. As soon as I receive them, I can act. As for you and your sister, it'll be a few months, I should think, before I can tell you if you're going to inherit, but from what I gathered from your aunt, neither of you is penurious, exactly. Between you and me, it won't be a fortune, after inheritance tax: there's the house, some investments and some cash; as you can see, there's no residual value in the business.'

'That doesn't bother me. But what about the remains?'

'They should be preserved. If an heir to Frank McGowan should turn up out of the blue, that person might want the right of disposal.'

I told him where they were, and that made him happy. I left him to call his courier, and got on with the nasty task that I couldn't delay any longer, telling Dawn and my father that they had two fewer relatives. I decided to clothe it as decently as I could, by telling them only that they'd been caught up in a forest fire.

Dad wasn't surprised, and he didn't buy my cover story. 'My darling girl,' he replied, when I asked him why, 'the day I can't tell when there's something seriously wrong in your life, I'll be in the box above your mother. It doesn't surprise me that the little bastard' . . . he spat the word out, with a venom I'd never heard from him before . . . 'has come to a sticky end, but it saddens me deeply that he took Adrienne with him. Probably inevitable, though. The boy inherited his recklessness from her; as witness, the circumstances of his birth.'

I didn't have to spin the same yarn to Dawn. Miles was at home when I rang and picked up, so I told him the unvarnished truth and left him to pass it on in whatever form he thought best.

And then I turned to my top priority.

Thirty-nine

The expression on Emil Caballero's face when he opened the front door of his massive white house . . . called La Casa Blanca, what else? . . . and saw me smiling on the step, is one that I'll carry with me for a long time. It began with naked fear, but as the seconds passed and I said nothing, it changed, passing through uncertainty until it reached belligerence.

'Yes?' he barked. 'It's Saturday. I don't receive people on Saturdays.'

'You'll receive me, though, Councillor,' I told him, still grinning. I'd been watching the place from my hire car, parked almost opposite, and I'd seen his wife and children leave.

'I'll call the police,' he threatened.

'I'd appreciate it if you did. Once I'm done with you, I'm going to see them, to make a complaint against you. Call them and save me the trip.'

'You complain against me?' he exclaimed, as if the idea was ridiculous. 'Of what?'

'Do you want a list? Listen, it's hot out here. Invite me in or I'll start screaming.'

'Oh, yes?' he challenged.

I took a step back. 'You bastard!' I yelled, at the top of my voice. 'You come to my club, you fuck three of my girls, and then you leave without paying. You owe me money, you owe them money!' I spoke English, but the message got through. He hushed me, and ushered me into a round marble hall.

'Okay.' He sighed. 'What is it that you want?'

'I just want to see you, before I bring you down. You asked for what. Attempted kidnapping, corruption and murder are three counts that come to mind.'

'You're a lunatic.'

'That's been said, but since we both know that you took me out of my hotel at gunpoint and tried to bundle me into the boot of your car, it seems to me that my sanity isn't in question in this instance.'

'It was an act,' he protested.

'It convinced me,' I told him. 'The gun was real enough.'

'She told me it was loaded with blanks. The woman Lidia; she gave it to me and that's what she told me. The whole thing was her idea. She said you were working for Roy Urquhart, trying to ruin the project. She wanted to frighten you enough to make you stop. All we were going to do was drive you to one of our less attractive districts, throw you out and make you walk back. Then that madman Urquhart, that thief, showed up, and it was you two kidnapped me. Mother of God, he shot my car! That bloody gun was loaded. Now you have the nerve to show up here and I let you in. No, you're right, you're not crazy, I am. Where is Urquhart now? Outside, waiting to come in and finish me?' He was in full flow; I let him rave on. 'You know how long it took me to get out of the fucking car, until I figured out that that luminous green strip was to open it? Two hours! Two whole fucking hours! You burned all my bikes, you and he. You stole my Suzuki, and it was four days before they found it, with the false plates. So go on, call him in and you kill me. You took everything else, you, he and that Bromberg woman. I invest a lot of money and a lot of goodwill in getting the permissions for the hotel and casino, and now it's all gone. Bromberg is gone, Urquhart is gone, Macela is dead, and all the money is gone. Worst of all, my good name is gone. I'm a laughing stock in the city, with a piece of land that's worth nothing, that I can't even use to grow sunflowers. So, yes, we call the police. You denounce me, and I denounce you.'

There was something about his tirade that was beginning to convince me. 'The man you call Urquhart,' I said. 'You described him as a thief.'

'That's what Bromberg told me, and Macela, when he could see straight. They said he'd been stealing money from the company, and they kicked him out.'

'Then they lied to you, or she did. And what did you mean about Macela seeing straight?'

'The man was a morphine addict, hopeless. All the time he was here, he lay in my mother's old house in Alvarez Quintero, shooting up.'

'Yes, because you kept him there, doped up, until you killed him.'

'Killed him? I never killed him.'

'Caballero, I saw you go into the house. I watched you. You came in with a bag and you came out empty-handed, and that same afternoon he died of an overdose.'

'I took him food!' he shouted. 'I fed the poor bastard. I didn't kill him, I kept him alive. Yes, he did die of an overdose, and that's the truth, but he did it himself. I checked very carefully with the police, believe me.'

'So where did he get his dope?'

'I have no idea, no idea at all. It must have been Bromberg.'

'I think you may be right,' I conceded. 'How much do you know about her?'

'I thought I knew everything. Now it seems I knew nothing. She came to see me, almost two years ago. She said she was a Swiss businesswoman, and that she had a project, a huge project, for which my property would be perfect. She offered me shares in the new company in return for my land, and for my services in securing all the necessary permissions to build and licences to operate. I agreed, we signed papers. Then Urquhart and Macela came to Sevilla to sell the project to investors. I never saw Bromberg again until a few weeks ago. She turned up and told me that Urquhart had gone bad on us, and that she would take over his role in the company until we were ready to start. We were supposed to begin in September, after the height of the summer was over. We had enough money to fund construction, she said. And that was all, until you turned up.'

'I came to find Frank,' I said quietly.

'Who the fuck is Frank?'

'The man you knew as Urquhart was my cousin; his name was Frank McGowan.' I thought of Moira's warning, but decided to chance it. 'He was a cop, undercover, working to expose the fraud. So was Macela. They were sold out; that's why Frank disappeared.'

Caballero frowned at me. We had stopped threatening each other; instead, we were having a conversation. 'So where is he now, this Frank?'

'He's dead, he and his mother, my aunt. They caught up with him.'

'Bromberg?'

'Not directly. Two men, North Americans, blond, smooth-looking.'

'I've seen them,' he declared. 'Once when I met Bromberg in Hotel Alfonso Thirteen, she had two guys minding her. Sounds like them.'

'When was the last time you saw her?'

'Last time I saw her she was rolling on the ground, screaming and holding her ass. After I escaped from the Chrysler, where you left me, I called her. But there was no reply. I haven't heard from her since. Beginning of last week, I called the company lawyer in Luxembourg. I told them that I needed Bromberg as we'd have to pay contractors some up-front money soon. They told me they had no means of contacting her, or the man Rowland, the chairman. They said also that the money had been moved beyond their control.'

'Have you ever met Rowland?'

'No, only her and Macela, and the man you say was really

called Frank.' He looked at me. 'Christ, we've all been set up, eh?' He sighed. 'Look, I'm sorry for what I tried to do to you. I'm sorry about your cousin and your aunt.'

There wasn't much I could do other than accept his apology. 'Where does this leave you?' I asked.

'Financially, not too bad. Politically, my party colleagues don't want to know me. Fuck 'em, I'll be all right. My barn was insured, and all my toys: I'll get new ones.'

'What's your business? Your main business?'

'I sell bridal outfits, for men and women. And religious robes, for priests and altar boys.'

'If I were you,' I told him, 'I'd go to confession.'

Forty

And that was it. I caught an evening flight back to Barcelona, and was home in time to have supper in Mesón del Conde with Alex and Gloria, with Marte in a pram beside the table. In Spain babysitters aren't in great demand: in our culture we tend to take the kids with us, from infancy, when we go out to eat.

Next morning, I awoke feeling completely drained, empty, devoid of purpose and alone. I hate being idle, and usually fight against it by doing something constructive with Tom or by getting involved with local projects, like the annual St Martí wine fair. But that Sunday I couldn't think of a single thing to do.

So I took the advice I'd given to Caballero. I went to midday Mass, even though I was baptised in the Church of Scotland, a country not famed for its ecumenism. Once the service was over, and as Father Gerard saw the congregation off the premises, I slipped into the confessional, remembering what he had said about never turning away sinners. When he took his place on the other side of the divide, I told him all that had

329

happened to me, from Adrienne's first phone call. I left nothing out. I described my meetings in London and Sevilla, and I told him of my encounters with Frank, on the train and in the pool. When I was done, I waited.

'I suppose you expect a penance,' he said. 'You're not getting one. I absolve you from the sins of fornication and taking the Lord's name in vain. You're clear on arson, since it was your cousin who burned those bikes, and in the circumstances the least Caballero could have done was lend you his Suzuki. As for the rest, soon the memories will not be so sharp.'

I settled for that and invited him to lunch.

The story broke in London next day, thanks to a press release issued by the Foreign Office. I had advance warning, courtesy of a guy in the Barcelona consulate who had been advised of my interest, presumably by Gomez. He sent me a copy by email. It seemed to me when I read it that the party line had been agreed between Whitehall and the Catalan tourist ministry. It said that Adrienne and Frank had died after being engulfed by a wildfire on hillside overlooking the Mediterranean. There was no hint that they had been used as kindling.

The animal that was once called Fleet Street was on to it in a flash. I had one or two calls, which I fended off, but I was small fry in story terms alongside my famous sister, who drew top billing in most of the red-tops, and whose grief was expressed in a statement issued, and probably written, by her husband's media spokesman. It did not hint at the truth, that she had barely known either victim, family members or not, but that wouldn't have looked too good. I read as much as I could on-line next day: Adrienne rated respectable obituaries in the *Telegraph* and *Times*, but not in the *Guardian*: I don't believe she'd have minded that at all.

For the rest of the week I was like a solitary black cloud in a clear blue sky. I moped around the house. When I couldn't stand that any more, I hung about the cafés, in turn, drinking coffee and frowning at any tourists who tried to make polite conversation. On the Thursday morning, I went up to Shirley's for some peace and wisdom, but I didn't feel comfortable there. The memory of that waterborne knee-trembler, and the promise I'd made to Frank in the summer-house, *Tonight, then*, were still too fresh in my mind. Finally, I found something to occupy me: driven by a force I still can't explain, I sat down at my computer and sketched out a synopsis of what had happened to me; it was the start of a process that led in time to what you're reading now.

The outline was pretty much finished on Sunday afternoon, when Conrad Kent arrived with Tom and Charlie. In front of the whole village I gave my son a hug of embarrassing proportions, which he tolerated before dashing indoors to fill a water-bowl for the dog, and probably to check that I hadn't damaged or pawned any of his possessions in his absence.

Conrad would have driven straight back, but I had prepared lunch and made him stay to share it with us. He didn't say much, but I could tell he wanted to. 'Spit it out,' I told him, in the end, as I poured him coffee on the front terrace, after Tom had been cleared for beach duty.

'You okay?' he asked.

'I'm fine.'

'I read all the reports: a real official stitch-up.'

'Very true.'

'What does Kravitz think about it? Have you asked him?'

'He's not thinking anything.' I lowered my voice. 'He's been told not to, like me.'

'Leaned on?'

'Hard.'

'Can I help?'

'If you could find a security-service operative who goes by the name Moira, and do something painful to her, I'd appreciate it. Otherwise, no, but thanks for the offer.'

'If Kravitz can't do that, neither can I, I'm afraid. The best you can do is forget about it, and concentrate on that lad of yours. He's looking more like his father every day; that means he'll be a handful.'

'Any advice?'

'Make sure you teach him the difference between right and wrong in black and white,' he replied. 'It was a grey area to Oz.'

I looked at him. 'I know that better than anyone in the world.'

'Of course you do,' he conceded. 'But he didn't do what you think he did.' After he had gone, I found myself wondering whether Susie had put him up to saying that, but decided he was sincere, and that he believed it. I wish I did.

Tom's return brought Planet Primavera back into its usual orbit: around him. I put the writing aside for a bit and asked him to draw me up a list of things he'd like to do. The water-park at Ampuriabrava featured high upon it. We went there a couple of times, we did some bird-watching at Aiguamols nature reserve, we hit a lot of golf balls on the practice ground at Gualta and we fished, morning and evening, off the long jetty that stretches out from the rocks below the village.

After a few days of that, I was happy again and the bad memories were fading, as my confessor had promised they would. And then, in all his wide-eyed innocence, my lovely son knocked the lid right off the can of worms.

Forty-one

We had just returned from the beach at Montgó, where we'd gone to escape the strong afternoon breeze that was stirring up the sand at St Martí. We were in the living room, drinking carrot and orange juice and Coronita beer respectively, and Sky News was on the box. I allow one telly in the house, and that's all, although sometimes I cheat by watching on-line.

I wasn't paying much attention as the evening bulletin began. The main story of the day came from Westminster, where the dour and unloved Prime Minister had attempted to freshen up his image by freshening up his cabinet.

One by one, the losers appeared, one or two with brave smiles, the rest about to trip over their long faces. And then the winners were paraded, in no obvious pecking order: third in line, the new Home Secretary, was . . . Justin Mayfield, MP.

An official photograph appeared on screen, and then the programme cut to live footage from the doorstep of a posh terraced house, a red-brick job in a *nouveau riche* suburb like Fulham or Herne Hill. There he was, the man I'd last seen being given a one-finger salute by Frank as we wished him goodbye, smiling haughtily alongside his smug-looking little wife, a stumpy blondette.

'I know her,' Tom exclaimed.

'Yes, I know him too. He's on the telly a lot, but I met him a couple of weeks ago.'

'Not him.' Tom sighed, in his be-patient-with-her voice. 'Her. I've seen her.'

I stared at him. 'You must be mixing her up with somebody else.'

'I'm not,' he insisted. 'I've seen her.'

'Where?'

'Here, in the village. It was her, I know it.'

Tom is brilliant with faces. I decided not to argue. 'When was this?'

'A few months ago. April, just after school started again. Remember the day the old car broke down when you were coming to pick me up, and I had to come home on my bike and wait for you in Can Coll?'

'Yes, I remember that.'

'It was then. I saw her then, and I spoke to her.'

'You mean she spoke to you?'

He shook his head. 'No, I spoke to her. I asked her why she was videoing our house.'

'She was doing what?'

'I told you, Mum.' I was trying his patience.

'As in, she was filming the whole village?'

'No, just here, so I asked her why, and she just laughed at

me and told me not to be nosy, so I told her it was our house, and that you wouldn't like it.'

'Then what?'

'Then she went away, out of the square, just as the man at Can Coll came over to see what was happening.'

'Well, isn't that something?' I murmured.

My telly is fed through a very clever little box. Among other things it lets you rewind programmes, and that was what I did with the *Sky News* bulletin, running it back until I saw that upwardly mobile house and its self-satisfied occupants. The box also lets me freeze frames. I'd never used the facility until then, but when I did I saw that it gave a clean, sharp image. I went right up to the screen and peered at Mrs Mayfield.

It took a second or two, but I realised I'd seen her before too. She hadn't been blonde then. She'd been dark-haired, and she'd been calling herself Lidia Bromberg.

I tossed the remote to Tom so he could watch what he liked, and dashed into the hall. I was about to pick up the phone, when I remembered Moira and thought better of it. I had reported my mobile lost and they'd given me another, but I still had Adrienne's. I used that to call Mark Kravitz on his.

'How are you feeling?' I asked him. Even as I spoke, my mind was working, adding pieces to a jigsaw.

'Perfectly all right. I have a condition, Primavera; I'm not an invalid. I've had an okay day, in fact.'

'Then I'm about to upgrade it to brilliant. Would you like to shove one up that Moira woman?'

'In the sense of retribution, yes.'

'Then dig up all you can for me about the wife of the new Home Secretary. I think my son has just made her day as bad as yours has been good.'

Forty-two

'You realise we have to be careful here,' said Mark, as he reversed his car into one of the parking spaces that had been cleared in front of the Mayfield house. 'We may know what we know, and you may suspect what you suspect, but this man is now the Home Secretary, not the middle-ranking ministerial wanker you met in Barcelona.'

'Yes, and that's good. But remember, the higher you climb . . . and all the rest of that metaphoric stuff.' I looked at him and saw his anxiety. 'I'll behave myself appropriately,' I promised him, 'but what about you? You were threatened along with me, and so was your business. If you want to stay in the car with Tom and let me do this, I'll be perfectly happy about it.'

He grinned, and I saw that his concern had been about me alone. 'You know what?' He chuckled. 'After you left I started thinking about Moira and what she'd said, and I realised that I don't give a toss about her and her crew. I'm comfortably off, I'm well insured against incapacity, and I don't have any dependants they can threaten. Anyway, what are they going to do? Sabotage my wheelchair?'

'In that case, let's go.' I turned to my son, in the back seat. 'We won't be long, love,' I told him. Don't worry, I had no intention of taking him in there to confront Mrs Mayfield. But when I'd known I had to go back to London, I'd realised I couldn't leave him in St Martí, not so soon after bundling him off to Monaco, so I'd decided to take him with me and make it a holiday for him. (We left Charlie with the guy in El Celler Petit; he has dogs and said that one more wouldn't make that much difference to him.) We'd done the Tower that morning, and Madame Tussaud's in the afternoon. He was quite happy to sit in the car and play with his Game Boy, while Mum did a bit of business.

For the purposes of that business, we were supposed to be researchers for an American television company that was planning a feature on the fastest-rising political couple in the land. Mark had made the appointment, using one of his cover names.

His wheelchair was in the luggage space of the estate car, but he left it there, and used elbow crutches instead. There were two uniformed police officers, one male, one female, on guard duty at the Mayfields' door. 'Mr Crossley and Miss Gregg,' Mark announced as we approached them, 'to see the Home Secretary.'

Our names were checked on a list, then the young lady officer . . . once again, it was with great sadness that I calculated that I was old enough to be her mother, if I'd got myself knocked up at around seventeen . . . announced us through a video-phone, and the door was opened.

We were met in the narrow hallway not by the new cabinet member but by a pallid woman in a mannish suit, middle aged, wedding ring but no other jewellery, bad hair day, with an intense expression and the hollow cheeks of a heavy smoker. 'Martina Smith, Press Office,' she announced, as Mark put all his weight on his left crutch to shake her hand. 'We spoke on the telephone. You understand the ground rules?'

'Sure,' he replied. 'We recite the list of questions I gave you, one by one, and they recite the answers you've drafted for them. That's how it works, isn't it?'

I had the impression that she didn't know whether to scowl or smile: she compromised by doing neither. 'There will be some scope for supplementaries,' she said stiffly, 'as long as they're appropriate and relevant. I'll be the judge of that; I'll be sitting in, as usual.'

She swung a door open and stepped into a drawing room, beckoning us to follow, like courtiers. Mark led the way, and I followed.

I was much better dressed than I had been in the Hotel Arts, and much better groomed, and so it took Justin Mayfield a few seconds to recognise me. When he did, the politician's smile was wiped from his face like chalk from a blackboard. He glared at the press officer, and I knew that somewhere down the line she was going to pay, big-time, for not checking out our *bona fides*. 'Thank you, Mrs Smith,' he murmured, in a tone that would have etched steel, 'we won't be needing you for this one.'

'But, Home Secretary,' she protested, 'it's standard practice.'

'This won't be a standard interview. Leave us.'

As Martina Smith obeyed, he turned back towards me. 'Primavera,' he blustered, 'what the hell is all this about? If you wanted to see me, all you had to do was ring my office.'

'It isn't really you I've come to see, Justin,' I told him. 'As soon as I saw Lidia on telly the other night, I knew we had to renew our acquaintance.' I smiled at Mrs Mayfield.

'My wife's name is Ludo.' If he'd been in the dark about the whole operation, I'd have known it then, by the way he said those words. But his tone was wrong, his simple denial. There was no bewilderment there. He knew exactly what I was talking about.

'Sure,' I said, nodding, 'short for Ludmila. But in Sevilla, and on the website of a fraudulent hotel and casino project, she calls herself Lidia Bromberg. When she and an associate tried to kidnap me two weeks ago, that was the name she was going under. She had a black hair job then, but the cut was the same as she has now. I'm pretty sure I could tell you who her hairdresser is. My sister goes to him every time she's in London.'

'Woman's mad,' Mrs Mayfield snapped, and turned her back on me, as if she didn't want me looking at her any longer.

I couldn't help myself. I forgot my promise to Mark, that I'd be cool, and I kicked her, hard, on the right buttock. She screamed, arching her back as her hand flew to her rump; I was glad that the door had looked exceptionally thick, so that the sound wouldn't carry to the outside. Mind you, she wasn't the only one who was hurting. I'd thought that my broken toe had healed, but it hadn't, not completely. A spear of burning pain tore into my foot.

'Hey!' Justin protested. 'I'm getting the police in.' He headed for the door but I stepped in front of him.

'No, you ain't,' I said, putting my hands on his chest to stop him. 'If your wife was to bend over and drop her pants, we'd see a healing knife wound on her arse, just where I booted her. That was a gift from Frank, when he rescued me from her and from Emil Caballero. He thought they were only going to teach me a lesson, but I suspect Lidia might have planned more than that.'

Mayfield sighed. 'Look, Primavera, I know Frank's dead. You must be upset, so I'll make allowances. Now stop this nonsense.'

'Haven't you seen her naked in the last couple of weeks?'

'Of course I have and, yes, she has a wound there, but she got it in London when she slipped in the street and landed on a broken bottle.'

'And I was there when it happened, was I, and knew exactly where to kick her? No, Justin, that won't work for a second. Let's all sit down,' I glanced at Mark, on his supports, 'especially my friend, and we'll talk you through it.'

The new Home Secretary gave in. 'Okay.' He sighed. 'Let's do that.' His wife's expression would have frozen others solid, but I guessed he'd seen it often enough before. 'Come on, Ludo,' he told her. 'Do as I say.'

She did, grudgingly. I looked at my companion, an invitation.

'I've spent the last couple of weeks,' he began, 'doing a lot of research on you, Mrs Mayfield. Your maiden name, or birth name if you prefer, is Ludmila Banovsky, a member of an old Slovakian family, one that in the past was rich and powerful. Your grandfather, Ondrej Banovsky, was an industrialist, a steel magnate, and a friend of President Benes, in pre-war Czechoslovakia. This worked in his favour, for in 1937 he was advised that bad times were coming, and that he should protect his assets. He was an astute man; he did this by setting up a secret trust, in Switzerland, moving his family and as much of his money out of the country as he could, before the Germans arrived. He might have moved it all back after the war, but the country was unstable, and Communism was on the rise, so he stayed where he was and ran his enterprises from a distance. But they were in poor shape. The Nazis had allowed him to carry on, for they needed the steel that he produced, so the mills had survived, but as the tide turned against them in 1944, raw materials became scarce, and they had gone into decline. So, as a form of long-term protection, your grandfather decided to establish a business base in Western Europe, by taking over a French mining company called Energi, with solid profitability and considerable untapped reserves of coal.' He paused and looked at Ludmila. 'All correct so far?' She scowled at him.

'By the time the Soviets were gone in their turn,' he continued, 'so were your operations in what became Slovakia, all failed, all closed. And so was Ondrej, long gone. He died in 1965, and your father, Pavol, became head of the family, and chief beneficiary of the trust. When democracy was re-established, he reopened an office of the Banovsky Corporation in Bratislava, but that was no more than a patriotic gesture, for by that time the only asset it controlled was Energi. Unfortunately for your family, it wasn't the cash cow it had once been. It needed good, strong management, but Pavol wasn't a patch on his father. Ondrej would have ensured that the company had continued reserves or that it diversified in time, but his son sat back and watched the seams being worked out, and old equipment being patched up rather than modern machinery installed. When he died in 2000, and you inherited, Energi was doomed. Worse than that, its borrowings were underwritten by the family trust, in Switzerland.' Mark stopped again; this time, it seemed, to recover his strength, and maintain his momentum. It was a long time coming; I decided to take over.

'That much we know,' I told the Mayfields. 'That much we can prove. The rest is what we believe. You seem to take after your father, Ludmila, rather than Ondrej, because you seem to have sat on your hands for five years and watched the decline accelerate. By last year the business was, in effect, insolvent, so you decided on one last gamble, one grand scheme that really was worthy of your grandfather in its scope and its imagination. You did some research and you found some worthless land in the south of Spain. You invented the persona of Lidia Bromberg and, as her, set up Hotel Casino d'Amuseo SA, a company based in Luxembourg. Then, through the Banovsky Corporation, you instructed the chief officer of Energi to invest its last twenty million euros, telling the banks that at last you had a diversification strategy.

'You commissioned designs for the project, and then, as dark-haired little Lidia Bromberg, you approached the owner of the land, Emil Caballero, an essentially greedy man, with good political connections, and you showed him a vision. He went for it and, as a bonus, offered you a mountainside that his wife's grandmother owns as an add-on ski resort.

'With all your preparations made, you recruited Frank McGowan, your husband's old friend, to sell the grand design to would-be investors. You didn't do it directly, though. You found another convicted fraudster, Hermann Gresch, and he brought Frank into the operation, so that you and Frank could never be seen to have come face to face.'

'Nonsense,' Ludmila growled.

'I don't think so. The last meeting, in Lithuania, was between Frank, Gresch and a Canadian named Sebastian Loman, whom you had hired as security for the operation. Once it was all set up, they were given new identities. Frank became Roy Urquhart and Hermann became George Macela, those people being listed as executives on the website, with another man, Alastair Rowland, as the supposed chairman.

'Frank did incredibly well as a salesman,' I went on, in full flow. 'He used the list of wealthy contacts he'd ripped off from the Cinq Pistes ski resort and built up an international network. In more or less a year, he had raised another fifty-seven million in funding for the project. Everything was going well. But there was one bloody great bluebottle in the ointment. Frank wasn't on your team. When he was in jail he had been recruited by Interpol, through the security service,' I looked at Justin, 'for which you are now responsible, Home Secretary. A couple of months ago, he reported to his controller in London that the time had come to pull the plug on the operation and round everybody up before the money disappeared. Macela was in the process of killing himself through a drug addiction, and an investigation would surely uncover Rowland's identity. But Frank was betrayed: there was a mole within Interpol, and word got back to you, Ludmila. Whatever you paid the person who tipped you off, it was worth it. If the scheme had collapsed, the money would have been returned to the investors. Your role in it all might never have been exposed, but Energi would have got its twenty million back, and that wasn't what you wanted. The company would have crashed anyway, to the tune of over fifty million euros, and the French bankers would have pursued your family trust for the loss, since your unfortunate dad, Pavol, had guaranteed it way back. It'll still go down, and they'll do that anyway, but it won't matter to you, Ludo, for you've got another fortune salted away.' I looked at Justin, who sat there impassively. 'Who owns this house, by the way?' I asked him.

'I suspect you know already,' he replied. 'The family trust does.'

'See?' I challenged his wife. 'You had no choice but to step in and see the fraud through to the end. Until then your personal involvement had been kept to a minimum, but you had to surface again. You had to become Lidia, and take over

Roy Urquhart's role in the scheme. You ordered Loman and his pal, Willie Venable, to take Frank out. Unfortunately he got the better of them and went into hiding. You were in huge trouble then. You had to smoke him out, but how? I reckon that your original plan was to kidnap my son and me, and use us as hostages. That's why you went to St Martí in April, and filmed my house; you were casing the place.' Again, the woman shook her head.

'But my son saw you doing it,' I continued, undeterred, 'and you backed off. Instead you bided your time, until an even better target offered herself up . . . Frank's mother. You kept tabs on her, until one day she wasn't at the agency. You called and her idiot assistant told you where she was. Willie Venable abducted her from my house, you and the poor sap Emil tried to take me for a ride, and when Frank got me out of it, you had Loman track us. He was good, too good for Frank in the end. Now he and his mum are in a cardboard box in Girona . . .' to my surprise, I heard my voice crack '. . . and your old man's the Home bloody Secretary!' I glared at Justin. 'No wonder you weren't too keen to help us in Barcelona.'

Occasionally, very occasionally, there are silences that you think you can touch, as if a glass bubble has encased you, one that no noise can penetrate. One of those had formed in that drawing room. The Mayfields sat, stunned. I sat, exhausted. Mark sat, recovered but waiting.

And then Justin shattered that almost palpable bubble of silence into a million shards. 'Primavera, Primavera,' he sighed, 'that was brilliant, it was sad, and it was deeply moving, but it was also very, very wrong. I love my wife dearly, but you identified the flaw in your own argument. Ludo is indeed as intellectually limited as her late father was. She isn't capable of coming up with a scheme like that.'

'Then who did? You?'

He shook his head. 'I'm afraid I don't have that sort of imagination either. But Frank did; your cousin, my pal. The whole project was his idea, from start to finish.'

'Come on,' I shouted, outraged by his attempt to smear the dead. 'He didn't have access to those Energi funds.'

'No, but I told him about the company's problems, and what it would mean for us when it collapsed, losing the house and maybe even my career going down the toilet.'

'But you dropped Frank as a friend, after he was jailed.'

'Who told you that? No, let me guess. He did.'

'In the Hotel Arts,' I countered, 'he had to threaten you to get in to see you.'

'Gretchen Roberts, you mean?'

I nodded.

'There's no such person; that was for your benefit.' He smiled. 'Look, I didn't exactly flaunt our friendship, but Frank was always my best mate. He was the only person I'd ever have told about Ludo's problems. A couple of weeks after I did, he came back to me and set out the whole scheme. The only difference from your account was that he said it would be legal. He did it all. Ludo didn't set up the company in Luxembourg, he did . . . as its records will prove.' I looked at Mark quickly, then back at Justin. 'Ludo didn't hire any security people; Frank did that. But that was much later in the day: I'm not sure when. The first we knew of them was when he sent them to a meeting Ludo had in Seville, with Caballero. As for Macela, he didn't recruit Frank; Frank recruited him. Hermann Gresch is a name I've never heard until now. We knew nothing about the man's background, only that Frank vouched for him. As for a meeting in Luxembourg with the man you called Loman, that's news to me also. I can't think why that would have happened.'

'When the project got under way,' I said, 'Frank took a false identity and still you thought it would be legal?'

'He'd been in prison. How would that have looked to investors?'

'So what was Macela's role?' I demanded.

'To be on the ground, showing the project to investors who chose to visit Seville, but he turned out to be useless, because of his addiction.'

'Frank told me that Macela controlled the money as it came in.'

'Nonsense. Frank controlled everything. I was amazed by him, by the level at which he operated, but it was all of his creation.'

'No,' I protested. 'No. I'm not having it.' I jabbed a finger in his wife's direction. 'You're trying to save her skin.'

'No, and I'll prove it. You still don't know who Alastair Rowland is, do you?'

'No,' I admitted.

He smiled again. 'I am,' he said. 'I signed the funds-transfer order that the Luxembourg lawyers received, and I used the company seal to do it.' He rose, walked over to a sideboard, and took something from it, then returned and handed it to me. It was blue, metal, hinged and heavy, a stamping device, and its base held a carved round symbol. I'd never seen one before, but I knew what it was.

'That was why Frank came to the hotel. When we were together on the club floor, before you came up to join us, he gave it to me, to keep it safe, and so that I could move the money into an account he'd set up. Our meeting was pre-arranged, before his mother went missing. If only he'd accepted my offer of help and not gone storming off, he'd still be alive, and so might she.'

Begged questions were being thrown at me as fast as I could process them. 'But if you still thought it was kosher, didn't the funds transfer seem odd?'

'Not at all. The plan always was to move the money out of Luxembourg before construction started, into a better tax environment. So I signed the transfer, to a bank in the Cayman Islands.'

'Hold on. Let's go back. When Frank had to disappear, didn't that alert you that all wasn't well?'

'It concerned me, I'll grant you, but he told us that he believed that his real identity had been blown and that he had to fade away, into the background. With him out of the picture, and Macela pretty much helpless, there was no choice but that Ludo should become Bromberg again.'

'And that she should film my house?' I sneered. Yes, I actually did sneer; I felt my lip curl.

'Frank asked me to do that,' Ludmila murmured, 'on one of my trips to Spain. He said he was considering hiding out with you but wanted to see how secure your place looked.'

'Where was he hiding at that time?'

'I have no idea.'

'Why? Where were you?'

'Most of the time I was in London. Calls to the land-line number in Seville were diverted to my mobile. Like when you called me. If I had to see someone I always gave myself a couple of days to get there.'

'And you and Caballero kidnapping me? I imagined that, did I?'

'Frank told me to do it. He said his security people had gone bad on him, that his mother had been kidnapped, and that you were in danger. He said we had to do something to get you out of the way, but to make it look convincing to those men so that they'd lay off you. So I recruited Caballero to help me: I told him that you were a conwoman trying to fleece us, and the clown believed me.'

'But, Ludmila, you still can't sit down comfortably,' I pointed out. 'Remember what happened to you.'

'I did not expect that,' she admitted. 'But Frank called me afterwards, full of remorse, and said that the whole thing had had to be as realistic as possible.'

'That's why he and I spent a little longer on our own in Barcelona than he'd expected,' Justin added. 'I didn't like that either. Frank and I were having it out, while you were waiting downstairs.'

'Jesus,' I whispered, apologising mentally to Him and to Gerard. The more I thought about it, the more I was coming, if not to believe them, then at least to see their account as a possibility. But there were still holes in it. 'Who gave you the gun?' I asked Ludmila.

'Frank did. It was loaded with blanks, wasn't it?' She looked at me nervously, and this time I did accept that her ignorance was genuine, since Caballero had said more or less the same thing.

'No,' I told her. 'It shot a very convincing hole in the upholstery of your friend's car.' I winced. 'That little bugger should have kept the damn thing, instead of chucking it in the flames when he burned Caballero's toys in that barn.'

'He set his bikes on fire?'

'Yes, but it did no good. None of it did. Sebastian and Willie got him in the end, and his poor old mum.'

'I'm sorry,' she whispered.

'The money?' I asked.

'Gone,' said Justin, with a huge sigh. 'Moved on from the Cayman bank, blind transfer; we don't know where it is now, and we never will.'

'When did this happen?'

He told me the date. I made a quick mental calculation. 'The day after he was abducted,' I said. 'They must have forced him to transfer it again, then killed him.'

'Poor little bastard.' I'd cried all mine, but the Home

Secretary was on the verge of tears. 'It was meant to be legal,' he said, 'I promise. As soon as we'd secured some additional funds through bank borrowing, the casino would have been built. As soon as the ground was broken, Energi investment would have quadrupled in value.'

'So why did both Lidia and Rowland vanish from the face of the earth?'

'We had to, as soon as the money went missing. I'd just been offered the post of Home Secretary: I couldn't be seen to be involved in any scandal.'

'But an investigation will be bound to lead to Ludmila.'

'But not to Lidia. Energi will be . . . no, Energi *is* just another victim of theft. You say fraud, but still I don't believe it. The money was honestly, if unconventionally raised, and stolen by the people who killed Frank and his mother.'

I knew that I'd like to go along with that explanation, but I wasn't ready to tell him. 'And you two? What happens to you?' I asked, not particularly kindly.

'We move house, or I buy it from the family trust before it implodes. I'd hoped to hang on to my job, but when those Luxembourg records become public, I'll be stuffed. My signature's there.'

'Funny you should say that,' Mark intervened. He told him about the robbery. 'Would I find MI5's fingerprints all over that, by any chance?' he added.

Justin blinked, several times. 'If they knew of this operation . . .' he murmured. (Mark and I could have told him they did, and how. That explained a lot about the hard line the security-service woman had taken with us: not just a minister to protect, but maybe a government if the scandal was messy enough.) 'But I didn't authorise it, I promise you.'

I thought about that for a while. 'If I accept all of that,' I said slowly, 'it means we're the only people who know of your involvement. Caballero can identify Ludmila as Lidia Bromberg, but he's more concerned with political rehabilitation right now. Anyway, he'd never make the connection.'

'I suppose it does,' Justin agreed. 'So . . .'

I beat him to the question. 'So what do we want? Only one thing. There's a woman in the security service who made some very nasty threats against me, and Mr Kravitz, here, my associate. She called herself Moira; blonde, early thirties, rat faced. I want her told to forget that she's ever heard of us.'

'That won't be a problem,' the Home Secretary promised.

'In that case,' I told him, 'good luck with your career, and God help the country.'

Forty-three

If I said that the meeting hadn't gone the way I'd imagined, that wouldn't be quite accurate. No, the truth is, when we went in there I didn't have the faintest idea how it was going to play out. But I hadn't expected my carefully constructed theory to be turned completely on its head, and for Frank to be revealed as the brains behind the whole business.

I might have had a strong suspicion that Justin and Rowland were one and the same, given what I knew about Ludmila, but the part about the seal had taken me totally by surprise. No wonder Frank had hung on to that rucksack as if his family jewels were in it. No wonder it had landed in Caballero's back seat with such a thud. No wonder I'd noticed a difference when I'd picked it up in my garage.

The rest of the scheme, though, that had been brilliant. What a pity, I thought, that he hadn't hired his muscle from Mark, who would have made sure that the guys were completely trustworthy. I told him as much as we left.

'With that sort of cash in the pot,' he replied, 'you can never be one hundred per cent sure.'

'What do you think, Mark?' I asked. 'Did it all happen as Justin said?'

'He believes that it did. His wife confirms that for me; she's way short of bright enough to do that sort of thinking for herself. Is it the truth? Maybe, but there's another possibility I can't ignore, and it's much the likelier, that as far as Frank was concerned, this was a fraud all along, only he told his hired hands too much and they turned on him.'

'I can't bring myself to accept that.'

'Think of the story he spun you.'

'Maybe he was an undercover agent.'

He held up a crutch. 'And maybe next week I'll sign for Chelsea.'

I laughed. 'As a Barcelona fan, I hope you do.'

Tom had been waiting in the car for an hour by the time we returned, but he had a supply of crisps and fizzy water, and the two police officers had been keeping an eye on him, as I'd asked them. He was fine and I didn't feel too guilty.

I did feel troubled, though, as Mark dropped us off at the Tower Bridge Hotel. I could understand why he thought Frank might have been on the con from the start, considering the story he'd told me. And that was where Justin's version really rang true, when I thought about it.

All of the core information I'd gathered about the whole d'Amuseo affair had come from Frank himself. Mark had done some digging, but the key details had been offered by my cousin.

The problem was I had believed it before, and I still did

then; and suppose he had embellished it a little, with the undercover stuff and his lies about Caballero being involved with Energi, and about the break-in. I convinced myself that he'd done it to keep the Mayfields' involvement secret and maybe also in the hope that I'd hang in there and help him, after Loman and Venable, his badly chosen security team, had turned on him.

What I did know for certain was what had happened to us after we were reunited in Sevilla, and what had happened ultimately to him and Auntie Ade.

So why had Ludo filmed my house? Since I had come to believe the rest of her tale I decided to accept her explanation, that Frank was thinking of hiding in St Martí. I wished I could ask him, but still I concluded loyally that he had indeed concocted a brilliant scheme to help his best pal out of a jam, and it had gone fatally wrong on him.

For the next couple of days, I focused on Tom alone. I took him to a cricket Test match at Lords . . . he knows all the players, and loved it; I slept through much of it . . . and for a cruise on the Thames . . . he's been nagging me ever since to buy a boat . . . before we headed back to Spain, back to our usual, humdrum, sun-splashed existence, filling in time before we were due to leave for California.

For his age, Tom's a great reader. In no time, he'd devoured all six books I'd brought him from Dad's. For my age, I'm not. I found the first of mine to be a struggle, which eventually I gave up and turned to the second, plucked in a hurry, and completely at random, from the shelf. It was called *Reverse*

Circle, by a guy named Michael Jacks. I sat down to read it one night, on the front terrace, when Tom had gone to bed.

I had reached page thirty when I began to feel a tingle. By page one hundred I was aware that I was sitting stiff and upright in my chair, reading as fast as I could, and that I couldn't stop. It was almost three in the morning when I put the book down. The square below was deserted, the mosquito population was well fed, my eyes were standing out like organ stops, and I was wide awake.

With certain subtle differences, I had just read the story of the Hotel Casino d'Amuseo scam, page by page. Ex-con comes up with a brilliant wheeze, recruits team in Italy, finds some Mafia interests to come up with front-end money, and the fund-raising gets under way. Then it all goes pear shaped, the Mafia figure out what's happening, ex-con's wife is kidnapped, and he's chased halfway across Europe before . . .

And that's why I found myself staring, gasping, and finally laughing, alone in the middle of the night. In the end, with the aid of a gullible accomplice, the ex-con and his wife get clean away.

By next morning, it didn't seem so funny. I sat outside Mesón del Conde with Tom, watching an American coffee with a little milk get cold before me, happy for my son to devour my croissant as well as his own, my brows knitted as I racked my brains thinking how I could prove what I suspected or, better, rid myself of my worst fears. And then I remembered. I replayed a scene in my mind, dialogue between me and . . .

I looked at my mobile. The signal was just strong enough for me to make a call. This time it didn't take me as long to get through to Intendant Gomez, and to make an appointment to see him in his office in an hour.

I took Tom with me. He would have stayed on the beach, but I wouldn't allow that. Normally I'd use the slower road to Girona, but that day I headed for the *autopista*, bombing down it and paying the toll at exit seven. Gomez was ready for me when I arrived. I asked Tom to stay in the waiting room, found him a magazine, and headed for the *intendant*'s office.

'Do you have the ashes?' I asked him.

'Of course. Do you want to take them away?'

'I want to see them.'

He looked puzzled, but he agreed. He led me along to a store room, issued an order to a clerk, then led me on into a second room, windowless, with a table set under a strip light. I waited, until the orderly entered with something a little bigger than a hat-box. 'This is all of them,' he told Gomez, shooting me a strange glance.

The *intendant* was equally puzzled when I took the lid off, peered inside at the greyish contents and started to sift through them with my bare hands, feeling for anything other than ash and bone chips. I worked away for ten minutes and more, until I was sure I had gone through everything, every last scrap of cremated tissue.

'Is this everything?' I asked.

'Yes,' he assured me. 'I supervised the recovery myself, I made sure there wasn't a single piece left there. Why? Are you going to tell me what you're looking for?' He was staring at my arms; they were grey to the elbow.

I swallowed, hard. 'Mr Gomez, my aunt had silicon breast implants. They would have survived the fire, altered perhaps, but they would have survived in some form. Also her front teeth were capped, steel-bonded porcelain on gold posts. Was there any melted gold?'

'No,' he whispered.

'Can I see everything else that was taken from the site?'

'Sure.' He left, returning ten minutes later with another, smaller, box. I tipped its contents on to the table and peered at them. I saw the remnants of my taser gun, two scraps that might once have been mobiles, and three shrunken relics that looked as if they had once been credit cards. They were fused to a metal clip that I recognised as having come from Frank's Gucci billfold. I checked them carefully, looking for a fourth, but there was no sign of it. Either it had been destroyed completely . . . or it had never been in the fire.

I was about to call a halt to my search, when my hand bumped against the melted taser. I turned it over and saw something small, sticking in it rather than to it. I hadn't been aware that I'd been looking for it, but as soon as I saw it I knew that I had. I pulled it out and held it up.

All the enamel had gone, but the metal had survived the blaze in more or less its original form. I looked at it under the light. It was still recognisable, as a lapel pin in the shape of a maple leaf.

'Do we have a problem?' Intendant Gomez murmured.

'I rather think we do. These ashes, they're not my cousin and my aunt. They're the guys who kidnapped them. Somehow Frank got the better of them, killed them, then did this to them, very efficiently, in the hope, well founded as it turned out, that we'd assume this was him and Adrienne. I don't know how he managed it, but that little sod's got away with everything.'

'Everything? What do you mean?'

'I mean he's stolen seventy-seven million euros.'

The policeman sucked his teeth. 'Maybe not everything,' he exclaimed, 'but damned close.'

'What are you going to do?'

'That's a very good question,' he conceded. 'But it could be better put. It could be, what are *we* going to do? Two deaths have been registered, by you. I have been chasing two murderers and now I find that they are dead, but so, officially, is the man who killed them. As for the money, was that stolen in Spain?'

'No.'

'Then I have no jurisdiction. That's not my business.' He looked at me. 'I believe that in English you have a saying, something about covering your backside. Is that correct?'

'It's slightly less polite than that, but you've caught the meaning.'

'Then that's what I'm going to do, by doing nothing at all. I suggest, respectfully, that you do the same. You can take those ashes away, if you want. Otherwise I'm going to take them to a hill that I pass on my way home and release them.'

I thought about the old Dylan song, 'Blowing In The Wind'. At that moment I couldn't come up with a better solution. I walked out and left him to it.

Forty-four

It nagged at me, though. The more I thought about it, the whole damn business nagged at me. Frank had conned everybody, from the word go. Justin, his best friend, had told him about his wife's problem. He had recalled that non-selling novel that his mother's client had written and that undoubtedly he had read, and he had stolen the plot, lock, stock and smoking barrel.

He had conned Justin, Ludmila, Caballero, Hermann Gresch, every-damn-body. Who had fed Gresch his dope in number forty-seven? Frank, of course, and I was willing to bet that the final delivery had been spiked. Where had he found him? I took a guess, one that wouldn't be hard to verify, with Justin's help: in prison, and if so, sure as hell, he'd had a drug problem there too. The guy had been a tool, no more.

But weren't we all? I thought back to the time I had spent with him. Most of all, he'd conned me: I'd been cast in the role of the gullible accomplice.

From the moment we'd hooked up in Sevilla, I'd been the softest touch of them all, falling for all the bluff and double-bluff. My fake abduction, set up on Frank's orders by the desperate Ludmila, the rescue, painful for her, the frantic flight across Spain, had all been fake, and its ultimate purpose had been . . . to make me an unassailable witness to Frank's death and, in the process, his ticket to a life of luxury. Yes, Ludo had been stupid, but what did that make me?

Yet, I realised, at the time it had all been real, so real that for much of my time as a 'fugitive' I'd been genuinely, authentically scared. My cousin had to be some sort of a dark genius, the king of the fraudsters.

Worst of all, the cunning, needle-dick swine had even conned me into screwing him on board that damn sleeper train, with that scared, trembling act of his. I was sure that if I checked back, I'd find out that ours hadn't been the last compartment available, as he'd claimed. Then there had been the next night, in the pool . . . only . . . No, I had to admit that maybe that was my idea as much as his, maybe even more.

And then there was Auntie Ade. He had conned her, too, into coming after him. Yes, of course he had. Except why, exactly, had he asked Ludmila to video my house? He'd had no intention of hiding out with me; clearly that was crap. So why had he done it? There could only have been one reason for that. He wanted to show Willie Venable the lie of the land when it came time for him to snatch Adrienne. But how had he known that she'd ever be there?

Because they both bloody well knew, that's why. My outrageous old aunt had been in on it from the start. Those ashes had shown she was no more dead than he was; she and Frank had run off with the loot together!

As I pieced it all together I looked across at my son; he was digging a hole in the sand a few feet away from where I lay on the beach. 'Tom,' I asked him, 'remember when you came back to the house and found that Aunt Adrienne had gone?'

'Yes.'

'Why did you take Charlie for a walk along the beach that morning? You know that dogs aren't allowed there at this time of year.'

'She told me to,' he replied. 'I told her that I wasn't supposed to, but she made me. She said I'd get no breakfast if I didn't.'

The old bitch! She'd bullied him out of the house so that she could pull her disappearing act with Venable, Frank's hired gun. Except . . .

Another huge 'but' exploded before my eyes. 'But why would Frank hire real hit-men if all they were doing was role-playing?' I asked, in a whisper. 'And if they were pros, how did he ever get the drop on them and kill them?' But, then, we'd all been Frank's tools, hadn't we?

That's when it stopped being even slightly funny and got scary again.

When we were done on the beach, and Tom was in the shower washing off the sand before we went to Can Roura for dinner, I booted up my computer and went on line. Just for fun, I Googled up the names 'Sebastian Loman' and 'Willie Venable'. I got no hits for hit-men, but I did come up with a fistful for Arthur Miller and Tennessee Williams, the great twentieth-century American playwrights. Take Willy Loman, from *Death of a Salesman*, and Sebastian Venable, from *Suddenly Last Summer*, switch forenames and *voilà*.

The two 'killers' were fictional characters. Which meant?

I entered both plays in the search bar, added Spain, and in an instant I found myself looking at something called the Toronto Theatre Arts Group. The previous winter it had undertaken a tour of expat communities across Iberia, bringing the joys of Miller and Hemingway to retired coppers and retired villains along the Algarve and the Costa del Sol, with a one week stop-over in . . . . Sevilla.

I was hot on the trail. It took me only a few more seconds to find the group's website. Its menu was extensive and included a section labelled 'Performers'. I clicked on it, and a dozen faces popped up, with a short biography below each one.

The guys I was looking for were there. 'Sebastian Loman' was, in reality, Jerry Martis, from Uxbridge, Ontario. 'Willie Venable' was Jeff Paton, from Rochester, New York. Poor bastards.

They were actors, hired to play unorthodox roles for big bucks, I guessed. And Frank had written the script. He had shown them to Caballero and Ludmila, by having them 'bodyguard' her in Sevilla. He had sent them to intercept me in the tapas bar, to drop me their names, and feed me the clue that had taken us to Masia Josanto where, of course, they had been careful to make themselves known in advance. He had told Jerry to be in the Mezquita for me to spot. He had planned Jeff's 'abduction' of his mother, with the aid of the video footage that the simpleton Ludmila had shot for him, and, no doubt, he had set up his own 'kidnapping', being careful to leave me his rucksack, with the mobile, so that it would be me who unravelled Adrienne's video clue. Finally, he had put the trap for me in place, the one that had fooled me completely, so terrifying had it been.

Those two guys had earned their money. They hadn't deserved the pay-off they'd been given. I knew what had happened. Just as 'Lidia' and Caballero had believed in Sevilla that their gun had been loaded with blanks, so had Jerry and Jeff, until they had handed it back to Frank and found out the terminal truth.

So that was it, the whole story. My cousin wasn't just a con-man. He'd done what he had to in bringing down the curtain on a superb performance. He'd become a killer too. And my aunt had been a part of it . . . unless, of course, her little bastard had buried her somewhere else. I wouldn't put that past him. I wouldn't put anything past him now.

Forty-five

I had two more calls to make, before I finally put the affair to bed.

En route to Los Angeles, Tom and I stopped over in Toronto, where I hired a car and drove for an hour and a half to the home of Mrs Lina Martis, of Uxbridge, Ontario. She was in her early fifties and she was worried to distraction about what had happened to her son, Jerry. She hadn't heard from him in months, not since he had told her that he and his boyfriend, Jeff, had been hired for this weird project by an English guy. He hadn't given her any detail, but said that there was a quarter of a million Canadian in it for each of them.

I didn't give her my real name. I called myself Lidia Bromberg. I did give her a distorted, but still recognisable lapel pin, and suggested that she contact Intendant Gomez of the Mossos d'Esquadra, to report her son missing, and that she also should let the Canadian Embassy know what she had done. I left the poor woman in a state of shock.

My second call was on the way home. We stopped off in London, and there, in Mark Kravitz's flat, I had another meeting with the rodent-like Moira from MI5. Mark had arranged it, at my request. This time the woman was polite, cautious, and curious.

I told her my story in every detail, save two. I invented names for Justin and Ludmila Mayfield. (Yes, an investigation might trip over Ludo, but very quickly it would look the other way, given who her husband was.)

I gave her my copy of *Reverse Circle*, by Michael Jacks, and advised her to read it. I told her how much Frank, and probably his mother, had got away with, in terms of cash and murder. I said that, although I had no proof, I believed that my cousin might now be using the name Jason Lee. Finally, I asked her what her service, if it was really interested in major crime, proposed to do about it.

'We'll look out for them,' she replied.

As far as I know, they're looking still.

Me? I'm watching the sun rise out of the sea, from my bedroom terrace. One day my Tom will deign to join me, but not yet, not yet. He's his own man.

Author's Note

There is no house in St Martí d'Empúries that corresponds to the one where Primavera and Tom claim to live.

Shirley Gash's home is fictitious also, as is Mark Kravitz's flat, Emil Caballero's White House, and the Mayfields' upwardly mobile terrace.

There is no such book as *Reverse Circle* and no such author as Michael Jacks, although my buddy Michael Jecks, the UK's foremost author of medieval murder mysteries, gets pretty damn close.

The rest of the businesses, scenery and locations described here are all real, if 'tweaked' on occasion.

Welcome to the laid-back world of St Martí d'Empúries, where the sun never sets unless it feels like it.

Visca Catalunya.

QJ

Death's Door

Quintin Jardine

'I'm pretty sure we've got a double murderer on our patch. And the scary question is, if we don't catch him will he stop at two?'

When two young female artists are murdered in what look like ritualistic killings, the pressure is on to find a highly professional murderer. Is there a link with the art world? Or is something far more sinister behind these attacks?

The arrival of the father of one of the victims, millionaire businessman Davor Boras, brings in the big guns of the Home Office, MI5 and the CIA. And it's not long before Deputy Chief Constable Bob Skinner gets called back to the frontline.

But what is Boras' real motivation: business or family? And are the grieving parents hiding vital information? There's too much at stake – there's going to be bloodshed – and Skinner's men are at risk of getting caught in the crossfire . . .

Praise for Quintin Jardine's novels:

'A triumph. I am first in the queue for the next one' *Scotland on Sunday*

'Well constructed, fast-paced, Jardine's narrative has many an ingenious twist and turn' *Observer*

978 0 7553 2911 3

headline

For The Death Of Me

Quintin Jardine

It's summertime in Monaco and Oz Blackstone, now an international film star, is idly gazing at Roman Abramovich's luxury yacht as it gently cruises into the harbour. Life doesn't get much better than this.

But when a struggling author sweet-talks him into buying the movie rights to his latest novel, a shocking trap is laid.

Oz travels all the way to Singapore to track down the owner of some incriminating photographs but he's in grave danger of over-exposure. And when organised crime muscles in on the picture, Oz is getting perilously close to losing a lot more than his wealth and reputation . . .

Praise for the Oz Blackstone series:

'Perfect plotting and convincing characterisation' *The Times*

'Jardine's plot is very cleverly constructed, every incident and every character has a justified place in the labyrinth of motives' Gerald Kaufman, *The Scotsman*

978 0 7553 2107 0

headline

Now you can buy any of these other bestselling books by **Quintin Jardine** from your bookshop or *direct from his publisher*.

FREE P&P AND UK DELIVERY
(Overseas and Ireland £3.50 per book)

Bob Skinner series

Aftershock	£7.99
Death's Door	£7.99
Dead and Buried	£7.99
Lethal Intent	£6.99
Stay of Execution	£6.99
Fallen Gods	£6.99

Oz Blackstone series

For the Death of Me	£7.99
Alarm Call	£6.99
Unnatural Justice	£6.99

TO ORDER SIMPLY CALL THIS NUMBER

01235 400 414

or visit our website: www.headline.co.uk

Prices and availability subject to change without notice.